DADDY'S GIRL

BELINDA WILLIAMS

DADDY'S GIRL: Freshwater #3

ISBN: 978-0-6488099-8-2 (Trade paperback)
https://belindawilliamsbooks.com

Edited by Laura Greaves
Proofread by Rebekah Groves
Cover art by Belinda Williams

Also by Belinda Williams

Read Between The Lines: Freshwater 1

Self Made: Freshwater 2

Don't Let Me Forget

Heartthrob: Hollywood Hearts 1

Heartbreaker: Hollywood Hearts 2

Heartbeat: Hollywood Hearts 3

Wild Heart: Hollywood Hearts 4

Heartstrings: A Hollywood Hearts novella

The Boyfriend Sessions: City Love 1

The Pitch: City Love 2

Modern Heart: City Love 3

Wish List: City Love 4

Anthologies

(available for FREE digital download):

Bad Things Come In Threes: Winter Heat – Six Sizzling, Fun-Size Chick Lit Stories

The Spring Clean: Spring Fling – Six Mini Chick Lit Tales

Dear Reader

This book is set in Australia, so I've used UK English instead of US English.

This means if you're one of my US readers, you might notice some differences in spelling: colour instead of color; towards instead of toward; realise instead of realize.

You may also notice other differences like my characters' tendency to call their friends "mate" or "mates". Hopefully the Australian colloquialisms are self-explanatory, but if you come across any that you don't understand, feel free to get in touch via the contact form on my website: https://belindawilliamsbooks.com/contact/

I've tried to refrain from using Aussie slang because this can seem like a language within itself! But if some usage has slipped in, I'll cop it . . . whoops, see? That means I'll take responsibility for it.

I hope you enjoy *Daddy's Girl*.

Happy reading,

Belinda

Chapter One

'YOU CAN SMILE, YOU KNOW.'

Em shot her sister an unimpressed sideways glance. 'That would suggest I'm enjoying myself. Besides, I've done my quota of smiling today.'

'The whole wedding has been so romantic. I don't understand why you aren't happy right now,' Ana gushed.

This time Em turned to look at her sister properly. They were both dressed in the same electric blue bridesmaid dresses, but with Ana's dark wavy hair, olive skin and wide brown eyes, it was difficult to tell they were sisters. Their parents regularly joked that Em took after the Irish side and Ana the Greek side of the family. Their height was the only thing they had in common looks-wise. Put bluntly, they were both lacking it.

'And we all know that you love romance,' Em told her.

Ana sighed, the long-suffering variety that spoke of a heavy burden she was forced to endure. 'And we all know that you don't. Come on, haven't you found today even slightly romantic?'

'Oh, don't get me wrong. Rosie and Tim are great

together, and it was a beautiful wedding. If you're into that sort of thing,' Em added.

Ana huffed. 'I can't believe you've been a bridesmaid this many times and it hasn't changed your opinion on weddings.'

It had changed Em's opinion of weddings, but not in a positive way, so Em chose her next words carefully. Ana was exactly the type of person who did go for this sort of thing, and this wedding was tame in comparison to what her own had been.

'You know it's not my thing. Even if I decided to settle down—'

'Which you won't.' Ana finished her sentence with another huff.

'Which I won't,' Em confirmed. 'But if I did, I'd probably just elope somewhere.'

'Over Mum and Dad's dead bodies!'

It was Em's turn to sigh. 'Look. You had the big Greek wedding. That should have satisfied Dad. Now you're starting a family.'

She gestured to Ana's cute pregnant stomach, which resembled a basketball. Fortunately, the bridesmaid gowns were loose and flowing, so Ana hadn't needed to worry about fitting into the dress.

'Dad's so over the moon about the baby, he might actually forget about me for a change,' Em finished. She could only hope, at least.

Ana smiled. The smile turned into bright laughter. Which morphed into a loud guffaw. Ana's eyes widened at her own outburst, and she smacked a hand over her mouth, but she didn't stop laughing.

Em cracked a smile. 'Yes, alright. I know I'm deluded.'

Ana coughed and cleared her throat, gaining control over her laughter. 'So deluded. But that's why we love you. You do know there's someone that Dad wants you to meet tonight, don't you?'

Em silently contemplated her need for another drink. 'There's *always* someone Dad wants me to meet. What's new?'

'What's new is that you're lacking your usual decoy,' Ana replied, her dark eyes gleaming.

'Please don't remind me. I'm still very unimpressed he cancelled.'

Em's long-term strategy of bringing unsuitable men along to family events or functions was a long-running joke in the family, as was their father's attempts to set her up at every available opportunity.

'What happened to man number three-hundred-and-forty-five, anyway?'

It really was very difficult to *not* roll her eyes at her sister sometimes, Em found. 'He had to work at the last minute.'

'At least that means he has a job. That's a good start.'

Em levelled a stern look at her sister. 'He's a doctor.'

Ana's eyebrows shot up in surprise. 'Ooh, exciting. It's nice that you're finally starting to see that it's important to date someone with a similar IQ.'

'Don't be so condescending,' Em replied. 'Just because I'm university educated doesn't mean the men I see have to be.'

'Em,' Ana said, and a pained note crept into her voice. 'You're not just university educated. You're an academic who is about to complete her PhD. I don't see how going out with all those surfer dudes and backpackers you insist on hanging around with can result in any sort of interesting conversation.'

Em's lips tipped up at the edges. 'That's because we don't talk much.'

'You. Are. Insufferable.'

Em grinned. 'But you still love me.'

'So would a decent guy if you gave him half a chance.'

Em put an arm around her sister's waist gently. 'You know a relationship isn't important to me. I'm too busy studying, and soon I want to apply what I've learned and researched in the real world. I don't need a guy for that.'

'Yes, but a guy might make you happy.'

Em tilted her head to the side, considering her sister's words. 'For half an hour or so, perhaps.'

Ana growled, a cute little growl that sounded more like a purr. 'You are so frustrating!' She waved a hand in front of her stomach. 'Don't you want this? Don't you want what Mum and Dad have?'

Em's expression softened as she surveyed her beautiful sister. She was like an image of a Grecian fertility goddess with her wavy hair cascading over her bare shoulders and her eyes lined in dark kohl.

'I don't long for it the way that you do. I'm so happy you've found it, by the way.' While Em didn't have the yearning to find a man and settle down like her little sister had, she was genuinely happy that Ana had found what she wanted.

'Stop changing the subject,' Ana said. 'I swear you don't *let* yourself look for a long-term relationship.'

Em shrugged. 'Unless one comes looking for me, I won't be searching for it. Just accept that we want different things, and life should be a lot more pleasant.'

Ana screwed up her nose. 'Tell that to Dad.'

'Any idea which eligible bachelor he has lined up for me tonight?'

'No, I don't. And I wouldn't tell you if I did, because you'd avoid him.'

'I love you, too. Oh well, it should be easy enough to spot him.'

'Why do you say that?' Ana asked.

'Dad has a type, you know.'

Ana giggled. 'He does, doesn't he?'

'Yep. Private school boys that went to a reputable school, then a good university. They also smack of enough arrogance to put me off my dessert because they've had the world handed to them on a platter. You're just lucky you and Theo met during high school, and that he's Greek.'

'That's not why I married him, and you know it. We know most of the Greek guys here tonight, so I wonder who he is?'

Em couldn't help but wonder as well. Many of the weddings they attended were for an extended family member. However, Rosie, the bride, was a long-term employee of their father's, as well as a good friend of Em and Ana. They'd grown up in the same street, spending weekends at each other's houses. This was why both she and her sister were part of the bridal party. Em and Ana knew most of Rosie and Tim's friends, so Em couldn't think who it was. Not that it really mattered, because whoever he was, he was sure to be her father's usual type.

'Oh my God. I have to go to the toilet again,' Ana announced. 'This is crazy.'

'Wait for the baby.'

Ana poked her tongue out at Em. 'Aunty Em will be the first person I call when I'm sleep deprived and need a babysitter.'

'No, that's when you call Mum.'

'Fine. After Mum. Damn it. I've really got to go. Here.' Ana shoved her glass of pregnancy-safe mineral water in Em's direction and scurried off.

Em looked at the glass in her hand. If it was alcoholic, she might consider finishing it. She set it down on a nearby table and sighed. If she weren't in the bridal party, she'd have made an excuse to leave by now. Her pregnant sister would probably end up on the dance floor like most of the other guests, so Em could hardly claim tiredness.

Except tired was exactly what she was. Em had spent most of the week before staying up late working on her PhD. She was so close to finishing it. She already knew the parts she needed to go back and rewrite. Lately, she often found herself doing chores like folding washing, only to stop and realise that she was silently going through the rewrites in her head.

If it weren't for this wedding, Em would have spent all weekend working.

'You party animal,' she muttered to herself.

It was definitely time for another drink, so Em turned and headed towards the bar. The irony was that she could be a party girl when the occasion called for it. When she was feeling less pressure to work, Em was the first to suggest a night out with friends. She also had no hesitation about heading to one of the bars near her apartment for a drink by herself.

But tonight Em wasn't in the mood to party. It must have been something to do with all the romance in the air. Unlike Ana, romance made Em grumpy.

Don't you want what Mum and Dad have?

Em increased her pace towards the bar. Damn Ana and her happily-ever-after fantasies. Ana didn't seem to understand that what her parents had was rare, and not everyone was cut out for long-lasting happiness. Ana was lucky that she had met her partner young, so of course she would expect that romantic happiness was achievable for everyone.

As far as sisters went, they really couldn't be more different if they tried. In Ana's case, the cuteness on the outside reflected the person on the inside. Whereas Em's fair Irish looks—her "gentle beauty" as her mother called it—constantly got her into trouble. Em knew a lot of men found her attractive, but they soon discovered that her exterior sweetness was at odds with her strength of character.

Too bold.

Too honest.

You look sweeter than you really are.

Wow, you're not what I expected.

Em snatched up a champagne flute from the bar and took a grateful sip, chasing the demons of men long gone out of her mind.

Well, damn those men and their outdated ideas of what a woman should be, which also included her father. Em wasn't going to change for anyone. And if that meant remaining single for the rest of her life, then so be it.

Chapter Two

EMILY GEORGIOU WAS NOT AT ALL what Joel expected.

First of all, she was a redhead. Joel hadn't anticipated that. Not with a Greek father like Chris Georgiou. When he'd visited Chris's office for meetings, Joel had met her sister—Ana was her name, he recalled—and her dark colouring reflected her father's Mediterranean background.

Emily was . . .

Joel still wasn't sure what Emily was, but he knew one thing already.

She was captivating.

This was particularly notable because Joel generally didn't notice women, let alone find them captivating. Not that he didn't like women. He liked them a lot. But he'd learned to shut that part of himself off, which wasn't all that hard when he had a business to focus on.

Except right now his business was the last thing on his mind, although that's exactly what had led him to this uncomfortable situation. When a promising new client slapped you on the back and suggested that you "get to know" his daughter at the upcoming wedding you were both attending, you agreed politely.

Having seen Ana that one time, Joel had resigned himself to a night of polite conversation and nothing more. Ana was beautiful, but not in the same way as Emily. Ana was cute and almost homely—and Joel didn't mean that in a bad way. He just knew that homely didn't suit him, like oil is opposed to water.

But Emily . . .

'Ah, shit,' he said softly, and already hated himself for approaching the bar.

Chris had made it quite clear that he would introduce Joel to Emily at some point during the night. But Chris was a social man, and the night was getting old. Plus, right now Emily was drinking alone at the bar and she had no idea who he was.

The idea of complete anonymity was more comforting to Joel than he would care to explain. In other words, he'd only explain if forced to. Every meeting and interaction he had as the face of his business always felt tiring to him because it meant that he had to maintain the persona he'd grown along with his business.

Despite the tempting idea of introducing himself as a stranger to Emily, Joel stalled at a table five metres from the bar just so he could watch her. He wasn't quite ready to break the beautiful illusion of her.

He'd been watching her since the moment she'd walked down the aisle during the ceremony earlier in the day. Her hair captured his attention straightaway, as he was sure it did for many strangers. It wasn't really fair to call her a redhead. Her hair was auburn, not red, and almost golden in certain lights. It contrasted her perfect pale skin, and when she'd looked at the guests and smiled, he'd caught a flash of intense blue eyes as electric as the dress she wore. Momentarily stunned, Joel hadn't registered how small she was at first. Another illusion. The elegant sway of her slim hips as she walked fooled him into thinking Emily was much taller than she was.

At that point, Joel had no idea who Emily was. It wasn't until Chris had come over to greet him after the ceremony and nodded towards his two beautiful bridesmaid daughters smiling for the cameras that the realisation had sunk in.

While Emily's classic beauty might be reminiscent of an early nineteen-hundreds screen siren, Joel was certain she'd be similar in personality to Ana, who didn't interest him in the slightest. After all, the two were related. Joel had Emily pinned as sweet, bubbly, and a little spoiled. Maybe a lot spoiled given she was still a student and dear old dad was maintaining the life to which she was no doubt accustomed. Chris had mentioned in passing the name of the development in which he'd "gifted" Em a penthouse apartment, so Joel had looked it up. She was definitely a daddy's girl living in a beachside property like that.

Emily went to push away from the bar, which set Joel into motion. He didn't want to lose his chance to introduce himself without Chris's overbearing presence. Joel genuinely liked Chris—and seriously respected him—but the man was a force of nature.

Emily stopped when Joel stepped in front of her. She blinked and her eyelashes fluttered like butterflies, drawing attention to eyes that were such a deep blue they were almost violet. Joel opened his mouth to say something, which was when he realised he didn't have the slightest clue what to say.

Fuck.

He watched, entranced, as Emily's eyelashes stilled and she observed him.

'I don't think we've met,' she said.

Her voice was rich and warm, and once again, nothing like

he'd expected. He'd only heard her speak a few words, but listening to it was like taking a sip of the finest red wine. Sweet but spicy.

When he didn't respond, Emily tilted her head slightly, still observing him. 'I'd remember if we had, I think.'

Say something, you idiot.

'Why is that?' he asked. By comparison, his voice sounded gravelly, like he barely used it.

Joel groaned inwardly. Why hadn't he said something more confident like, "I'd remember if we'd met, too"?

She gave him a slow smile. 'Because I'd remember you.'

What was that about not being able to speak? Now Joel found his lungs were tight as well. What was happening to him? He didn't act like this, and women never affected him this way. He used all of his internal willpower to get a grip.

'I hope in a good way,' he said smoothly, feeling more himself.

Emily nodded approvingly. At least Joel thought it was an approving nod. It was possible he was losing it altogether.

'I'm Em. How do you know the bride and groom?' she asked.

Good. Small talk. Joel could manage small talk. And Em, not Emily, Joel noted with interest. Chris always referred to his daughter as Emily.

'Through work, actually,' he replied, being deliberately vague. 'You?'

'I grew up with Rosie. We were neighbour buddies. Not neighbours anymore, but still friends.'

Joel knew his body was working overtime being in close proximity to Em, but now his mind was a blur of thoughts, too. She was confident and self-assured. Direct. Joel had antici-pated demure. His heartbeat ratcheted up a notch, becoming more erratic.

'I noticed you in the bridal party.' Joel felt like slapping a hand to his forehead for stating the obvious. Or for sounding like a stalker, he wasn't sure which.

'Hard to miss us in these dresses,' Em replied, either not noticing his obvious statement or pretending not to notice. 'Do you know many people here?'

Hardly anyone.

'A few,' he replied. Vague. He was good at being vague.

Em leaned in as though they were co-conspirators, and his pounding heartbeat halted momentarily. 'Then you won't know that this is the twelfth time I've been a bridesmaid and I'm over the entire thing—no offence intended to the happy couple. I was honoured to be asked, of course.'

'Twelve times? Surely you can start charging?'

Em's smile widened. Joel wondered if she usually chose not to smile with her teeth or if her closed-lipped smile was because she was still reserved around him. He had a feeling it was the latter. He also had a feeling she was assessing him carefully. He was curious about what he'd need to do to pass the test, because whatever it was, he wanted to know.

'It's not the way it works, I'm afraid,' she said.

'Then at least you'll have your choice of bridesmaids when the time comes for you. Either that, or the biggest bridal party in history.'

Em's lips parted in surprise. 'Oh. I'd never considered that. Probably because I have no intention of getting married.'

'What?'

They both stared at each other in shock, except Joel's shock was pained while he considered that maybe his first impression hadn't been accurate.

He went to clear his throat, but Em spoke first.

'Not everyone wants to get married, you know. Or be Cinderella for a day.'

'I know. I've never wanted to be Cinderella. I'm more of a big bad wolf.'

Em quirked an eyebrow. 'Interesting. Is this your disguise?'

Joel knew it was just teasing—perhaps even flirting—but something about the conversation cut too close to the bone for him, so he returned the focus to her.

'So why don't you want to get married?' he asked. 'Or if that's too personal, feel free to change the subject.' The truth was, Joel was fascinated. This woman was turning out to be very different to her sister.

Joel might have been wrong, but she appeared disappointed. Or was he misreading the way the sparkle in her eye dimmed?

Em shrugged. 'I'm not into big weddings, for one. If you want the honest answer, I've got too much to do.'

'And you can't do that with a partner?'

Em frowned slightly. 'You sound like my sister.'

He held up his hands. 'Hey, I'm not advocating marriage. I'm not interested in it either. It was just an observation.'

'You don't want to get married?' Em asked with obvious interest.

'Like you, I've got too much to do.'

Em's smile returned and Joel felt stupidly proud that he'd put it there.

'And what is it you do, Mr. No Name?'

Oh, God. He hadn't introduced himself. What was happening to him?

'Joel Scott. Scott & Morris Architects.'

Em stared at him. 'You're an architect?'

'Last time I checked, yes.'

'And it's your firm?'

'Also yes, last time I checked. Along with my business partner.'

'Huh.'

Huh? What did that mean? In fact, what did any of this mean? Joel wasn't interested in a relationship, that was for sure. So why was he standing here wanting to get to know this woman better?

'Huh,' Em said again.

'Is there a problem with my choice of profession?'

Em shook her head. 'I'm sorry, no. I had you pinned as doing something else.'

'Like?'

'Finance, maybe? Or perhaps a lawyer.'

'I didn't realise I looked that serious.'

'Huh,' Em said a third time. 'What sort of architecture work do you do?'

'My passion is high-end renovations, but we also do large scale residential developments.'

'You mean you ruin the environment for the sake of money?'

If Joel had a drink, he would have choked on it. Instead, he cleared his throat. 'We try to avoid adversely impacting the environment, and strangely enough my employees like getting paid.'

'But if you do high-end renovations, I'm sure those clients have plenty of money to spend.'

'Yes.' Joel drew the word out, still choosing his words carefully.

Holy hell, she wasn't cute and bubbly like her sister at all, and that demure exterior hid a feisty personality. Joel was way more turned on than he cared to admit.

'But those high-end clients like to know that we have expertise,' Joel continued. 'And if we're competent and respected enough to work on major developments, they'll trust us with their homes. It's got to do with credibility.'

Em set her drink down on the table nearby and glared at him, those blue eyes so dark they'd lost their violet tinge. They were more like a stormy sea.

'Name me one credible large-scale property development in this city,' she demanded. 'To my knowledge, there aren't any. They're all conceived by developers like my father who are only interested in profit and approved by councillors who put economy before environment time and time again.'

What on earth? Joel stared at the blazing redhead—and she most definitely was a redhead at this moment. It was like her hair had become brighter to reflect her mood.

'And you would know this how?' Joel asked, both amazed and perplexed.

Em narrowed her eyes at him. 'Aside from being related to my father, I've spent several years writing my PhD on the built environment, with a focus on environmentally sustainable growth for cities. That's how.'

Joel gaped openly at her now. Far out. Chris had failed to mention what it was that Em had been studying. Or that she was a PhD candidate. In fact, Chris had made it sound as though Em's study was a stopgap until she settled down. Like it was something she did to fritter away the time because she didn't know what else to do.

The next words that came out of his mouth stunned both her and him.

'Dance with me.'

They both fell silent and stared at each other.

'Why?' Em asked eventually.

'Because you're nothing like I expected.'

It was like a wave crested and crashed onto the shore in those deep blue eyes. Abruptly, she turned away, her hair flaming behind her.

'Wait.' Joel reached out and caught her arm.

He wasn't sure what he'd said, but he wanted to fix it. He didn't resist when she shook him off, but the diversion was long enough for him to get his next words out.

'What I meant to say, is that you're better than I expected.'

Em stilled and blinked at him. 'You're the guy my father wanted me to meet, aren't you?'

'For the record, I only said yes because saying no might mean I lose his business.' And didn't that sound so many layers of wrong? Like he was no better than those unscrupulous developers and councillors she clearly resented. He rushed on. 'Not that I make a habit out of this. I figured I'd say hi, maybe share a drink and some polite conversation, and that would get me off the hook.'

'Then why ask me for a dance? Is that to impress my father, too?'

'No. It's because I'd like to dance with you.'

She fell silent again, and Joel didn't dare breathe in case he scared her away. Not that she scared easily by the looks of it, but he'd obviously hit a nerve earlier.

'Fine. One dance, but that's it. Then maybe my father will leave both of us alone.'

A part of Joel wanted to protest again that it wasn't why he'd requested the dance, but he was smart enough to keep his mouth shut. He'd been in business long enough to take a win when it presented itself.

But this had nothing to do with business right now, no matter what Em might say. It had everything to do with her and him, and a part of him he'd long discarded as useless and unnecessary.

Given the skeletons buried in his past, his reaction to her should have frightened him. It definitely should have worried him. But he was too entranced by Em Georgiou to care.

Chapter Three

AS THEY WALKED to the dance floor side by side, Em tried to get a hold of herself. She was equal parts angry and mystified. And if she was being truthful, she wasn't angry at Joel. She was angry with herself.

When Joel had come into view it was as if everyone else in the room had faded, and Em's thoughts had been reduced to one pathetic word.

Oh.

Em wasn't a stranger to the opposite sex, and she made a point to enjoy them on occasion. So after a quick evaluation of the man in front of her, her brain arrived at the same positive assessment that her body had already jumped to.

Tall, but not too tall. Maybe just shy of six foot? His bronzed skin hinted at a natural olive complexion rather than too much sun exposure. Dark eyes. So dark they had the sort of depth you could get lost in. A five o'clock shadow that Em guessed was a fixture. All of those things weren't remarkable within themselves. It was two other qualities that had elicited the unexpected "oh".

His hair. Or lack thereof. He clearly wasn't balding and had dark hair the same shade as his deep brown eyes. But for whatever reason, he chose to keep it cropped short. Not just short, but shaved, Em suspected. Like he was too busy to worry about the nuisance of longer hair.

Em's reaction to his absent dark locks surprised her. Usually she went for men with lots of hair. Wavy hair. Shoulder length hair. Tousled hair. Because, as a general rule, she like to run her fingers through it. Now she found herself wondering what it would be like to trace her hands over this stranger's scalp.

Which sounded creepy. So she'd moved her focus to what he was wearing, and there it was again . . .

Oh.

The man wore his suit like it was painted on. Like it was the most comfortable thing in the world. It moulded to broad, muscled shoulders that hinted at strength but not obsession over his looks. Likewise, his trim waist and strong thighs. A man like that obviously worked out, but as the hair already suggested, it was something he did efficiently, not self-consciously.

It was only when he'd told her what he did for a living that the doubt had started to creep in. This couldn't be the man that her father had wanted her to meet, could it? The more they talked, the more it fit. Plus, the suit. The men her father suggested were always corporate types in suits. Admittedly, all the men here tonight were wearing them, but they didn't wear a suit like this man wore a suit.

Of course, none of this mattered because there was no way she was interested in a man that her father put forward. Especially not a man involved in developments like the ones cropping up all over the city. In Em's educated opinion, they were not only ugly but a blight on the environment.

Then the man—Joel—introduced himself and asked her to dance. And now Em was standing at the edge of the dance floor. It went against every aspect of her better judgement, except for several softly spoken words.

You're better than I expected.

Joel's fingers brushed her arm to catch her attention, and Em experienced an involuntary shiver.

Who was this man? And why was she reacting to him like this?

Em noted the music and the shiver still tingling down her spine morphed into hesitation. She turned to face him, suddenly awkward. 'We can sit this one out if you'd prefer?'

The side of Joel's mouth quirked as he listened to the low-key song the DJ was playing. *Better Together* by Jack Johnson.

Em didn't mind the song. What she minded was the way people were slow dancing to it.

'I can do slow,' Joel said. 'You?'

Em hesitated again, not trusting herself to speak. Sure, she could dance slow. But with this guy? At this wedding, where everyone knew her? Her dad was also around here somewhere, and if he saw her dancing with his latest eligible bachelor, he was likely to become unbearable. Then again, maybe it would shut him up for a while. Em had never welcomed any of the men he'd suggested before. Perhaps he would finally leave her alone if she showed some mild interest.

'Em?' His voice was like the low bass note of a cello, hushed and lilting, but impossible to ignore.

Em darted a look in his direction, hating that she was coming across as shy, because she was never shy around men. She could rationalise and overthink all she liked, but deep down Em wanted to dance with Joel. Usually the men her father introduced her to were cocky to the point of brazen, their voices as loud as their egos, but not this man.

Em stepped into his waiting arms and, after an awkward moment where they seemed to hold their breath, they both exhaled. He chuckled and Em smiled.

'How long will it take for your father to spot us?' Joel asked.

His voice drifted down to her as if caught on a gentle breeze, and Em pretended to be completely unaffected.

'He's probably taking pictures.' She felt Joel stiffen, so she shoved him lightly on shoulder. 'I'm joking.'

'Strangely enough, I can imagine him doing exactly that.'

Em eased back to look up at him. His brown eyes were smiling, and she could feel the warmth in her toes. 'You know my father well, then.'

'I know he's driven.'

'And you aren't?' She was fishing for more information and he probably knew it, but Em found it impossible not to be interested in this man.

'Not like your father. I run a business. Your father oversees an empire.'

Em found herself laughing. 'You *do* have my father figured out. I'm impressed.'

The other men her father suggested would have preened at her compliment. Instead, Joel seemed unmoved by it.

'Your father is always open about his objectives. So I don't think you should give me any bonus points for figuring him out.'

'Not always. When he really wants something, he's prepared to be discreet about it.'

Joel's dark eyebrows rose. 'Interesting. I'll make a note of that. And I have a feeling you're speaking from experience?'

'Plenty of it.' She smiled again, but this time it was a little forced. 'Please tell me he didn't convince Tim and Rosie to invite you for the sole purpose of us meeting tonight?'

'You can relax. I actually know Tim through cycling. He was the one who gave me a business introduction to your father.'

'You ride with Tim?'

Em knew Tim rode regularly, but didn't know much about it as Rosie made her distaste of the sport well known: *Why can't he just kick a ball around a field like a regular guy instead of getting dressed up in lycra and endangering himself on the road?* It wasn't that Rosie didn't like Tim taking the time to keep fit, she just thought that cycling was dangerous.

'Reasonably regularly. So you're doing a PhD?'

The change in the conversation was swift and smooth, but Em immediately recognised his strategy.

He doesn't like talking about himself.

It didn't matter. Em had put up with her father's obstinacy for too many years to count. She was used to dealing with contrary men.

'You caught that?' she joked. 'I thought you might have missed my rant on the evils of high-density developments.'

'You make a good point.'

Choosing not to hide her surprise, she eased back again and looked into those mysterious eyes of his.

'What?' he asked. 'Can't I have an opinion on the matter?'

'And what's your opinion?' Em asked, suddenly on edge.

Please, please don't let him be another money hungry corporate type.

'I think,' he said slowly, 'that high-rise developments have their place.' He held up a hand when Em involuntarily slouched. 'But only if they are considerate of lifestyle and environmental factors. Developments near a transport hub are proven to be good practice. Where it falls down is when aspects like green space and community facilities are neglected or the designs themselves aren't geared towards being as carbon neutral as possible.'

'Go on.'

His lips twitched slightly, and he kept talking.

'I also think that we have a long way to go before we create developments that don't cause long-term harm to the environment. Which is why my firm is actively trying to integrate sustainability into our designs.'

'Because you've figured out it's good for business, am I right?' Em asked.

Increasingly architects were becoming more environmentally focused, which wasn't a bad thing. But usually they were all about creating single dwellings that showcased clever environmental considerations into their designs. It was more about their egos and their back pockets.

'Are you always this cynical?' he replied, sounding more interested than offended. 'Our firm *only* creates sustainable designs. It's our speciality.'

Em gaped at him. 'Then why on earth are you talking to my father?'

Joel shrugged. 'We've been invited to tender for one of his projects.'

Em bit her lip.

'You think we're making up numbers?' he asked.

'I didn't say that.'

'You didn't need to. Everything you've said about your father tonight tells me that's probably the case. Except from the five firms invited to tender, it's now down to the last two and we're one of them.'

'It must be something else about your design then,' Em concluded.

Em couldn't see Joel's face because she was facing his shoulder, but she saw the way his chest expanded and felt the soft rumble of laughter tingle through her arms.

'If it goes ahead, it will be the first sustainable development on his books,' Joel said. 'That's what I'm aiming for, anyway.'

Em stepped out of his arms. 'I'm not trying to be mean, I'm just being honest. My father doesn't do sustainable. He does profit.'

Joel shrugged. 'All I know is that we're talking about it and he's considering it.'

Em released a breath, her initial scepticism replaced with respect. 'Well, if you get him to agree to it, I'll be impressed.'

'That's our plan. I just need some time.'

Em shook her head again and moved closer. 'I don't envy you. I try to avoid taking my father on head-to-head if I can help it. That's not to say I've never won a battle. More like I'm battle-worn.'

Joel didn't say anything, but she could imagine those lips quirking again.

The Jack Johnson song finished and another one came on, with a toe-tapping beat this time. They broke contact, and Em studied him openly.

'Why would you want to work with my father if the environment is so important to you?' she asked him.

'Because what's good for the environment is better for us, only not everyone sees it right now. It has to start somewhere.'

Em stared at him. This man was a unicorn, that's what he was. Fabled to exist, never actually seen. 'Where have you come from?' she asked before she could help herself.

'Western Australia,' he replied simply.

'You know that's not what I meant.'

'I know.' He smiled properly this time, and the transformation rendered Em speechless.

When he smiled, his entire face smiled. His eyes went from mysterious to a warm brown, and the fine lines on his face that had made him seem serious a moment ago were now attractive laughter lines.

Em looked away, slightly dazzled. She wasn't sure why, but she had the impression Joel didn't smile all that often. So when he did, it was something to be treasured.

Em's back prickled with annoyance. Sure, she lusted after guys occasionally, but she didn't do dazzled. That wasn't her style. But then, she'd never met a man like Joel before. Not only was he easy to look at, he was obviously well educated and smart, too—Em didn't necessarily view them as the same thing.

'Emily! Joel! I see you've found each other already.'

Em turned slowly at the sound of her father's voice, the annoyance becoming more intense.

Her father addressed Joel and not her. 'So, what do you think of my eldest daughter?'

Em wondered if it was possible for a twenty-seven-year-old woman to die of embarrassment. She could feel her cheeks turning an unsightly shade of pink, but she had no choice but to stand there and wait for Joel's answer.

Chapter Four

JOEL DIDN'T NEED to look at Em to know that she was
annoyed. He could feel it. He still couldn't help himself from
glancing over at her. The sight of her blue eyes alive with
anger, and her pale, creamy complexion glowing a pretty pink
had him quickly diverting his gaze again.

'I can see why you wanted us to meet,' Joel said, careful to
keep his tone professional. 'Em's very accomplished.'

'Ha!' Chris huffed, like the last part was a joke. 'I suppose
close to a decade in the university system is an accomplish-
ment, but I value real world experience myself.'

Joel looked between Chris and Em. It was hard to believe
that Em was his daughter. This brash Greek developer with his
combed back salt and pepper hair, shrewd brown eyes, and
shiny olive complexion creased with deep wrinkles. Really, the
only thing they had in common appearance-wise was their
short stature. But where Em was sleek and elegant, Chris was
stocky and stout.

'Well, it's certainly something to be proud of,' Joel replied.
'Knowledge like Em's is valuable.'

Chris winked at his daughter. 'That's my Emily. A rare diamond. Don't you think, Joel?'

'Dad, stop,' Em told him. 'If Joel's firm is tendering for a project with your company, you shouldn't have made him feel like he has to meet me to be considered.'

Joel suppressed the urge to loosen his tie. So much for avoiding the elephant in the room. Em seemed perfectly happy pointing directly at it. He was caught between admiration and awkwardness.

'Now, Emily, no need to jump to conclusions. I simply thought you two might have something in common given your interest in sustainability.' Chris almost appeared hurt, but judging by Em's glare in her father's direction, she wasn't buying it.

Joel decided that was his cue. 'And you were right, Chris. We do seem to share some similar opinions.'

'See?' Chris said, his chest puffing out a bit like a peacock. 'Your father knows better than you think he does, Emily.'

Em crossed her arms and raised an eyebrow at her father. 'So you're seriously telling me that you're considering signing on for a sustainable development? Why the change of heart?'

Joel gritted his teeth. Impressive or not, if she wasn't careful, Em was about to destroy all the hard work he and his team had done these last few months in getting the tender to this point.

Joel took a step closer to Chris. 'Your father's company is smart, Em. He can see the benefits of a sustainable approach.'

'Only because of the money involved, is my guess. Sustainability is the new bandwagon. Isn't that right, Dad?'

How could one woman be so alluring and frustrating at the same time? Frankly, Joel couldn't care less if Chris Georgiou signed on with Scott & Morris because he was ticking a box. If that was what it took for him to get a foot in the door with one of the city's biggest developers, he'd take it. Joel understood that these old dinosaur developers were never going to choose his firm solely for the good of the environment. He had to be realistic and patient.

'Now, darling,' her father said, and the condescending note in his voice made Joel's shoulders tense. 'Let me deal with the business side of things. You stick to writing your papers.'

Ouch. Joel's annoyance at Em eased a bit. A PhD wasn't merely writing some papers, as her father put it. It was years of research and hard work, and it sucked that her father couldn't see that. Joel had always fancied the idea of further study himself. Except it had taken everything he'd had mentally and financially to complete his architecture degree, so it had never been on the cards for him.

Em chose to ignore her father and turned to face Joel again. The earlier anger was gone and replaced with something much worse, in Joel's opinion. Resignation. The flush from her cheeks had faded and now her skin looked much too pale against the brightness of her hair.

'On that note, I'll leave you to your business discussions. It was a pleasure to meet you, Joel. Best of luck with the tender.'

With that, she left Joel and her father staring after her.

Chris let out a hoot of laughter. 'Well, there you have my Emily. She's quite a character, isn't she?'

Joel had the distinct feeling Chris made a habit out of underestimating his daughter, but highlighting that fact wasn't going to do Joel any favours.

'It was nice to meet her.' As a rule, Joel hated the word "nice". He disliked it even more now, but he was trying to be diplomatic. Em wasn't nice. She was mind-blowing and fascinating and so much more than nice.

And she probably hated him thanks to his desire to work with her father, but he wasn't going to ruin his chance for this contract. Maybe Chris was right that Em lacked commercial experience, but it was understandable if she'd been studying all these years. It perplexed him that Chris hadn't involved Em in his business more, given her area of study.

Joel jumped when Chris nudged him in the side, then nodded in the direction of his other daughter, Ana, who was dancing. 'Chalk and cheese, my two daughters. But they're the best of friends. You know what they say, you can't choose your family. I think I did alright, though.'

Joel tried to keep his expression neutral. Chris certainly had done all right. He was one of the lucky ones.

'You've never mentioned your family, Joel. I like to think that I work with people that recognise the importance of family as well as business. Otherwise, what's all this hard work for?'

A loaded silence followed, and Joel knew that Chris was waiting for him to speak. Joel recognised that this was another test. He'd been jumping through hoops ever since the tender process had begun.

'I agree that family is important,' Joel said neutrally. 'I haven't been as fortunate as you. My father died in my teens and my mother when I was in my early twenties. I have a sister. She's still based in Western Australia, so we don't see each other much.'

If "based" meant jumping from one destructive relation-ship to another, which usually involved chasing the latest loser male to some new place. Joel had lost track of the number of times his sister, Mia, had moved in the last fifteen years. Last time she'd been in contact, she was living near the city. But that had been six months ago. Joel half expected her to be living in a small rural town by now.

Chris nodded sympathetically. 'I lost my parents early on,

too. It can be rough. All the more reason for you to build the life you want for yourself.'

'That's the plan.'

Well, building a business was the plan, anyway. Joel had no intentions of having a family. Not everyone was a family man. It wasn't in Joel's blood, but he had no intention of telling Chris that. Nate Morris, his business partner, was the sort of family man Chris was referring to. Joel would make sure to drop that into conversation at the next meeting somehow.

'Well,' Chris said. 'I'm going to go and ask my lovely wife to dance. Hopefully she might humour this old guy if I'm lucky.'

Joel smiled, but it didn't touch his eyes. He was tired all of a sudden and planned to leave unnoticed after Chris was gone.

Chris slapped him on the shoulder. 'Hey, do me a favour, will you? If I know Emily, she's going to try to escape soon because she can't stop thinking about that bloody PhD of hers. I hate the idea of her being in a cab alone, and she never listens to me. Can you escort her home?'

Joel resisted closing his eyes. What was one more uncomfortable favour for the good of the potential contract?

'Of course,' he replied. 'But do you think she'll agree?'

Chris grinned. 'Just tell her that I said so.'

'Something tells me that won't convince her.'

Chris let out a bark of laughter. 'Too true. Tell her this, then. Aunt Sophia is a bit tipsy and needs someone to accompany her home. Emily will leave with you, no questions asked. Trust me.'

Joel suspected Aunt Sophia was the pint-size, raucous old Greek lady who had been ogling and cooing at the young male waiters all night.

Joel nodded. 'I'll see what I can do.'

Chris slapped him on the shoulder. 'That's why you're on

my shortlist. You come to me with solutions. Goodnight, mate.'

Joel held up a hand as Chris retreated, then dropped it by his side in defeat when he was out of sight.

Joel had a feeling there were no solutions when it came to Em, only questions. If Em threw the offer back in his face, well, at least he'd tried to make good on his promise.

For the first time that night, Joel grinned to himself. He wasn't someone that gave up easily, and Joel suspected half the fun would be in trying to convince the spirited beauty that she needed a man to escort her home. She'd probably take it as an insult.

For reasons Joel didn't quite yet understand, his pulse spiked at the thought of her being annoyed with him, and he set off to find her.

Chapter Five

EM WAS JUST ABOUT to exit via the side entrance when she felt a presence behind her. Damn it. She'd been caught trying to leave. The only way to leave a wedding early with this many Greek guests was to sneak out. Actually going over to people and saying goodbye was the kiss of death. The next thing you knew, you'd wind up on the dance floor traditional Greek dancing despite your better judgement.

It was a man's presence, judging by the scent. Woodsy and warm with a hint of spice. Oh crap. She knew that scent.

Em whirled on Joel. 'What do you want?'

Joel raised both of his hands in a peace gesture. 'Whoa. I didn't mean to scare you.'

'You didn't scare me,' Em hissed. 'But you're ruining my escape.'

'I was planning on leaving now, too.'

She narrowed her eyes at him. She suspected this was some sort of evil ploy given he wanted to work with her father, but right now she didn't care. It was more important to take her chance and leave while she still could.

She grabbed him by the lapels of his suit and his eyebrows leapt upward in surprise. Then she pushed him roughly through the door off to their left.

Out in the hallway, she looked left and right. Thank God. There were no stray guests mingling that might see them.

'Come on,' she said in a low voice. 'If you want to get out of here before midnight, I suggest you hurry up.'

Joel kept pace beside her as she power walked along the hallway in her stilettos. She considered kicking them off, but it would take too much time to stop and pick them up.

'It's only eleven now,' Joel told her.

'My point exactly.'

'Why do I get the feeling you've done this before?'

'Because you're a smart man, that's why.' Em hadn't meant to compliment him. It had just come out.

They reached the end of the hallway and Em halted before they turned the corner to the foyer. Joel stopped beside her.

'What is it?' he asked.

'Shh. Can you hear that?'

They listened as the sound of voices carried towards them. Em risked a look around the corner. As she'd suspected, a few women were returning from the bathroom. Em tapped her foot impatiently on the carpet as they waited.

When it was quiet again, Em tugged Joel's sleeve, and they hurried across the empty foyer out the front door into the cool night air. She didn't wait to see if he followed and headed along the driveway at the same quick pace.

'Em! Wait,' Joel whispered. 'Where are you going?'

She kept walking. 'Outside. To the next block if I can make it, to call an Uber.'

'Why on earth?'

'Because,' Em told him, 'this isn't my first rodeo. Waiting

out the front of the reception venue for a ride doesn't guarantee you'll be there to accept that ride when it comes. Trust me.'

'I'm lost.'

She knew he wasn't referring to where they were. 'Let's just say you can still end up drunk and singing along to bad eighties songs half an hour after your Uber was due to pick you up if you're not careful. It's best to remain out of sight and not talk to anyone.'

'This is a Greek thing, isn't it?'

Em shrugged, her heels clicking loudly as she walked. 'Who knows? It's an extended family thing, at least. Anyway, why are you still here? You don't need to follow me anymore.'

They reached the end of the driveway facing the busy main road with three lanes of traffic flowing in either direction. Em breathed a sigh of relief tinged with exhaust fumes.

'Freedom,' she muttered, then turned to Joel. 'Seriously, I helped you escape, now it's best if we split up in case we look like wedding guests.'

His lips curled in that almost smile that Em was now recognising as a Joel thing.

'You're wearing a bright blue bridesmaid dress.'

'It's not like I'm carrying my bouquet.'

'Here.' He shrugged off his suit jacket and went to put it over her shoulders, but she jumped out of his reach in alarm.

'What are you doing?'

He tilted his head. 'Disguising you.'

'I don't need—'

At that exact moment a carload of idiots whizzed past and yelled out the window at her.

'Marry me, sweetheart!'

Em assumed they were young men, but they were obviously idiots whatever age they were. She glared at the retreating car, which gave Joel the opportunity to drop his jacket onto her shoulders. Damn her bright hair. It always made her noticeable, but she supposed the stupid dress didn't help either.

'Fine,' she said. 'Can we just walk? The further away we are from here, the better.'

She fished her phone out of her bag while they walked and opened the Uber app.

Joel captured her wrist gently. So gently, that his fingers barely brushed the delicate skin. Her pulse jumped erratically, and she reflexively let go of her phone.

Joel caught it easily, and in one swift motion slipped it into his trouser pocket.

Em skidded to a stop on the pavement, her heels wobbling precariously under her. 'What did you do that for? Give me my phone back.'

'I'm driving you home. I promised your father.'

Em's jaw dropped open. 'No way. Now give me my phone back.'

Joel studied her openly under the fluorescent streetlight. 'He was quite insistent.'

'I'm sure he was,' Em ground out. 'But I'm a grown woman and—'

'Or if not, apparently Aunt Sophia needs escorting home.' He gestured with his thumb in the direction of the reception venue behind them. 'So I can call you an Uber and go back and get her if you like.'

Em's glare turned into something more dangerous. 'You wouldn't.'

He grinned and his teeth flashed at her. Big Bad Wolf, indeed. It did strange things to her stomach.

'I would,' he returned easily.

Em put a hand on her hip. 'You really want to win this contract, don't you?'

He appeared to consider her words. 'Yes, but that's not what this is about.'

She let out a huff of frustration. 'Bullshit. That's the only thing this is about.'

He kept staring at her, and Em shifted uncomfortably on her heels.

'I wouldn't let you go home by yourself either,' he said softly, so softly she almost didn't hear him against the roar of traffic.

'Oh, great. Another traditionalist, just like my father. I should have known.' She huffed for the second time and looked around. 'Let's get it over with then. Where's your damn car?'

He caught her wrist again and this time his fingers slid down to thread their way through hers, leaving a trail of fire in their wake. She stared in shock at their hands woven together. She should shake him off, but somehow Em didn't have the willpower to do so. His confidence should have been off-putting. She hated arrogant guys with a passion. But for some strange reason, his hand holding hers didn't feel like a gesture of arrogance. It felt more like an act of good faith.

He waited until she looked up again to speak.

'It's not traditionalist to want to keep something precious safe. It's just common sense.'

Em blinked and looked down at their hands again, then looked away at the cars passing them on the road because that seemed safer.

'Fine,' she said again. 'Where's your car then?'

He tugged her hand gently, indicating they should walk again. 'Parked just around the corner and up one block.'

They walked in silence, still holding hands. Em frowned.

She couldn't recall the last time she'd held hands with a guy. Maybe in high school or during her undergraduate degree? She'd had a couple of steady boyfriends back then—mainly to keep her dear old dad happy. But since then, all the men in her life were transient. They kissed. They had sex. But affection wasn't part of the deal. What was the point in having affection when the relationship wasn't serious?

The realisation had Em quickly removing her hand from Joel's, and she pretended to adjust his jacket like she was worried that it might slip off. She felt his eyes watching her, but he didn't say anything. Em dropped her hand to her side, her fingers still tingling.

As they kept walking, Em tried to guess the sort of car a guy like Joel drove. Something European, like an Audi, BMW or a Mercedes, she suspected. Something that communicated executive style and success. Whether he was successful or not, Em had no idea, but guys who drove those sorts of cars liked to think they were successful.

They turned the corner when they reached the end of the next block, and Em saw Joel reach into his pocket. A moment later a car up ahead flashed and beeped. Joel led her to it and Em stared at the car, and then him, in surprise.

'That's yours?'

'Last time I checked.'

Em turned to study the car again. It was a light silver blue and Em had to admit it was gorgeous. 'It's a Porsche 911, am I right? I don't know much about cars, but I'm guessing it's a classic. I always noticed this model when I was a kid due to the round headlights.'

Joel reached down and opened the door for her. 'She's a 1982 911 coupe. And yes, she's a classic.'

Joel waited while Em lowered herself into the front passenger seat. The smell of old but well-cared-for leather hit her nostrils, and she found herself grinning as she surveyed the dash. It was all so nineteen-eighties, but gosh it was cool.

He got into the driver's seat and Em looked over at him.

'What is it with giving cars a female identity? I've never gotten that.'

'Something this beautiful? It's got to be female.'

Without waiting for her reply, Joel started the engine. It didn't roar to life as Em expected it might. It purred.

'If you're used to luxurious, this isn't that,' Joel told Em over the warm thrum of the engine. 'She's more about enjoying the drive.'

With that, he pulled out smoothly and Em fell silent, listening to the sound of the engine. She could never recall noticing how a car sounded before, but something about this car made her want to listen.

She darted a glance in Joel's direction. He looked comfortable in the driver's seat. At ease. It made Em realise that he hadn't been at ease earlier in the night. He'd been in control and confident, but not at ease.

'Do you drive this car all the time?' she asked.

'Mostly. I've got another more practical vehicle, but I drive this whenever I can.'

Em found herself wondering what "a more practical vehicle" looked like, then silently reprimanded herself for letting her thoughts get away from her.

'I haven't told you where I live. It's—'

'On the headland at Freshwater, I know.'

Em twisted in her seat to face him. 'Please tell me my father told you that?'

'I already told you. I'm the Big Bad Wolf.'

She swallowed as he flashed that wicked smile again, an unexpected thrill travelling down her spine. Em turned back to the road and eased back into her seat.

'Yeah, alright,' he said, grinning at her with more humour than wickedness this time. 'He told me. You can relax. I'm not some creepy stalker.'

'No. I didn't think you were,' Em told him, and sneaked a look at his profile for a quick second.

A strong nose, but from this angle she registered with a shock that it wasn't quite straight. Had it been broken at some point, perhaps?

She returned her focus to the road. No, Joel Scott certainly wasn't creepy in any way. But was he dangerous?

Something twisted again in Em's belly, curling then unfurling suspiciously like desire, and it told her that he might be very dangerous indeed.

Chapter Six

EM SMELLED of sweet jasmine and the ocean. Joel figured it was her, because usually the scent of the Porsche's leather overpowered everything else.

Joel glanced at Em as he checked the road for traffic. He was relieved that she didn't look uncomfortable. More curious than uncomfortable, anyway.

Joel still wasn't sure what had possessed him to hold her hand before. It hadn't been a conscious decision. Her hand was there, and he'd simply felt compelled to. Like he felt compelled to stare at her now, but that would be weird, so he made another attempt at conversation.

'What's it like living near the beach?' he asked. Joel generally hated small talk, but he was prepared to make an exception if it gave him some further insight into what Em was like.

Em kept her gaze fixed out the window. 'Nice, I guess.'

Joel waited a beat before replying, then figured *to hell with polite conversation*. Em hadn't seemed all that concerned about niceties earlier in the night.

'You do realise you live in a penthouse overlooking the Pacific Ocean, don't you?' he asked.

Em sighed and turned to face him. 'It hasn't escaped my notice, but I usually try not to dwell on it.'

Joel fell silent and returned his focus to the road.

'That makes me sound like a spoiled daddy's girl, doesn't it?' she said.

'I didn't say that.'

'Trust me, that's why I don't think too hard about where I live, or I'll throw the keys at my father and flounce off to some inner-city dive to make a point. But I've been there, done that.'

'I know I started the conversation, but you don't have to explain yourself to me.'

Em fell silent again, and Joel wondered what she was thinking.

'You're not judging me,' she said after a while. It was a statement rather than a question.

'Why would I judge you?'

'Because most people do.'

'When you've been judged yourself, you learn not to do the same thing to others.'

Em looked over at him in surprise. 'What would people have to judge you about?'

Joel chewed his bottom lip. He'd said too much. It had been a long time since he'd said too much to someone about his past. But he was well practised at deflecting attention, so he simply shrugged. 'I don't know. People who judge always find something.'

'You've got that right.'

Em didn't seem to notice that he'd slipped up and said something he wasn't planning on.

She tapped her finger thoughtfully on the door handle. 'When I first started my university degree, everyone was really complimentary because Ana had chosen not to go. "Oh, isn't that nice, dear," they'd say. Then when I went on to do my Masters, I'd get looks of confusion as if to say, "hasn't she studied enough?" By the time I decided on my PhD, I'd become an academic too scared to get a job in their minds. Or worse, I should be settling down and not focusing so hard on my studies. I can't win.'

'No, you can't. That's why you ignore them.'

Em arched an eyebrow in his direction. 'Easy for you to say. You're not related to my father.'

No, his family situation had been way more fucked up.

Instead, he said, 'True. What does your mum think?'

Em sighed again. 'Mum's more understanding than Dad. She'd still like me to find a guy and settle down, but she understands my desire to study. She always wanted to, but never had the chance. So she supports me. But quietly.'

'While your dad is louder?'

'Ooh, yeah. You got that? And for the record, I did live in an inner-city dive during my undergraduate degree.'

Joel cocked his head to one side. 'Nope, I can't imagine it.'

'What was that about not judging?' she threw back, but didn't sound offended.

Joel realised that was one of the things he liked so much about her. She had a thick skin.

'Promise me you didn't go all alternative, too?' he joked.

Em's lips curled. 'No, I didn't have the time. I was too busy studying and working late nights at a grocery store to pay the rent on the shitty terrace house I shared with five other people.'

'You just described my undergraduate degree,' he said.

'It sucks, right? I was tired and hungry all the time, and I still can't stand the smell of two-minute noodles.' She shuddered as if to make her point.

'It's burgers and fries for me. I worked in a burger joint to get by, and that damn oil smell gets me every time.'

Em nodded. 'My grades started to suffer. That's why I was weak and relented when Dad wanted to mollycoddle me. I already knew I wanted to do a Masters degree, but if I didn't perform well, I'd ruin my chance.'

'Wanting to achieve something isn't weak,' Joel pointed out.

'Maybe not. But I didn't put up as much of a fight as I should have. When Daddy dearest learned of my living situation, he was horrified. He'd been depositing a monthly allowance into my bank account that I refused to touch.'

'I wouldn't have thought attempting to support yourself was a bad thing.'

'When it involves working in an area renowned for junkies and brothels, it's not great.' Em shrugged. 'I never really minded it. I avoided the junkies, but the girls came into the supermarket and most of them were nice. The brothels were all legit, and it was a career for most of them. They'd walk me home sometimes to make sure I got there safely.'

Joel's chest constricted at the thought of Em walking home alone late at night in that sort of area. He knew what it would have been like because he'd lived in places exactly the same growing up.

Joel glanced in Em's direction when it was safe to take his eyes off the road. 'Did your dad know about that?'

'Not the girls that I befriended—he probably would have had a coronary—but he found out about the area. I might have told him a white lie about where I was living when I first moved out.'

Joel swallowed a laugh, and Em shot him a grin.

'It was my little sis who sold me out,' she said. 'We tell each other everything, and she slipped up.' Em raised a shoulder in an offhand shrug. 'I can never stay mad at her.'

'Is that when your dad gave you the penthouse?' Joel asked.

'Not straightaway. I'm weak, but not that weak. He ordered me to come home, but I refused. There was no way I could live and study under the same roof with him—we'd just get on each other's nerves too much. So I relented and quit the grocery store job and used the allowance he gave me, but I still didn't move out of the shitty house. Then Ana got married, and he "gifted" them a house. The next thing I know he's handing me the keys to my penthouse, saying he wants to keep it as an investment and I may as well live in it.'

'Wow. Maybe you should be stubborn more often.'

'It's not forever,' Em said firmly. 'Just until I finish my PhD. Once I have full-time work, I'll find my own place. I've already started applying to places.'

'With your expertise I'd have thought you could stay working in the university system?'

Em screwed up her nose. Joel found the expression immeasurably cute, but he didn't dare tell her that.

'I could, I suppose. But the reason I've studied what I have is so I can encourage change. I believe I'm better off doing that in the commercial world.'

'Do you have any commercial experience?' Joel asked.

'None,' Em said bluntly. 'Unless you count customer service in a grocery store.'

Joel gripped the steering wheel tighter. Chris's protectiveness of his eldest daughter might be understandable, but he'd really done her a disservice. As the daughter of one of the city's biggest developers, Em could have been working part-time for him and gaining valuable corporate experience.

'How heavy is your PhD workload at the moment? Do you have time to work part-time?'

'In another few weeks I will. Like I said, I'm already looking.'

'Our sustainability consulting arm of the business is growing. I've got a woman leading it who is extremely capable, but we need someone to work under her. Why don't you come in and talk to her sometime?'

The GPS indicated that Em's building was a few hundred metres up the road, so Joel slowed the Porsche. He brought it to a stop near what looked to be the driveway to her complex. When he pulled on the park brake and twisted to face her, she was staring at him.

'Yes?' he asked.

Her eyes narrowed at him. 'You're only saying that because you want to win this contract with my father.'

'Yes, I do want your father's contract. But no, that's not why I'm saying it.'

'I don't believe you.'

Joel gave her what he hoped was a level look, trying to hide his own surprise at the offer he'd made spontaneously. He was rarely spontaneous.

'I'm not offering you a job,' he clarified. 'Just an opportunity to talk. We need to learn more about your research. You need to see if what we do interests you.'

Her eyes were still narrowed. 'I suppose it's unlikely to come to anything. Plus, if you really wanted to look good to my father, you'd offer me your hand in marriage, not a job.'

Joel released a tight breath. 'Are you always this suspicious of people?'

'Only when it comes to things related to my father.'

'Fine. Don't come and talk to us. It makes no difference to me.'

'Are you always this indifferent?' she shot back.

Joel may have been wrong, but in the dark of the cabin he thought he saw her eyes glinting with a challenge.

'Calm and indifference aren't the same thing,' he replied, looking out the window and easing back into the driver's seat to give her some space.

His statement was ironic given the way his heart was dancing wildly in his chest. If he'd been calm, there was no way he would have suggested that she come to his office. He would have determined that it was a bad idea given the link to her father. While Em might claim he'd suggested it for that exact reason, Joel knew if things didn't go well with Chris—or Em—the situation could blow up in his face.

But of course he hadn't thought about it, because the fact that she was sitting less than a foot away was doing crazy things to him. It was probably just as well that she'd refused his offer. Now he could say goodbye and try to forget about how his body reacted to this woman. Try being the operative word.

'Joel?'

It was the first time she'd addressed him by name, and the way it sounded coming from her lips didn't settle any of the craziness still crackling like electricity through him.

'Yes?' He didn't turn towards her.

She reached over and touched his thigh tentatively to get his attention. Joel's pulse spiked and he felt himself harden. He tried not to shift in the seat. He wished like hell he was wearing his jacket, but it was still covering her shoulders.

He met her eyes again, his crotch painfully tight, but fortunately she was focused on his face.

'You know,' she said softly, 'I've never once liked any of the men my father has introduced me to.'

Joel stayed silent. Despite the obvious tension in the car, he had no idea if he was included in the category of men that she was referring to.

Her hand hovered in the space between them, like she wanted to touch him again. He didn't so much suck in a breath as stop breathing altogether.

'But you're different,' she murmured, 'and I'm not sure why.'

He caught her hand and lowered it onto her lap. Let go. 'Probably best not to overthink it.'

'Probably,' she agreed. 'It's weird. I don't know anything about you, so I can't explain why you're different.'

'No,' he said, his voice low.

If she did know about him—really know about him—she wouldn't be happy about the differences. This train of thought served to ease some of the discomfort below his belt.

Her gaze dropped to his hand, which was now resting on the gear stick.

'Good strong hands,' she observed. 'I can see those hands building a house, not designing one.'

'I did.' He swore silently. Why had he said that? That period of his life was something he didn't need to draw attention to.

'When?' she asked.

'I worked on a few building sites before I started my degree. It made me realise I'd rather design houses than build them.'

'So you did.'

'So I did.'

She smiled at him, and Joel suddenly knew what it was like to be an ice cube on a hot day. The temperature must have fried his brain, because he didn't stop to think about his next words.

'Do you have a bathroom that I can use?'

Em blinked. 'Sure. You can use mine if you want. Or is that just your way of asking to see my apartment so you can critique my dad's work?'

It was neither. Joel discreetly readjusted his collar. He hadn't been thinking that strategically. The only thing he'd been thinking was that his skin was boiling hot and he needed some fresh air. Then it occurred to him that his request could be construed as something else equally strategic but less honourable, like trying to invite himself into her apartment to be close to her.

'If you're not comfortable, I can go elsewhere,' he told her.

Her smile returned, reaching those blue eyes, and they appeared to glow in the moonlight. 'If I wasn't comfortable, I wouldn't offer. Big bad wolves don't scare me.'

Joel nodded and looked away, then grabbed the keys from the ignition. Em bent down to grab her clutch, and they got out of the car in silence.

Only Joel's thoughts weren't silent, and he wished for an internal volume control.

He knew he'd never let Em get to know him well enough to know the truth. But it still didn't stop him from thinking that old, well-worn thought that haunted him like a recurring nightmare.

Yet. She isn't scared of me yet.

Chapter Seven

EM WAS FAIRLY certain that Joel hadn't invited himself into her apartment for dishonest reasons. His request to use the bathroom had seemed genuine.

Then why did lust-filled thoughts keep entering her mind?

Like when they were in the lift together, she imagined stepping in front of him and placing her hands on his hips. Then she would draw him against her to see what his chest felt like pressed against her breasts. If the cut of his shirt was anything to go by, his expanse of chest would feel muscled and firm.

Or when he followed her out into the hallway from the lift. There she imagined him hooking an arm around her waist from behind and capturing her to lay his lips on the back of her neck.

By the time Em unlocked the front door, she was almost panting. This was why she didn't look back as she kicked her heels off and pointed in the direction of the guest bathroom off to the right.

She heard Joel close the bathroom door with a gentle click, and Em released a tight breath as she entered the open-plan living and kitchen area. She went straight to the floor-to-ceiling glass sliding doors and pushed them open so she could step outside onto the balcony overlooking the ocean.

The cool sea breeze made goosebumps appear on her bare arms, but Em didn't care, she just needed the fresh air.

She'd never been attracted to a man her father had suggested before. Ever.

Em's stubborn streak should have ensured that this fact alone would prevent her from thinking about Joel romantically. But as her thoughts in the lift and hall had already proven, she was most certainly entertaining the idea.

Em heard the bathroom door open and she didn't turn around. 'I'm out here,' she called back to Joel.

Not long after Joel had stepped onto the balcony beside her, he whistled quietly.

Em glanced over at him. 'OK, so I might have lied a bit. I do kind of like living here.'

He kept looking at the Pacific Ocean. Tonight it appeared to be slumbering beneath a clear but moonless sky. Despite the gentle breeze—there was always a breeze up here—the night air was calm, and the sound of the waves meeting the sand below was a soft hush.

'How do you lie a bit?' Joel asked. 'Either you're lying or you're telling the truth.'

'Rookie,' Em teased him. 'I spent my teenage years perfecting the art of truthful lies. Like, "Dad, I'm spending the night at Rach's house. Yes, her parents will be there". The fact that *we* wouldn't be, and we were going to a party down the road that Dad would never let me attend, was beside the point.'

'Sneak,' Joel shot back. 'So you were a rebellious teen?'

'I was never a true rebel. I lived in a loving, supportive home, so I didn't go too crazy. I always kept my grades up and mixed with the "nice" girls. I just had an overprotective father, particularly when it came to boys.'

'Uh oh.'

Em smiled, recalling a humorous memory from the past. 'At my sixteenth birthday party, my father did a toast announcing that I was sweet sixteen and never been kissed. My girlfriends and I dissolved into fits of giggles. We pretended it was because we were embarrassed about my dad talking about me kissing boys instead of the fact that I'd been dating boys without him knowing since I was thirteen.'

Joel's lips curved into a slow smile, and Em turned to focus on the water again. Gosh, what was it about that smile? Part wicked and part good guy all rolled into one. Em couldn't decide which part she liked more.

'How about you?' she asked. 'Were you a rebellious teenager?'

Em sensed something in Joel shift. It was like a cloud had cast a shadow over them, but the sky remained clear.

'I did my fair share of lying. Mainly to get by. I didn't grow up in as loving a family as you did. I don't like to talk about it.'

'I'm sorry.' It was an obvious response, but Em still meant it. 'Do you keep in touch with any of your family?'

'Both of my parents are dead, and that leaves me and my sister. We're not close.'

Em's skin prickled, feeling colder all of a sudden. *Dead*. Not "passed away", Em noted. Like death hadn't just taken them, but they were actually dead to him.

'I'm sorry,' Em said again. 'I must seem all the more spoiled complaining about my dad. We do love each other, for what it's worth. Most of the time, anyway,' she added, trying to lighten the mood, because it was obvious Joel wasn't keen to revisit his past.

'Yeah, I got that. Don't worry. And I don't think you're spoiled.'

'What *do* you think of me?' Em asked.

The question hung in the air between them.

Em pressed her lips together so that she didn't say anything else. She was known for her honesty, but this was bold even compared to her usual behaviour. She was obviously fishing—not for compliments, exactly. But Em wanted to know—no, *needed* to know—what this man thought of her before the night was over. That way she could return to life as normal tomorrow morning.

Em had already determined that Joel's quiet confidence meant that he'd be honest with her. Plus, she was almost certain he'd figured out that she wasn't offended by frank discussion.

So if he could just tell her that perhaps she was too young —he was obviously in his thirties. Or too outspoken. Or too bold. Whatever it was, once it was out in the open then she could relegate him to being like all those other men and move on. Because frankly, the curiosity was killing her like the proverbial cat, and the sooner he dismissed her the better. That way she could conclude her thoughts were fun little fantasies and nothing more. It wasn't like he'd actually enter- tain the idea of sleeping with her given the contract her father was dangling in front of him, anyway.

Joel pivoted silently to face her and tilted his head to one side.

'What do I think of you?' he whispered, more to himself than her. 'I think you're dangerous.'

Em stiffened and blinked at him, because that was the same thought she'd had about him in the car earlier. 'Me? You're the one calling yourself the Big Bad Wolf.'

'Yes, but I've made no secret of that. You? You're wrapped up in a million contradictions.'

Em raised her eyebrows at him. 'I've been called plenty of things before, but never a contradiction. I'm not sure I follow.'

There was that slow smile again. 'See? This is why you're so dangerous. Most women would be offended by this point, but you? That clever brain of yours wants to know why so that you can analyse the answer and make your own mind up.'

'Well, I *am* an academic,' Em drawled, making a joke out of it, but secretly pleased by his response.

He shook his head. 'Not for long. You'll hit the ground running in the commercial world before you know it.'

'Do you think?'

Joel's dark eyes became more intense. 'You doubt it?'

'I don't doubt it. It's just that I haven't been there like you yet. It's the unknown, I suppose.'

'You're impressive in every way, Em. A future employer will see that.'

'Thank you,' Em said, genuinely flattered, but then she narrowed her eyes at him. 'Don't think that you can throw compliments at me to escape explaining your original answer. Why am I a contradiction?'

Joel laughed, soft and low, and Em resisted sighing at the sound. If she was the curious cat, right now the Big Bad Wolf was stroking her.

Joel stepped in closer and Em's breath hitched.

'You're captivating, but frustrating,' he said.

She released a huff. Honest. She liked honest. 'Go on.'

'You're highly intelligent, but still a little innocent.'

This time Em laughed. 'Yeah, I'm not sure my last hook-up would agree with you on that one.'

Joel's eyes were so dark in the dim light she couldn't tell

where his irises were. 'You're experienced when it comes to men, but your heart is still pure, then.'

Em's smile faded. 'That sounds like something someone would say if their heart had been tainted.'

His expression stayed unreadable. 'We're talking about you.'

'You don't like talking about yourself.'

'No.'

They continued to stare at each other, and the breeze turned warm somehow. When he lowered his eyes to her mouth, Em instinctively bit her lower lip.

'Don't do that,' he told her softly.

She released her lip. 'Why?'

'Because it makes me want to kiss you.'

Honesty. When had a man been so honest with her? The guys she hooked up with were fun, but they always danced around the truth. Usually because they weren't into long-term relationships and they were practised at lying to girls on a regular basis. It's not that they were bad guys, necessarily. Just scared that she'd turn out to be a clingy woman despite making it clear that wasn't who she was.

She threw some of that honesty right back at him. 'Then why don't you kiss me?'

His eyes returned to her face. 'You know why.'

'My father,' she replied flatly.

'Yes.'

Despite the tug of disappointment in her stomach, his answer told her something very interesting. It was so interesting that the tug of disappointment morphed into a surge of desire.

'You don't want a relationship,' she stated, rather than asked.

'No.'

'You don't want to court me. Because that's what my father wants. For a man to court me like an old-fashioned romance story.'

'No,' was all he said. His eyes were still unfathomably dark, and Em found them fascinating.

'But you do want to kiss me,' she concluded.

His gaze returned to her lips. A beat of silence passed. 'Yes.'

She wanted the very same thing, and to hell with her father wanting a man to treat her like a piece of property to be bought and sold.

'I want to kiss you, too,' she announced.

Neither of them moved.

'Do you want to know why?' she asked him.

The side of his mouth twitched. 'I think you're going to tell me.'

'Damn right I am. Because you're sexy and you're smart. And I didn't know I liked classic cars until I saw you driving one, but it makes you unquestionably cool, which makes me sound like a teenage girl, but so be it.'

'You don't know anything about me,' he said, and there was that dark cloud again.

'I know enough. I know you're not some horrible architect just out to make money, and that you actually care about how what you create impacts the environment. And I can see you're worried that some of your Big Bad Wolf vibe is going to rub off on me, but don't worry, I'm not as sweet as I look.'

'No, you're not, are you?' he said. 'You're . . .' He stepped in closer again.

'I'm what?' Em challenged. 'I'll take intelligent. I'll even agree with you that I'm a contradiction. But that's not enough to make you want to kiss me. So what am I then?'

'You're . . .' He reached over and cupped her cheek in his hand, then ran his thumb lightly over her lips.

Em inhaled a ragged breath, her chest rising and falling in response. When he ran his thumb back over her mouth a second time, she moved her tongue out to stroke it.

He paused and looked at her again. She could make out his pupils now he was so close and they were impossibly wide. He wasn't so scary after all. Just so seductive that it hurt.

'You're . . .'

He glanced down at his thumb pressed against her bottom lip, his forehead creasing as though he couldn't quite make sense of her. He met her eyes again. Em was sure hers held a challenge.

He cleared his throat softly. 'You're devastating.'

It wasn't the answer she was expecting. In fact, Em had no idea what she expected his answer to be. But she was pretty sure it was far better than anything she could have dreamed up.

So Em kissed him.

Chapter Eight

JOEL HAD no idea what he'd been thinking touching Em. Stroking her cheek like that. When she'd flicked her tongue out and licked him, he'd discovered that he wasn't capable of thought anymore.

Then she'd kissed him.

It was like his entire world evaporated. After one hell of a dangerous explosion that he was lucky to survive. Because that's what she was. Dangerous. Devastating.

And he wanted more. Not just more, but as much as he could handle.

They shifted together towards the glass doors, still kissing, like they were performing a silent dance whose moves they already knew. When they reached the doors, Joel pressed Em up against the cool glass.

Holy hell. Those lips. That tongue. He was breathless and in need of oxygen, but he needed Em more.

She kissed him confidently, like she was sure of her appeal. Or perhaps she was just as lost as he was, and he found himself secretly hoping that was the case. Her kisses were deep and dizzying. He stroked her face and her neck. Buried his fingers in her auburn hair, setting a few pins loose so they fell with a metallic tinkle onto the balcony tiles.

Em moaned softly as his hands caressed her back, following the curve of her spine. The dress was backless, revealing a tantalising view of her fair skin, and she inhaled a ragged breath as his fingers travelled lower.

She arched against him, and in response he gripped her hips tightly, his arousal painful. Em moaned again, this time throwing him a killer smile, those blue eyes sparkling in the moonlight.

'I want you,' she whispered.

Jesus. He'd only just met her, and it made no sense, but he wanted her, too. The only thing that he'd ever come close to wanting this much was the drugs he'd been tempted to try to lose himself to when he was a teenager, and Em was better than any drug.

Her hands came down to rest on his hips, and she pressed so hard against him that he could feel the outline of her panties.

'Shit.' He broke off their kiss and stepped back before he lost control completely. He wasn't sure if it was the memory of his past or the taste of her that scared him more.

Em's lips were swollen and even more devastating than before. 'What?'

'We can't,' he said gruffly. 'Your father—'

'Doesn't need to know,' she finished firmly. 'How we choose to entertain ourselves is our own business.'

His eyebrows rose. 'Entertain ourselves? Is that what you call this?'

'Yes.' She reached over and trailed a finger down his cheek.

He caught her wrist. 'I knew you were dangerous.'

'You don't want a relationship. I don't want a relationship. What's dangerous about that?' she said simply.

What she said was true, yet he still hesitated. There was nothing wrong with mutual pleasure between consenting adults. The women he occasionally sought out always held similar beliefs to Em. No strings, just pleasure. But Joel was having trouble assigning that role to the woman standing in front of him despite what she said, and he wasn't sure why.

'Joel.' Em stepped in and slipped her hands behind his neck. 'No one needs to know. What happens between us stays between us.'

He closed his eyes and breathed in her intoxicating scent. That hint of jasmine and the freshness of the ocean filled his nostrils. It seemed more intense somehow, but that could have been from the actual ocean. Whatever it was, it was infiltrating all his senses, not to mention his defences.

She pressed her forehead to his. 'What do you say?'

'The things I want to do to you . . .' He let his voice trail off.

So far, they'd joked about him being the Big Bad Wolf, but the risk of her actually discovering the darkness in his soul made him experience a panic he hadn't felt in years.

'I can't promise I'll be gentle.'

She eased back, her eyes impossibly bright in the dim light. They revealed no fear, and she smiled. 'I don't want you to be.'

'Fuck, Em. You deserve—' *Someone better than me*, he wanted to say, but she placed two fingers over his lips.

'I'm no shrinking violet, Joel Scott. I know what I like, and I'll tell you so. And I want you. Trust me.'

The war he'd been waging inside himself settled, but he asked again anyway. 'Are you sure?'

She tugged gently on his tie. 'Come inside.'

Then she turned and stepped into the apartment.

'I'll be in the bedroom,' she called after him, and disappeared down the hall.

Joel stood on the balcony, inhaling the smell of the ocean to calm himself. It didn't smell the same without Em here.

He could still leave. He still had the chance to put this down to a momentary lapse of judgement.

He swiped a hand across his face. Joel had a feeling this wasn't what Chris had in mind when it came to "getting to know" his daughter.

He swore to himself. If he did this, he could risk the entire contract. As stunningly beautiful and alluring as Em was, there was nothing more important to Joel than his business.

No one needs to know.

But if Joel wasn't going to say anything, and Em wasn't going to say anything, then what was the harm? Joel had a feeling there was a great deal that Em's father didn't know about her. Besides, it was one night.

'You're insane,' Joel muttered to himself, then stepped inside. If his mind wasn't fully made up, his body already was.

EM HEARD footfalls coming down the hall and forced herself to release a breath. Logically, she knew that if Joel rejected her she would survive—but tell that to the rest of her.

Joel appeared in her bedroom doorway. 'Em?'

'Yes?' She tried to keep her voice neutral and looked over at him from her position sitting on the edge of her bed.

'I'll stay. But what happens here tonight stays between us.'

'Agreed.'

They both rushed for each other and met in the middle of the floor, centimetres apart, but didn't touch.

Joel reached over and brushed a strand of stray hair away

from Em's forehead, then leaned in so his lips grazed her earlobe.

'So apparently you know what you want and what you like. Mind enlightening me?'

Em hid a grin and stepped back, then turned so her back was to him. 'First things first. I need help getting out of this dress.'

'I can do that.'

They were standing opposite her full-length mirror, and Em watched as he found the zipper at her side and undid it. Em shrugged off the shoulder straps and stepped out of the dress. She didn't turn around.

Em watched his eyes darken in the mirror as they roamed her body. There wasn't much to the lace panties, and she wore no bra.

Joel stood close behind her and wound an arm around her waist so his palm rested on her stomach. In the reflection, the position appeared possessive. Em couldn't say why she liked it so much. Then he dropped his chin onto her shoulder.

'Now what?' he whispered.

She could feel the length of him pressing into her backside and her lips curled.

'I think you must have some idea,' she suggested.

'Too many to count,' he shot back lightly. 'But let's start with this.'

The hand on her stomach travelled downwards, disappearing beneath her panties. His fingers slid easily against her slick dampness. Rather than being embarrassed, Em tilted her hips to invite Joel to explore further.

He inhaled a tight breath, dropped his mouth onto her shoulder and bit down gently on the bare skin. Em squirmed as his finger slipped inside while he made lazy circles with his thumb.

'Do I taste good?' Em teased, wondering if she'd have bite marks on her skin.

Big Bad Wolf indeed.

Joel lifted his head and looked at her in the mirror, pinning her to the spot with his dark gaze. 'I don't know. Do you?'

He gave her a dangerous grin, then removed his hand and dropped to his knees in front of her.

Oh boy. She obviously didn't need to tell him what she wanted. He already had a pretty good idea.

He dragged her panties slowly down her legs, the deliberate motion making her ache with need.

Em kicked off the panties and waited.

And waited.

His eyes were taking her in, like he was memorising all the important details.

'So, um, you know what to do next, am I right?' she joked to hide her impatience.

'I think I've got some idea.'

He offered Em his hands, and she took them, her eyebrows raising in a question. Then he tugged her forward.

Em's mouth rounded in a silent "o" as his tongue found her. He was gentle. Gentler than she'd expected. He took his time, watching her to see what she liked. Em's hips bucked with need, and she thought she saw him smile.

He let go of her hands and held her from behind, increasing his pace, but it still wasn't enough for her. She moaned, a combination of desire and frustration.

'More,' she demanded.

Joel eased back on his heels and grinned at her. 'More?'

'That's what I said,' Em ground out.

He chuckled and inserted two fingers inside her, returning his mouth to her. Em sighed, but the sense of relief didn't last long. Soon she was rocking above him, desperate for him to go deeper, harder.

It made no sense. Outside he'd been intense, almost out of control. Now he was so patient and calm it was driving her crazy.

'It's not enough,' Em told him, grabbing his shoulders.

'I know.'

Em stilled. 'What did you just say?'

Joel stopped and looked up at her. This time there was no smile and his expression was serious. 'You heard me.'

Em gasped. She hadn't meant to. 'You're doing this deliberately?'

Joel stood slowly, not taking his eyes off her. 'You told me I had one night. You think I'm going to let you come easily?'

A surge of lust shimmered down her legs, and she shoved him lightly, not sure if she was annoyed or turned on. 'You bastard.'

'Really? Tell me you haven't been with guys before that go too hard, too fast.'

Em bit her lip. He had a valid point. 'That may be true, but that doesn't extend to torturing me. And you're still wearing your clothes.'

'Easily fixed.'

Em watched as Joel loosened his tie, not taking his eyes off her. What was it about those eyes? Em sensed that they held secrets, but right now he was making no secret of his desire for her. When he shrugged off his shirt, another flicker of lust shimmered through her. He was olive-skinned and toned, with a sprinkling of dark hair across his chest.

'More,' she told him.

'Bossy.' But he unhooked the belt on his pants, which was when Em's patience ran out.

She stepped in, shoving his hands out of the way, then

unzipped his trousers. They kissed again—quick, desperate kisses—as she thrust his clothes off. Once he was naked, she pushed him against the wardrobe door with a dull thud.

'Stay there,' she ordered, then turned to get a condom out of her bedside drawer.

'I wasn't finished with you yet,' he told her when she came back and handed him the packet.

'One night doesn't have to mean only once,' she shot back. 'We have plenty of time for that.'

If it was possible, his eyes darkened even more as he opened the packet and got ready for her.

Gosh, he was beautiful to look at. Muscled, but not over-done. It was like the practicality she'd sensed in him earlier in the night extended to his physical attributes, too.

'Come here,' he said softly, and Em all but threw herself into his arms.

He caught her with a muffled laugh and swallowed the sound with his mouth on hers. The feel of her bare skin on his shot waves of lust through her, but she just couldn't get close enough. She closed a hand around him, his firmness telling her everything she needed to know, and she ran her hand up and down the length of him.

He broke off the kiss and dropped his head against the wardrobe door, breathing hard.

Em couldn't explain it. Usually she liked to be in control, but the thirst she had for him made her want to be dominated by him. Taken by him. Wherever that would end up, she had no idea.

'Swap places,' she whispered, and they shuffled so she was facing the door.

She glanced over at him in the reflection of the mirror and saw him taking in the sight of her. Em arched her back. An invitation.

Joel blew out a long breath and ran a hand across his head. 'Are you trying to make me lose control?'

Em considered his question. 'In every way possible.'

Their eyes met in the mirror. Then he stepped in close so his arousal pressed against her.

Em arched further, and Joel swore. The tip of him found her, and when he hesitated, Em eased herself back onto him. He grabbed both of her hips and shuddered as he entered her. They were still for a long moment.

'So much for foreplay,' he growled into the back of her shoulder.

'Nonsense. What's tonight been? Foreplay is as much mental as physical.'

He growled again, and it reverberated through her like a warning. Em's answer was to push against him, positioning him deeper. With that, she sensed something in Joel snap. Whatever patience, whatever resolve he'd had, evaporated, and he pinned her to the door and drove into her. Again and again, deeper and deeper, punctuated by Em's little yips of pleasure.

Before long, sweat coated both of them and the tremors rocking her body made it difficult to stand.

'Oh, no you don't,' Joel whispered, and he caught her wrists, bringing them above her head. 'You're mine.'

She wasn't just his, she was lost altogether. She mewled like a satisfied cat as with every stroke of their lovemaking he reached the part of her that was longing for release. She squirmed impatiently. Dangerously close, but not close enough.

As if sensing she needed more, he kept hold of her wrists with one hand and dropped the other between her legs.

'Oh, yes,' Em breathed, bucking helplessly in front of him.

If Joel was out of control now, he didn't show it. He kept

stroking her inside and out like it was the only thing that mattered in the world.

When their eyes locked on to each other in the mirror, and Em registered what she was seeing, it uncovered another layer of craving she hadn't known existed. The sight of him, all powerful and hard, and her, rosy and flushed, twined together in the most erotic way, sent a shockwave of longing through her body.

'That's it,' he breathed. 'Keep watching what I'm doing to you. Don't take your eyes off the mirror. I want you to watch yourself come.'

Em was glad Joel was holding on to her because she might have slid to the floor. She was destroyed. He was destroying her, and nothing had ever felt so good. She writhed against him, and he met her stroke for stroke, insistent and uncompromising.

'*Oh. My. God.*'

It was too much. He was too much. But Em knew that meant she was close, and she surrendered to him.

As the need built, unfurled and overflowed, Em moaned long and loud, not caring who heard. She didn't take her eyes off the mirror like he'd instructed, and as she clenched around him, she saw his own need take control of him. He drove into her, wringing the last drops of pleasure from her, and in doing so, found his release. He dropped his hand down and gripped her waist like he was holding on for his life. Like he'd been destroyed, too.

When the aftershocks faded, they both looked at each other in the mirror. Em couldn't help her self-satisfied grin, and Joel huffed.

'Holy shit,' he said. 'If I move, I might fall over.'

Em's grin intensified. 'Come on, the bed's just over there. We can make it.'

They shuffled over to it together and then collapsed on top of it. Joel lay on his back, staring at the ceiling.

'Holy shit,' he said again. Then his expression flickered with something, and Em recognised it as that dark cloud she'd seen earlier. 'Did I hurt you?'

Em rolled onto her side to look at him. 'Did it sound like you hurt me?'

His face was serious. 'No. But how do you feel now?'

'Sublime.'

Joel released a tight laugh. 'I don't feel too bad either, come to think of it.'

Em lay on her back. 'You know, this might be the best wedding I've been to.'

Joel laughed properly. 'Me too. Shame we can't tell anyone about it.'

Em frowned at the ceiling. Damn it. She'd thought one night would be enough with this man. That she could get him out of her system and be done with him. The realisation that this was a one-off made her stomach clench.

She glanced over at him again. Well, the night was still young. She'd just have to make the most of it.

With that, she climbed on top of him, determined to make every moment with Joel count.

Chapter Nine

WHEN EM WOKE the following morning, she hurt. Not in the way Joel had feared, but in the best sort of way that spoke of a night that would be long remembered. She could still feel his fingers digging into her hips. His teeth on her shoulder. Em brought her hand to the shoulder in question, secretly hoping he might have left a mark as a sort of memento.

Em released a sigh. 'Now you're getting sentimental.'

She rolled over with a huff, deliberately ignoring the empty side of the bed. Em had no idea when Joel had left. They hadn't actually discussed it. She assumed he'd waited until she fell asleep or left before she woke up. Em wasn't remotely offended—it was pretty standard behaviour and she'd done it herself a few times when the roles were reversed. Yet this was the first time she recalled feeling a bit sad, which struck her as strange.

Ignoring the inexplicable sadness, she got up and headed for the kitchen. She'd have a shower in a minute, but first she needed a coffee and the ocean view so she could indulge in the post-coital glow still lingering in her system. She padded down the hall barefoot and stopped in shock when the view came into sight.

Out on the balcony, Joel sat cross-legged with his back to her.

What the hell?

A frisson of annoyance and maybe even a little bit of fear zipped up her spine. Not allowing herself to think, Em marched towards the open doors, ready to blast Joel for over-staying his welcome.

Em opened her mouth, then promptly shut it again when she registered the scene in front of her more closely. Her "what the hell?" became a silent "what on earth?" Em stood staring at the man who had brought her an unexpected amount of pleasure the previous night like she'd never seen him before.

He appeared to be meditating. His eyes were closed against the bright morning sunlight and his hands were resting on his knees. His breathing was slow and steady. She knew this because he wore only boxer shorts and his white shirt was open at the front, and she could see the rise and fall of his muscled chest. It was nothing like the ragged breaths he'd been drawing in and out last night.

Em stepped backwards silently, careful not to alert him to her presence. When she'd put enough distance between them to ensure that she hadn't disturbed him, she turned and went to sit on one of the stools next to her island bench.

Em watched Joel for a few minutes, fascinated. This wasn't quite the morning-after behaviour she'd expected. A couple of times she'd had guys smoke cigarettes out on her balcony, which she hated. One of her favourite guys, Armando, had become a regular thing a while back. But not a relationship, because he was Spanish and on a short-term visa. He had occasionally spoiled her by cooking breakfast.

But meditating? That was new.

Em had tried meditating a few times. Before a couple of big exams, or when she was going through some particularly rough patches with her father. She'd found it helped, but the habit had never really stuck. That Joel was meditating out on her balcony suggested it was more of a habit for him.

After five minutes, Em grew restless. She wasn't comfortable leaving him out here while she had a shower, in case he left without telling her. Em wasn't sure why that was a problem all of a sudden, but it was.

She decided to make coffee. It would involve some noise, but not what Em considered offensive noise, and it would at least alert Joel to her presence. So Em set to work, flicking her glance over to him every few seconds, waiting to see what happened. It felt like a reverse of the "freeze" game you played as a kid, but instead of everyone freezing when the music stopped, you waited for the other person to move.

When Em put a mug of coffee down on the bench, Joel angled his head left and right in a stretch, then rolled his shoulders backwards. She waited, full of curiosity, as he took his time standing. Finally, he turned towards the kitchen and when his eyes met hers, they were bright. Until now, Em never would have described his dark eyes as bright, but that's what they were.

'Hey,' he said. 'You're awake.'

'Hey,' she replied. 'You're still here.'

His lips quirked at her honesty, but she wasn't rewarded with a smile. It disappointed her somehow.

'Did you think I'd leave?' he asked.

Em shrugged, feeling cagey all of a sudden. 'Most guys would have.'

'I'm not most guys.'

No, he wasn't. A fact that hadn't escaped Em's notice.

'I'm not cooking you breakfast, just so we're clear,' she told him.

Another quirk of the lips. 'How about a coffee?'

She shoved the one in front of her towards him and turned to make another for herself. Em had no idea if milk with one sugar was how he liked it, but this was her apartment, and at this stage her hospitality only stretched so far.

'Were you meditating?' she asked. She wasn't embarrassed about what had happened between them last night, but for some reason she felt nervous. Maybe because in the morning light she worried that he wouldn't be as good as he'd seemed the night before.

'Thanks.' He came over to the island bench and sat on the stool facing her. 'Yes, sorry if it freaked you out, but you were still asleep and it's such a fantastic morning.'

'I'm not freaked out,' she said, turning back to face him with her own coffee. 'Why do you meditate?'

'Why does anyone meditate? It centres me, I guess.'

'And I threw you off centre?'

His eyes danced with laughter, but again his mouth didn't follow through with a smile. 'You could say that. It also helps me to be in the moment when I'm thinking too much.'

'And what were you thinking about this morning?'

The laughter in his eyes disappeared. 'You.'

Oh. It was a fair enough answer, Em supposed.

'And that it didn't feel right to leave,' he added. 'But maybe I should have.'

Em decided not to reply, because suddenly she wasn't sure what he should have done either.

Joel took a sip of the steaming coffee, continuing to look over the top of the mug at her. 'But I'm still here,' he said after he had swallowed. 'I'm not entirely sure why.'

'Usually a guy hangs around because he wants more,' Em pointed out.

He raised an eyebrow. 'You're telling me that you don't want more of what we shared last night?'

'That's not possible,' Em shot back, deliberately avoiding answering the question.

Joel nodded slowly. 'Too risky, then.'

'I would have thought that was obvious.' Em hadn't meant the words as a reprimand, but that's how they came out, so she rushed to add, 'And I thought you didn't do relationships.'

'I don't. And neither do you, apparently. But I would be up for . . . more.'

Em placed her palms on the bench. 'What are you suggesting?'

Joel cocked his head to one side, regarding her openly. 'You on this bench naked would be a good place to start.'

Em's eyes widened involuntarily.

Before she could think of an equally smart reply, Joel's lips twitched again, and this time he threw back his head and laughed. When he was done, he winked at her. 'You can't blame a guy for trying.'

Em felt increasingly unsteady, and she gripped the edge of the bench. Seeing Joel laugh hit her hard every time, and she was beginning to appreciate that the more she knew about this man, the more she had to learn. One minute he was quiet and serious, the next he was teasing and fun. And there was always that edge of the unknown about him.

'I guess not,' Em said. 'But are you serious? Not about the bench. The . . . more.'

'Only if you're comfortable, but I understand if you're not. I know my business relationship with your father may be too close for comfort.'

'Way too close,' Em replied. But . . . but she couldn't bring herself to say no outright. Like he'd already pointed out, more of what they shared last night wouldn't be a bad thing.

Joel stood, the stool scraping on the hard floor. 'Hey, I didn't mean to make you uncomfortable. I should get going.'

'Wait.' Em's hand shot out and covered his hand that was resting on the bench. 'I mean, what are you suggesting? That we see each other again?' Em wasn't even sure why she was entertaining the idea, but he'd started it. She might as well understand what he was proposing.

He cocked his head to one side again. 'The details are up to you entirely. You make the rules. I'll follow them.'

Em looked away and took a drink of her coffee. He had been quite good at following her instructions in the bedroom last night. And when he hadn't . . . he'd been mind-blowing.

She cleared her throat, balancing on an imaginary cliff she wasn't aware existed until a moment ago. Seeing Joel again had never entered her mind. Em supposed she'd had a few similar arrangements in the past with other guys. Rob, in her final year of her undergraduate degree. They were better friends with benefits than just friends, so it had worked perfectly. Or Armando. Now Em thought about it, they'd had a sort of informal arrangement, too.

Em shook her head at herself. She was being crazy. Her father was potentially going to sign a contract with this man standing in front of her, and if he ever caught wind of something going on between them . . . Em almost shuddered. There were only two ways that could turn out. With her father forcing Joel to propose or Joel losing the chance to work with her father. Em didn't want to be responsible for the latter, as it was blatantly obvious how hard Joel and his company were trying to win the contract.

'Em?'

She opened her mouth to tell him what her brain was

certain of, but her phone pinged on the bench in front of her. Em glanced down at it in annoyance. Whoever it was could just wait. But when she saw the message preview on the screen, she swore.

'Sorry,' she muttered, and snatched up the phone.

It was from her friend and downstairs neighbour, Kat.

You still up for our exercise session with Jess on the beach this morning? I thought we said we'd meet at mine. Or judging from the noise coming from your place last night maybe you're too tired . . .

Em swore again, and quickly typed a reply.

No, I'm coming. Give me five minutes and I'll be downstairs.

'I'm really sorry, but I've got to go,' Em told Joel.

He held up his hands. 'I get it. I'll get out of your hair. But before I do, let me give you something. One sec while I grab the rest of my clothes.'

Em tapped her fingers impatiently on the bench while she waited for Joel. She needed to throw some exercise gear on and get going sooner rather than later. And once Joel left, she wouldn't have to reply to his question that she didn't know the answer to.

He appeared a minute later fully dressed and came over and slid a card onto the bench. Em had no idea how he looked neat and tidy, but he did.

'Here,' he said. 'So you know how to contact me. And I was serious about that offer of you speaking to my colleague.'

Em's heart sank. 'And about sleeping with me again?' she replied in disbelief. 'I don't see both working well.'

'You get to decide the rules. Not me,' he reminded her. 'And no pressure. You can still talk to my colleague and not see me again if you choose.'

'I'd see you again if I worked for you,' Em pointed out.

His eyes filled with amusement. 'I can control myself around you, you know. And I can also handle rejection.' He nodded at the card. 'I'll go now. Bye, Em.'

He walked down her hallway and not long after she heard her front door close.

'Shit,' Em breathed.

What the hell had just happened? The guy she'd slept with wanted to sleep with her again, but only casually, of course, which suited Em just fine. But he was also offering her a chance at a job and could potentially be working with her father before too long.

In the space of one night, Em's life had just grown a lot more complicated.

'It's not complicated if you don't see him again,' Em said to herself.

But that was the thing. A big part of Em *did* want to see Joel again, and she had absolutely no idea what to do about it.

Chapter Ten

EM WAS RUNNING SO LATE after Joel left that she arranged to meet her friends on the beach instead. She half jogged, half power-walked the five minutes down the hill to Freshwater, or "Freshie" as the locals referred to it. By the time she arrived, she'd already worked up a sweat.

'Well, good morning, sleeping beauty,' her neighbour and friend, Jess, called out, waving in Em's direction.

She was waiting with Kat near the path that led to the sand. They appeared to be doing stretches and chatting—probably more of the latter.

Em smiled to herself. Despite feeling tired, flustered, and seriously considering going back to bed, Jess's enthusiasm was catching. Jess's enthusiasm was *always* catching, which was why her fitness business, Hi-Jinks, was going from strength to strength. It also didn't hurt that Jess looked like an advertisement for healthy living with her toned body and bouncy blonde bob.

'Hey,' Kat said when Em stopped in front of them, giving Em a raised eyebrow.

Em pretended to ignore her and started to stretch. 'Sorry I'm late. I forgot to set my alarm.'

'I bet you did,' was Kat's reply.

Em continued to ignore her, making a show of stretching.

Jess and Kat couldn't be more different if they tried. Jess was cute and bubbly, while Kat was waif-like with sleek dark hair and knowing brown eyes. She was also the host of a renowned evening news show, and Em wished that Kat's razor-sharp tongue and keen skills of observation weren't focused on her right now.

Em saw Jess shoot Kat a questioning look.

Kat's expression turned incredulous in response. 'Tell me you didn't hear the sounds coming from Em's penthouse late last night.'

Jess's mouth formed a small "o" and her bright blue eyes widened with excitement. 'Ooh, did Em have a man over? I stayed at Ant's.'

Em grabbed on to the thread of a different conversation. 'I thought Ant was moving in with you?'

Ant was Jess's boyfriend, as well as Kat's co-host on the evening news show. He was a seriously funny guy and Em was looking forward to him living in their building. Plus, even for a non-relationship person like Em, she could admit that Jess and Ant were perfect together.

'Don't answer her,' Kat ordered. 'She's trying to change the subject.'

Em decided to try ignoring Kat instead. She turned to face the horizon, doing some more stretches. Like the night before, the sky was still cloudless, and it made for a brilliant morning. Past the waves and out to sea, yellow reflections danced playfully on the surface of the water. Em supposed it was a particularly serene morning to be meditating.

'Em?' Kat's impatient voice cut through Em's thoughts.

'Huh?'

Kat smirked. 'Some man.'

Jess gasped. 'Better than Armando?'

Kat snorted. 'Unlikely. There's been no one before or since like Armando.'

'He was better than Armando,' Em said without thinking, and immediately snapped her mouth shut.

Shit. Where had that come from? So much for her tactic of ignoring the conversation. Then a worse thought occurred to her. Em wasn't supposed to tell anyone about Joel, so she *really* needed to change the subject.

Taking a leaf out of Jess's fitness coach book, Em clapped her hands together. 'Right. What are we going to start with this morning?'

'Oh, no you don't,' Kat said, grinning. 'You can't drop a bomb like that and pretend nothing happened.'

Em sighed. Maybe a half-truth would work instead. 'Fine. I had a man over. He was incredibly awesome, but it was a one-off.'

'Who was he?' breathed Jess, obviously still affected by the revelation that he was better than Armando.

'No one special,' Em replied.

'Oh, come on, Em,' Kat shot back. 'With that amount of noise? It totally killed the vibe of the movie that Matt and I were trying to watch last night.'

Em blushed. 'I'm sorry. I must have left a window open or something. I didn't mean to disturb you.' Or to broadcast her late-night hook-up.

Em really had gotten carried away. After embarrassing herself with her neighbours on a few occasions due to Armando, Em had been careful to be discreet ever since. Until now. Whoops.

Jess brushed Em's arm to get her attention. 'He must be somebody if he was that good,' she persisted.

Em smiled. Jess really was a sweetheart. She fell into a similar category to her sister, Ana, in that she was always eager for everyone to find their happily ever after.

'Alright,' Em relented. 'He's somebody, I'll give you that. But he can't be my somebody. It's just not going to happen.'

'And why not?' Kat asked.

Em thought for a second before answering. When she'd agreed with Joel that no one could know about them, it was in relation to her father. Em observed her friends with amusement. Kat stood with her arms crossed and Jess's hopeful expression was endearing.

'Look. I can't tell you who he is—' Kat opened her mouth to protest and Em held up a hand. 'It's better if I don't, alright?'

'Is he someone famous?' Jess whispered.

Em chuckled. 'No, thankfully. But my father knows him.'

'Oh,' Kat and Jess both said together, understanding immediately.

Em's father's ongoing efforts to interfere in her life were something Em regularly vented to her friends about.

'See why I can't go there?' Em told them.

'Are you sure?' Jess asked. 'I mean, just because your father knows him doesn't mean—'

'Dad introduced me to him.'

Her friends fell silent and Em didn't bother saying "see?" a second time. They knew all about her father's continued efforts to marry Em off to inappropriate men.

'Hang on,' said Kat after she'd digested this information. 'You're telling me you actually like a guy that your father has put forward?'

Em gave her friends a desperate look. 'I know, right? You can see why I can't tell *anyone*. Except you, of course.'

'Yes, you can!' Jess cried. 'Your dad would be over the moon.'

Em shook her head. 'If we wanted a relationship. Which neither of us do,' she said firmly. 'And I'm pretty sure if my dad finds out this man had a "sleepover" at my place, things wouldn't go well for either of us.'

'What's he like?' Kat asked, always the first to want to find out more.

Em supposed there wasn't any harm in talking about Joel if he remained anonymous.

'He's . . . different. Like no one I've been with before.'

'Interesting,' replied Kat. 'In what way?'

'He seems to have a similar world view to me,' Em said vaguely, not wanting to allude to the fact that Joel was an architect. 'But he's kind of mysterious, too. He doesn't seem to like talking about himself or his past.'

'Uh oh. Bad sign. Maybe a tough upbringing? Or he's hiding a wife and family somewhere,' Kat guessed.

'God, I hope not.' Both of those options sounded equally bad. Em prayed it wasn't the latter, although Joel had already mentioned his family in less than glowing terms, so Kat was possibly on to something.

'In my experience,' Kat went on, 'when people deflect, they're hiding something. I tried it with Matt because I wasn't ready to deal with my issues.'

'Do you think he might have issues?' asked Jess, looking worried.

'Honestly?' replied Em. 'I have no idea. I only met him last night. From what I've seen so far, he's confident and capable. He doesn't appear to have any hang ups, and he strikes me as a pretty straightforward guy.'

'Matt suffers from post-traumatic stress disorder, and he's a capable guy,' Kat reminded her. 'How we present ourselves to the world doesn't always accurately reflect what's going on inside.'

'He meditates,' Em told them. She wasn't sure why she said it.

Kat frowned. 'He told you that? Seems like an odd way to pick up a woman.'

'No,' Em corrected. 'He was meditating on my balcony this morning before I kicked him out.'

Jess grabbed Em's arm in excitement. 'He didn't go home?'

Em shrugged. 'That doesn't mean anything. We didn't really discuss it, and we both fell asleep before we agreed on how to . . . say goodbye. I think he was just being polite.'

'No way. He wanted to be there,' Kat said. Her voice held a degree of certainty that Em didn't feel, although she had suspected the very same thing when she'd found Joel still in her apartment.

'I don't think so. He's not the sort of guy to want a relationship.'

'And nor are you,' Kat agreed. 'But I'd bet my life that he wants to see you again.'

Em hesitated for a beat, then couldn't resist telling her friends more. It wasn't like she could share any of this with her sister.

'He did sort of suggest something like that.'

Both women stared at her, waiting for her to elaborate further.

'I'm not sure,' Em hedged with a huff. 'He said it was up to me, but I still don't think it's a good idea. I mean, I'll occasionally see the same guy more than once. It's always been a casual thing, though. And they didn't know my father.'

Kat's face broke into a wide smile. 'You want to see him again, don't you?'

Em didn't answer, and Kat turned to Jess.

'She wants to see him again.'

'I didn't say that,' Em told them. 'Even if I wanted to, it's too risky because of my dad.'

Jess grinned at her. 'A forbidden romance. How cool.'

'No. Not cool. Stupid. It would be really stupid.' If she kept telling herself that, she might start to believe it.

'But you're thinking about it,' Kat finished for her.

'You're really annoying sometimes, do you know that?' Em said it kindly, but she didn't hide her exasperation.

'I know. Just ask Matt. Actually, don't. He'll probably try to swap "Kat is a know-it-all" stories, and I don't want that. But back to you. Can't you just keep it under wraps? If it's not a relationship, then I'm assuming it's sex, and that's not something anyone needs to know about if it's in the privacy of your home.' Kat's lips twisted into a wry smile. 'Except us, when you're too vocal.'

Em rolled her eyes. 'You make it sound so simple.'

Kat shrugged. 'It's sex, Em. What's to arrange other than a time and a place?'

'Surely it must be more than that?' Jess interrupted, ever hopeful that Em would one day entertain the idea of a relationship.

'It's sex,' Em confirmed bluntly.

'Then how is that different from any of the other guys you've ever been with?' Kat reasoned. 'So he knows your dad. Big deal. If you like him, see him again.'

Kat had a valid point. Things between her and Joel weren't really all that different to the previous guys she'd seen. Provided her dad didn't know about it, that was.

'You're encouraging me to have a salacious affair,' Em joked.

'Hey, what you get up to in the bedroom is your business, not ours,' Kat replied. 'And that includes your father, too. It's none of his business either.'

When Kat said it like that . . .

'I'll think about it,' Em relented. 'But right now, I really need to clear my head. So, Jess, what are we doing today?'

Jess beamed, always in her element when she was talking about exercise. 'Let's warm up with a couple of laps of the beach. Come on.'

They followed Jess down onto the beach, Em thinking how glad she was to have such good friends that she could talk to.

Chapter Eleven

JOEL COULDN'T STOP THINKING about Em.

Which was bad, very bad, because Joel didn't get distracted easily. Especially not by women. As a general rule, Joel always chose when and where to be distracted by women. He could admit to himself that sounded a bit . . . detached. But detached was exactly what he chose to be with the opposite sex —until now.

That approach was proving harder to maintain with Em, because she was so damn . . . devastating. If they hadn't already slept together, Joel probably could have fooled himself into thinking that his preoccupation with Em was due to not knowing what she was like in the bedroom. But that was just the problem. He knew *exactly* what she was like in the bedroom, and it physically pained him to think about it. And not in a bad way, but a now-I-know-what-I'm-missing-out-on kind of way.

Joel pushed away from his desk with a huff. Sitting here mooning over Em wasn't going to get the presentation ready for their final tender meeting. They had the rest of this week to finalise it, and that should have been plenty of time, except Joel was convinced they were missing something. The nagging feeling had him leaving his office and knocking on his partner's door.

Nate Morris glanced up from his computer when he saw Joel. 'What's up?'

'The same thing that's always up lately. The Georgiou job.'

'It's not a job yet. We have to win it first,' Nate corrected him with a wry smile.

Joel came into the office without waiting for an invitation and seated himself in one of the chairs opposite Nate's desk. His partner looked tired, but he often did lately. With a business to run, two teenage daughters, and what he and his wife lovingly referred to as their "extension project"—meaning their two-year-old toddler—Nate was a busy man. But he always had time for Joel.

Nate pushed his grey hair out of his eyes. It had been dark when they'd first met over a decade ago in the architecture firm they'd both been employed by at the time. He still wore it long, and with his twinkling blue eyes, somehow the grey hair didn't seem to age him at all. Joel often wondered if he'd still look that youthful in his early forties.

'You haven't had the chance to tell me how the weekend went,' Nate said.

'Ah, the wedding,' Joel began. His thoughts had long since moved on from the event. They were currently stuck on what had happened *after* the wedding. 'Yeah, it went fine as far as I can tell. I jumped through some more hoops for Chris, like the trained seal that I am.'

'Degree of difficulty of the hoops?' Nate asked.

This made Joel smile, as there'd been some banter between them about what Chris's daughter would be like prior to the wedding. Nate had suggested that the night might be challenging if said daughter was in need of her father's match-making attempts, which Joel now knew couldn't have been further from the truth.

'Not as expected,' Joel stated. Or was that understated? 'Keeping my hands off the daughter proved to be the biggest challenge of the night.'

Nate blinked and eased back in his seat, his mouth curling into a surprised smile. 'No shit?'

'I shit you not.'

Joel's commitment to his bachelor status was legendary around the office, so for a woman to turn his head was some-thing. He supposed the conversation wasn't very mature for the two leading partners of a respected Sydney architecture firm, but Nate and he were more like brothers when all was said and done. Joel couldn't imagine going into business with anyone else, and he probably wouldn't have if it weren't for Nate.

Nate frowned after he digested this bit of information. 'I trust you behaved like a gentleman,' he said, sounding more like the executive he was.

Joel pondered his reply. He hated lying to Nate, but it was better not to mention where the night had ended up.

'When have I ever been a gentleman?' Joel shot back, but added, 'Don't worry, she didn't hate me by the end of the night.' Far from it, Joel hoped. 'But Chris did imply that having a firm that understands the importance of family was a non-documented requirement. Obviously I have nothing to recommend me in that area, but you do. We need to make sure that we can work that in somehow.'

Nate blew out a breath. 'Interesting. Why don't we invite Chris to our Friday evening drinks? I can have Amanda and the kids drop by. Well, at least two of the kids. Nadia is apparently too grown up to be seen with her family anymore,' he said, referring to his oldest daughter.

They generally held company drinks once a month in the reception space of their offices. It wasn't unusual for partners or family members to join them, especially if they were picking up their spouse from work so that they didn't have to drive home after a few drinks.

Joel tapped his fingers on the arm of the chair. 'Yeah, I suppose that could work.' They often invited long-term clients to join them, too. Chris wasn't exactly a long-term client, but they hoped he soon would be.

'Why not suggest he brings the daughter along? What's her name?'

'Em.'

'You don't sound sure.'

How did Nate do that? Joel had only said one word and his friend managed to sense his hesitation, but that was the sort of bond they had.

'I wouldn't want her to feel awkward,' Joel replied carefully, not adding why she might feel that way.

Nate shrugged. 'That's up to her to decide. I just thought if we're seen to be including Georgiou's daughter, it could bode well.'

Damn it. There was nothing polite about what he and Em had gotten up to the other night. Or about the extremely X-rated thoughts he'd been having about her ever since. But Joel was an adult, and if he had to, he'd act like one.

'Yeah. Good point. But I draw the line at a proposal,' Joel joked.

'Like that will ever happen,' Nate said with a laugh. 'Perpetual bachelorhood suits you.'

'I think so,' Joel said standing up, his mind working quickly. 'Actually, while I think of it, I'm not sure anything will come of it, but I offered for Em to come in and speak to Sasha about that position we've got going.'

Nate frowned. 'Why?'

'Chris failed to mention that his daughter is about to complete a PhD in the built environment with a focus on sustainability.'

Nate's eyebrows rose. 'Seriously?'

'She's one smart cookie,' Joel confirmed. 'But she's a bit wary of getting a leg up from Daddy dearest. She's the independent type. I just felt it was too good an opportunity to pass up.'

'No, that's good thinking. Once word of that offer gets back to Chris, it can only help our case, even if she doesn't take you up on it. That strategic mind of yours is why I hired you.'

It was an ongoing joke between them because they were in partnership and neither had hired the other. Joel's return joke was that he hired Nate for his human resources skills because he was better at that side of the business.

'Right. I'm going to stare at this damn presentation some more,' Joel announced.

'Not too hard, I hope. You don't want to wrinkle that pretty face of yours.'

'Smart arse,' Joel muttered as he left Nate's office, but he was grinning.

TWO DAYS later Em had come to a decision. After way too much time thinking about Joel, Em decided on the mature course of action. There was no point in continuing their casual fling when neither of them was interested in a relationship, so Em would take Joel up on his offer of coming in to talk to his colleague. After all, her career was more important than a guy.

It also wouldn't hurt Joel's chances of winning her father's contract, not that she'd ever admit it to him. The idea of her dad's company finally being involved in a sustainable project was almost too good to be true. So if Em could do something to make that a reality, she was damn well going to try.

Em also needed interview experience if she was ever going to get a job. It wasn't like she'd have to see Joel again, anyway. Em had her doubts that she'd even want the job, or that they'd want her—it was too much of a long shot. What sort of university academic got the first job they went for in the corporate world? Maybe she'd see Joel in passing when she came into the office, but ultimately she'd be there to talk to his colleague, not him.

To Joel's credit, he was equally mature when she texted him. He had his colleague contact her afterwards to arrange a time for the meeting and there had been no suggestion of he and Em seeing each other on a personal level again. This was good, as it confirmed Em had made the right choice.

The sensible choice.

Em had it all planned out in her head. She'd go in, talk to this woman, Sasha, then leave and that would be the end of it. Interview experience gained, and a sneaky little push in the right direction for her father achieved.

Easy.

'Oh no,' Em murmured.

Except now it wasn't looking quite so simple after all.

'Dad, why do you always do this to me?' Em whined.

She was in her apartment and no one could hear her talking to herself like a crazy person.

'Damn it, Dad!'

Em threw her phone on the sofa and paced the living area

of her apartment. Why was her father always meddling in her life and ruining her plans? Why? And when would she officially be old enough not to warrant this sort of heavy-handed interference?

Em growled and returned to the sofa to retrieve her phone.

'Fine,' she said. 'But I'm doing it for Joel and not for you, Dad, not that you'll ever know that. And for the good of the environment, of course.'

She re-read her father's message.

I'm attending drinks at Joel's company on Friday afternoon from 4pm. Do your old man a favour and come along with me. Then maybe I won't be so insistent about you staying in the penthouse when your PhD is done.

Well, if he was going to order her around and use blackmail, Em could play that game. She hit reply and started typing.

As it turns out, I'll be there already. I'm meeting Sasha, one of their managers, about a position they've got going. So it will work well. See you there x

The sign-off with a kiss was perverse on her part. But Em had learned that sometimes it was best not to show her father how annoyed he made her, because he was clueless anyway. His reply was swift and highlighted this fact.

That's my girl! x

'Ugh!' Em groaned. 'Perfect, just perfect.'

Somehow her responsible decision of attending an interview had backfired on her. Now she'd have to stand around and make small talk with Joel in front of her father and the rest of his office, pretending like nothing had happened between them.

Wouldn't that be fun?

Chapter Twelve

JOEL WAS NERVOUS. Joel was never nervous. But then he hadn't been in the position of entertaining a potential client and his daughter who he'd slept with. Suddenly Em's and his "no one needs to know" agreement didn't seem so smart after all.

It wasn't the first time that Joel had mixed business with pleasure. He'd had a casual office fling at the last firm that he'd worked at with no problems. He'd even gotten to know the woman's fiancé when she became engaged later on. They'd continued to keep it a secret that they'd slept together with no issues, because it hadn't seemed relevant.

Unfortunately, the situation with Em felt different, and Joel was having a hard time figuring out what that meant. The idea of working with Em was actually extremely attractive—but only if he could be with her again. The thought of not being able to touch her was maddening. Or worse, being introduced to another man involved with Em. That thought made him feel physically sick.

'Stop it,' Joel muttered to himself as he adjusted his tie.

He was killing time in his office before the afternoon drinks. Staff were already gathering downstairs and Nate was down there chatting to Chris. They'd agreed it would be smart for Nate to greet Chris on arrival so that he could make a point of talking about his family. Meanwhile, Joel had hovered restlessly by his computer, giving them some time together.

He'd missed seeing Em when she'd arrived earlier for her meeting with Sasha. He'd been on a conference call with a client, and Sasha was more than capable of introducing herself.

It was probably better that way. The last thing he wanted was to make Em feel uncomfortable. That was why, when she'd messaged him, Joel had kept it friendly but professional. She'd set the tone by requesting to go ahead with the meeting. Given that she hadn't mentioned the possibility of getting together with Joel again, he'd left it. Not that he hadn't wanted to ask. He'd been dying to ask to see her again ever since that night, but like he'd told her, he could handle rejection.

He just hadn't thought it would sting so damn much.

After another few minutes of impatient waiting, Joel set off downstairs. Some of their staff greeted him when he arrived. They invited him over to have a drink, but just then Sasha and Em came into view. Joel stalled midway to the group, pretending to check a message on his phone while he watched the women approach.

Sasha appeared at ease and was focused on talking to Em, who was listening intently. It gave Joel a moment to watch them unnoticed from his position on the other side of the foyer. Em wore a fitted knee-length navy blue dress that could be described as professional, but it still didn't manage to tone down her bright hair. And even though the dress had short sleeves and came up to her neck, it didn't succeed in quelling

Joel's thirst for her. If anything, the demure quality of the dress only made him want her more.

'Who's that?' asked Damian, one of their junior architects who'd just entered the foyer near Joel.

Joel cleared his throat. 'Em Georgiou. Chris Georgiou's daughter. She's talking to Sasha about that position we've got going.'

'Sweet,' Damian said, nodding in their direction. 'I wouldn't have guessed that she was a Georgiou. It will be nice to have some more young blood around here.'

Joel had the odd urge to snarl at Damian like a lion protecting its territory and tell him that he was too young for Em. Joel had no idea why. Damian was a nice kid, almost sweet at times, so there wasn't anything untoward in his attention towards Em. He was merely being curious.

Instead Joel said, 'I don't know if it will happen yet. It will depend on Sasha.'

'Cool,' Damian replied. 'Would you like a drink?'

'No, but thanks. I'd better mingle first.'

Damian nodded and joined some of the other employees. Joel inhaled a steadying breath, fully intending to go over to Nate and Chris, when he saw Sasha wave him over.

Here we go. Showtime. He supposed that he couldn't avoid Em forever.

Joel hoped that he looked relaxed as he crossed the room, when inside he was overthinking everything again. He knew he shouldn't have skipped his meditation session earlier today. Today of all days, he needed it.

'Joel,' Sasha greeted him in her no-nonsense way.

With platinum hair pulled back in a neat ponytail, her light blue eyes never missed a thing. She was the epitome of well-kept. Joel knew that she was nearing fifty, and she still turned heads.

Sasha nodded at Em, who was standing quietly beside her. 'I'm impressed. I'm also surprised she hasn't been snapped up already by another firm.'

'That's nice of you to say,' Em replied. 'But I've only just started looking seriously.'

Her light skin had a rosy hue to it, and Joel knew that meant she was embarrassed. Or turned on. When she'd become worked up by his touch the other night, she'd gone that same colour.

Joel coughed politely into his hand and nodded at Em, forcing himself to focus on the here and now. 'That's why I thought the two of you might like to talk. I'm glad it's been worthwhile.'

'Our biggest issue will be convincing Em that she wants to work here,' Sasha went on. She was known for speaking her mind, but on this occasion Joel would have preferred that they discuss Em's potential employment status in private.

'It's not that I don't want to work for you,' Em began.

Sasha waved a hand in the air. 'I know. You need to look around. I get it. You can't just settle on the first job you find. I would like to talk to you again, though. I'm putting it out there now.'

'Thank you,' Em said, appearing genuinely flattered. 'I'd like that. And I don't want to come across as not being keen—'

'I get it, don't worry,' Sasha finished for her again. If Em did decide to work here, she'd have to get used to Sasha's confidence. Joel suspected it wouldn't be an issue, though, from what he knew of Em already.

Joel also hadn't anticipated things would progress so quickly. His throwaway comment about Em coming to have a chat with Sasha had been intended as generous, and admittedly a little self-serving given her father's upcoming development. Joel hadn't actually thought through the reality of Em working here full-time. It was extremely stupid on his part not to have, and also unlike him given he was usually very business-minded.

'Anyway, I'll leave you two to chat,' Sasha announced. 'I need to take a couple of calls before I indulge in an end of week drink. We'll be in touch, Em.'

With that, Sasha walked off towards her office, her high heels tapping purposefully on the marble tiles.

'So it went well, then?' Joel asked.

'As far as I can tell,' Em replied. Then after a beat added, 'Well, this is awkward.'

Joel found himself smiling. 'You aren't very good at avoiding the elephant in the room, are you?'

'Why avoid her? She's pink after all.'

And just like that, all the tightness in Joel's body eased. 'I would have hoped we could come up with a more up-to-date colour scheme for our elephant. We have a team of talented interior designers on our books.'

'Pink is timeless.'

'Ah, a classic elephant then? I guess I can live with that.'

They fell silent again. They were both facing the now crowded room, and Joel stole a glance at her. The tightness returned. What was it about this woman? When he was away from her, all he could do was think about her. Now she was here, he had the odd desire to run in the opposite direction. After secreting her away somewhere so that he could be alone with her first, of course.

Yep, he really could have done with that meditation session, because his thoughts and desires made absolutely no sense whatsoever.

He decided to go with her approach of tackling things head on. Honesty was what had started things between them, so it only seemed appropriate.

'Seeing as we're addressing the elephant in the room, it might be worth acknowledging that there is more than one,' he told her.

'Oh?' Em turned to face him.

Joel swallowed with the full force of her attention on him. He imagined being a kid again, tapping her on the shoulder and yelling, "Tag, you're it!" That way he could run away from her, but at least she'd be chasing him.

'Joel?'

Damn it. *Focus, Joel.*

'The other elephant is related to the job. Do you want it?'

Em opened her mouth. Closed it again. Then narrowed her eyes at him. 'Was that a job offer? Because if it is, I'd say no on account of the fact my father is standing right over there and it seems a little too staged for my liking.'

Joel swore silently at himself. He was usually much better at communicating than this. 'Sorry, no. It wasn't a job offer. If it comes to fruition, there will be a few more hoops to jump through first.'

Em nodded, noticeably relieved by his explanation.

'I was asking you if you could see yourself working here,' he clarified.

Em bit her lip, obviously thinking. Then, when she saw the way Joel's eyes were watching her mouth, she quickly released it.

She smoothed the front of her dress with her palms. 'I'm not sure yet. I like what I've seen so far. But even Sasha seemed surprised that I might want to work here when I could take a position doing town planning or the like.'

'Is that what you want?' Joel asked.

'I'm not sure,' Em admitted, 'and that annoys me. After this long studying, you'd think that I'd know exactly what I want now I've got the chance to work full-time.'

'Not necessarily. Sometimes you don't know how much you want something until it lands right in front of you.'

Em stiffened beside him, and Joel clenched his fists. What the hell had he been thinking saying that? The double entendre was undeniable and it wasn't how he'd intended for it to come out.

Holy shit. Maybe he'd meant it more than he'd realised. Still, the last thing he wanted was to scare Em away.

'I didn't mean—' he began.

'I knew what you meant.'

More silence. Then Joel figured *to hell with it* and turned to her again.

'Em? Maybe I did mean it that way a bit.'

Those blue eyes rounded. 'What are you saying?'

'I think you know what I'm saying,' he said deliberately, keeping things vague, because they were in a room full of his employees and her father was nearby. 'But like I said before, it's up to you.'

'What about this?' She held out her palm to gesture to the foyer in front of them.

'This company? The job? That's a completely separate issue in my mind, and what we're discussing now won't have any bearing at all on your prospects here.'

'I'm not sure that I believe you.'

'I don't say things that I don't mean.'

But there's plenty that you don't say.

Joel clenched his fists tighter. That little voice inside his head was quieter these days, so when it did make itself known, it always took him by surprise.

Em didn't appear to notice Joel's inner musings.

'Neither do I,' Em told him. 'So I'll say this. I need time to think about the job.' She appeared to hesitate and cast her gaze around the room.

Joel wished he knew what she was thinking. 'And the other . . . matter?'

Em's luscious lips curved slightly. 'It's . . . tempting.'

Tempting.

It may not have been a green light, but it wasn't red either in Joel's opinion. His chest constricted to the point where he felt the need to loosen his tie, but he resisted the urge.

'Is there anything I can do or say to sweeten the deal?' he asked, keeping his voice low.

She licked her lips and Joel squirmed. This time he was the one to look away and survey the room. It was partly self-preservation and partly making sure that he maintained the appearance of talking to a business associate.

'I don't know.' She slid her eyes in his direction. 'Try me, I suppose.'

The imaginary light was almost green, but that was probably just repressed sexual tension on his part.

'How about this?' he suggested. 'I take you out for a drink after this is done. Then you can decide whether the matter is worth pursuing further.'

Em smiled this time. 'Fine. It's a deal. Now where are your toilets? After that we should probably chat to my father. If you think that's wise?'

Joel was almost one hundred per cent sure that none of this was wise, but it didn't change how much he wanted it.

'Good idea. I'll meet you over there in a few minutes.'

Joel watched her retreat, waiting for his heartbeat to steady. He wasn't sure what had possessed him to invite her for a drink. If it was just casual sex they were both after, then they wouldn't have even bothered with the formality, but there were no rules when it came to Em. He'd snatch any opportunity to be near her in public or private, and the idea of chatting to her one-on-one over a drink sounded damn good in his opinion.

Her mind was just as sexy as the rest of her. They could consider it foreplay.

He definitely wouldn't consider it breaking every rule he'd ever had about women, because Em was in a different category to any woman he'd ever known.

What that category was, he had no idea, but he intended to find out.

Chapter Thirteen

BY THE TIME Em returned from the bathroom, Joel had already joined Nate and her father. When her dad waved her over, there wasn't exactly anywhere else she could go, especially given she didn't know any of the other staff.

For the first few minutes the discussion centred on various developments around Sydney, mostly by her father's competitors. Usually during a discussion of this nature, Em would find herself challenging her father's more traditional views of progress in favour of the environment. Interestingly, this time the topic seemed to be about how the competition could have improved their designs in regard to sustainability. Em was so gobsmacked that her father was even having the conversation that she kept her views to herself and let the others talk.

Along with her amazement, Em felt a bit of jealousy. What had Joel and Nate done to make her father finally listen? And why hadn't he heard *her* all the other times that she'd tried to bring the subject up? She was so busy pondering the situation that she almost missed the change of topic.

'Well, what do you think of Scott & Morris, Em? Good

enough to tempt you away from a life of academia?' her dad asked her.

Em shot him a firm look. 'I'd say that's a question to consider if I'm offered the job.' The last thing she needed was her father throwing his weight around. It was important that she be offered a job on her own merits, not because of who Chris Georgiou was.

'But would you like to work here?' he persisted.

Em wished the glass of wine in her hand wasn't empty, as what she'd had so far wasn't enough to take the edge off her father's brashness. Before she could answer, Joel spoke up.

'I think Em still needs time to think about it,' he said smoothly. 'Today was only an initial discussion and not a formal job interview.'

Chris tapped the side of his beer glass with a finger. 'Ah, but I'm sure my Emily is so bright that you'll consider it, am I right?'

Em glared at him. 'Funnily enough, I'd say that's up to them and not you.'

'Now, darling, don't jump down my throat. I'm merely showing my support.'

'And putting Joel and Nate's company in a difficult position, seeing as they're tendering for a contract.'

Her father raised his free palm. 'A completely separate matter, I assure you. Now I'd better get home to your mother. She's got a dinner party planned. I do appreciate the invite, though. It's been good to get a feel for your company's culture.'

Em stood back while the men shook hands, then Chris nodded in her direction.

'Do me a favour and make sure Em gets home safely, won't you, Joel? If I know her well, she will have left the car at home in favour of a more environmentally-friendly transport option.'

Em smiled at her father through gritted teeth. 'It was a nice day.'

Ordinarily, Em would have asked for a lift, but then that would prevent her from having a drink afterwards with Joel. Not that she wanted her dad to know that. But on the bright side, now she and Joel could leave together and no one would think it was strange.

Once Chris had left, Nate nodded in the direction of his wife Amanda. She was chatting to some of the other staff on the opposite side of the foyer. A toddler dangled off one arm, tugging on it roughly. 'It looks like my ride home is expiring fast. It was nice to meet you, Em. I hope we'll get a better chance to catch up properly another time.'

Em smiled at Nate, watching as he crossed the foyer in a few long strides thanks to his lanky frame. When he arrived at Amanda's side, he scooped up his son, who erupted in fits of giggles as his father tickled him.

'Distraction techniques,' Joel told Em. 'You should see that kid have a meltdown. He makes your father's determination look weak.'

Em grinned. 'I'd like to see him take on my dad.'

Joel considered it for a moment. 'My bet's on the kid.'

Em laughed, then sobered when Joel's fingers brushed her hand as he took her glass. She ignored the tantalising chill that ran up her spine. 'I've got to say, after tonight my bet's on you, actually. I can't believe Dad was listening with an open mind to your suggestions.'

'It's taken time, but we're making progress,' Joel replied— humbly, in Em's opinion.

Or maybe he just didn't appreciate the magnitude of change it represented. Either way, Em was impressed.

'The first drink is on me,' she told him, noting that he hadn't had any of the alcohol on offer tonight, probably because he was driving. 'And wherever we end up, you really don't have to drop me home again. I'm capable of making my own way.'

Joel's dark eyes watched her, and Em had no clue what they were thinking. She still hadn't decided if his mysterious expressions added to his sex appeal or frustrated her slightly.

'I'm well aware of that,' he said. 'But you don't live far from me, so it's no problem.'

'Oh?' Em's eyebrows rose. It hadn't even occurred to her that Joel could live close by, but then she'd been too distracted to ask until now. 'Whereabouts are you?' she asked.

'The eastern side of Manly.'

He was right. It wasn't that far from Em's, maybe only a ten-minute drive in busy traffic.

'That's a nice area.'

Em's comment was an understatement. Houses in that part of Sydney's Northern Beaches ran into the many millions, so she figured Joel's business was doing well with or without her father's contract. Whether he owned or rented a house in that area, the cost would be steep.

Joel swallowed a laugh. 'The area is, but the house isn't.'

'Really?'

'I bought it for a steal a year ago and have been doing it up ever since. It had really been let go.'

'Huh.'

Joel raised an eyebrow in her direction. 'You say "huh" when you're thinking something.'

'I'm just wondering if an architect's house is ever finished,' Em joked, secretly trying to imagine what it was like. Apart from a love of the environment, the other thing that had attracted her to her area of study was her love of beautiful houses.

Joel surveyed her again, and Em really wished that she could read his mind.

'I can show you if you like?' he offered, to her surprise. 'I have plenty of wine in the basement. We can enjoy it on the part of the front balcony that isn't about to collapse.'

'Alright, now I definitely want to see it,' Em told him.

By the sounds of it, the house was old, and Em adored old houses. The older the better—they were usually the ones with the best bones and the most potential.

Joel's hand hovered over the back of her waist as he guided her from the foyer, using his free hand to wave to a few people as they went. Em ignored the questioning glances a few staff shot their way. She'd let Joel explain her presence another time. Em found herself wishing that he would just place his whole damn hand on her back. She knew that he was keeping things polite for the office, but having him not touch her made her physically ache.

By the time he'd led her down to the basement garage and they'd both gotten in his Porsche, the ache had become almost unbearable.

They both spoke at the same time.

'Joel—'

'Em—'

They laughed.

'Sorry,' Em said. 'You first.'

'No, you can—'

'It wasn't important,' she told him.

If wanting to climb over the gear stick and sit on his lap to kiss and touch him wasn't important. It was a bold thought, even for her. She held her hands together in her lap so that she wouldn't be tempted to touch him.

'All I was going to say,' he said, 'was if you're not comfortable coming to my place, then I understand. I don't want you to think that I'm inviting you there with the express intention of . . . you know.'

The words he didn't say hung in the car between them. He started the engine, which filled the silence, but it didn't ease any of the tension in Em's shoulders.

'That's OK,' Em said. 'I'd genuinely like to see your house.'

Joel angled a serious look in her direction as he drove out of the basement garage, appearing to accept her answer.

And you. I wanted to see you again. But she didn't say it.

Chapter Fourteen

THEY DROVE in silence for the majority of the journey to Joel's house. It wasn't so much uncomfortable as it was painful. At least it was for Joel. Having Em beside him in the close confines of the car was like a sweet sort of torture. She'd added another layer of perfume to her usual jasmine and ocean scent—something spicy—that had him resisting the urge to pull the car over and nuzzle her neck to breathe her in.

It seemed weird that he should feel nervous around her after everything they'd done the other night, but he still did. Their evening together had been defined as a one-off, so hoping for anything more than that felt like too much.

By the time he navigated the tight backstreets of eastern Manly, which were lined with parked cars, he wanted nothing more than to remove his tie and get some fresh air. Usually the narrow, parked-out streets didn't bother him, and the Porsche ordinarily zipped through them easily. But tonight he felt the need to be careful and drove slowly.

'I've never been up here,' Em told him as they made the final ascent towards the dead-end street he lived in. 'I've been to the little harbour cove beaches nearby, but I had no idea it went this far.'

They reached the top of the long, gentle rise and Joel directed the car the last fifty metres towards his home.

'Oh, wow,' Em exclaimed, as she took in the row of double level weatherboard terraces facing a bush reserve overlooking the harbour. 'These have to be original to the area.'

'I believe so.' He turned into his front drive and pulled on the park brake, but left the engine running. 'Wait here.'

He got out of the car and opened the picket fence gate that led to the under-house garage, then went over and pushed open the garage door. An electric gate and door opener were on his long list of to-dos for this place.

Joel returned to the car and drove the Porsche inside carefully. The garage was only wide enough for one car plus some storage shelves on one side. He didn't miss the way Em gazed up at the facade of the house as they drove in, and it did weird things to his stomach.

He cut the engine off and twisted to face her. 'Drink or tour first?'

'How about a tour with a glass of wine?'

'I like your thinking, but you'll need to get rid of those,' he said, nodding at her feet. 'It's a worksite upstairs. I've got some old sandals you can throw on instead.'

Em looked at her black high heels, then back at Joel, her lips curling in a slow smile.

'What?' he asked.

'I must be strange. You mention the words "worksite" and I'm turned on.'

Joel cleared his throat. 'You like old houses?'

She grinned at him. 'I *love* old houses.' Then she leaned in and planted a kiss on his lips with a loud smack.

When she eased back, Joel sat staring at her with a stunned expression on his face.

Em winced. 'Too much?'

'Not enough,' Joel whispered, and in response Em's eyes flared an impossibly bright blue in the dim light.

'Don't tempt me,' she murmured.

Joel bit down on his tongue or else he would have released a tight groan. The thought of having Em in his arms again was so tantalising, he ached.

Shit. He rubbed a hand over his cropped hair and thrust open the door. He wasn't sure if bringing her here was a good idea after all. If they'd been sharing a drink in a public place, he'd be forced to control himself and his thoughts. Now his brain was calculating exactly where and how he could do more of the things they'd done the other night. But Em hadn't agreed to anything like that—yet.

Em got out of the car too and stared at the space in surprise. 'You live down here?'

'For now.' He walked towards the end of the garage that had enough length to house three cars, but he only ever kept the Porsche in here. Down the far end he'd set up a small living area with a sofa, coffee table and television, plus a king single bed off to one side because that's all there was room for.

'Oh my God, it's the ultimate man cave,' she said, taking it all in. She turned to face him. 'Are you telling me that you sleep down here with your car?'

Joel smiled in spite of himself. 'Something like that. Come on. I'll grab you those shoes and we'll take a look upstairs.'

EM WAS PRETTY sure that she'd died and gone to heaven. She'd never really believed in the idea of a perfect man. How could one person totally fulfil another's requirements? But if she'd had a list, it might have included a man that appreciated architecture and was good with his hands. Em already had proof that Joel was good with his hands, plus he was an architect, so she supposed that made for a tick on both counts. Not that she was counting.

The amount of times that Ana had told Em to stop going out with those surfer dudes who had no drive to get anywhere in life and find herself someone with some passion . . .

Passion was writ large in every part of this house. Every wall that had been stripped bare. Every floorboard that needed sanding. The house had literally been reduced to bare bones to make way for . . . what? Em wasn't sure, but she had a pretty good idea it would be spectacular when Joel was done.

Em stood in the middle of the now open-plan dining and lounge area trying to take it all in. She looked upwards in amazement.

'You've removed the ceiling?' she asked. The top storey of the house started further back, and this room's roofline dominated the front of the property.

'Yeah, it's still in progress. The picture rails will stay, but I'm going to do away with the flat ceiling altogether and open it all up to make it cathedral style. It was that or put a loft in up there, but this way is better for the environment. I plan to add feature windows in the eaves over there. It will help keep it cool in summer and let the north facing sunlight warm the house naturally in winter. Plus, I like the feel of it this way.'

'It's going to be magnificent. Who have you got working on it?'

'Me mostly, plus a few tradesmen I trust.'

Em lowered her gaze and looked at him. 'You? You're doing this?'

Joel shrugged. 'Most of it. I told you, I used to be a builder.

Whatever I'm not capable of, I bring one of my guys in to handle. It's slow going, but it works.'

Em went over to the fireplace and skimmed her fingers across the top edge. It was missing a surround, but Em could imagine the style that would suit the room perfectly. It would be sophisticated without being too stuffy, giving the room a sense of presence.

'When do you work on it?' she asked.

'A lot of nights. Most weekends. What can I say? I have a killer social life.'

'Gosh, you'd never tear me away if this place was mine,' breathed Em.

'Really?'

Em turned back to face him again, although it was an effort because every time she looked around she noticed some new detail about the house that captured her imagination.

'I'm not some precious daddy's girl who spends my weekends partying when I'm not studying. I do know how to pick up a paintbrush, you know.'

Joel walked over to her and tucked a strand of her hair behind her ear. He looked into her eyes, and Em's knees went weak. This time she asked the question instead of wondering it silently.

'What are you thinking?' she asked.

'I'm imagining you with a paintbrush.' Then he leaned in and brushed his lips against hers, making Em release a soft sigh.

His hands slid down to grip her waist and she deepened the kiss, pressing herself against him. Yes. This was what she had missed. His firm body. His sure hands. The way he kissed her like she was precious, yet he knew that she wouldn't break easily.

Joel broke off the kiss and blew out a long breath. 'Far

out.' He pointed up the hall. 'Keep walking that way towards the kitchen or we'll never get there.'

Em debated fighting him on his need to do anything else other than what they had just been doing. She was as entranced with this house as she was with him, but she wanted to see more, so the house won out this time.

They arrived in a medium-sized kitchen area with cupboards that obviously weren't original. They even looked new enough to keep.

'Too bland,' Em murmured, 'for a beauty of a house like this.'

'My thoughts exactly,' agreed Joel. 'But I'm leaving it until last so I still can use it while everything else is being done.'

He showed her a second living area behind the kitchen that led outside to a small courtyard space, then upstairs to the three bedrooms, all in various states of disrepair. They returned to the kitchen where Joel located a bottle of wine and poured each of them a glass.

'The best place to enjoy these will be the front balcony,' he said. 'Follow me.'

Em hesitated. If he had been a different guy, Em probably would have already ended up in the bedroom with him by now. Once she knew she liked a man, she usually didn't waste time with formalities. While the idea of being in the bedroom again with Joel ignited every one of her nerve endings with a delightful sense of anticipation, there were two problems with that idea.

The first was that the bedrooms weren't usable, although Em was sure they could come up with a creative solution for that issue. It was the second problem that had Em biting her lip in indecision.

'Em?' Joel called back, waiting in the front hall for her.

Joel was different to any other guy she'd been with in

recent years, Em realised. She liked all those other guys well enough, but Joel? She wanted to spend time with him. To sit outside and talk. To learn more about him and this sleeping beauty of a house that he was bringing to life.

It was curiosity that had her making her way outside, wine in hand, instead of pulling him in for another kiss. Although she planned to do that again soon, too.

Chapter Fifteen

EM HAD GROWN silent during the last part of Joel's house tour. He'd noticed, but chosen to ignore it. She seemed unsure of herself, which Joel suspected was a rare occurrence for Chris Georgiou's daughter. Joel wondered if he should give her the opportunity to leave, but then she'd followed him willingly outside and now they were sitting on his front porch taking in the view.

'This almost rivals my view of the Pacific Ocean,' Em teased. Her eyes danced in the fading light, watching the slumbering harbour cove tucked into the headland.

'Almost,' Joel agreed. 'Where did you learn to paint?'

Em turned to him in surprise. 'You're really fascinated with my DIY skills, aren't you? Dad taught us when we were kids. He started out as a builder, too. So when my sister and I proposed sickening shades of lilac and pink for our rooms in our pre-teens, he made us do it ourselves.' Em smiled at the memory. 'It wasn't the neatest job, but we were both pretty proud of ourselves.'

'So just that one time?'

'No!' Em nudged him with her free hand, making the wine slosh in the glass. 'You might have noticed my big Greek family? I've been involved in lots of family projects over the years when my cousins have moved or bought their first house. I even tried painting my shitty rental room that I lived in while I was studying my undergraduate degree, but the paint didn't make much difference. It was that bad.'

'Did you prep properly?' Joel asked, still trying to imagine Em with a paintbrush. The image was becoming more and more enticing the more he thought about it.

'Yes! Mr. I-Can-Restore-My-Own-House. I know what's involved, thank you very much. How about you? Did you do much renovating when you were a kid? Or did you learn on the job later?'

Joel set his glass down carefully on the small table sitting between the two Adirondack chairs that he'd splurged on. He'd figured that if the inside of the house looked like a bomb while he renovated it, the outside could at least still look inviting.

'Joel?'

He knew he was avoiding the question. Joel was an expert at strategically avoiding those parts of his life that were unpalatable. It had become second nature to him. For some reason, instead of avoiding it completely by simply lying and saying he had learned on the job, he answered half-truthfully.

'My family didn't really do the renovation thing when we were growing up.'

'I get it,' Em replied. 'Not everyone wants to do it themselves.'

'No, it wasn't that.' He picked up the wine again, eager for his hands to have something to do. Was he really going to continue this conversation? He should just shut it down right now.

Em remained silent. It was almost like she was giving him the space to collect his thoughts.

'I grew up in a rough neighbourhood,' Joel said eventually.

'I wondered,' Em said softly. 'You talk about your family as though . . . as though you'd prefer to forget them.'

The fact that there was no judgement in her tone, only empathy, had Joel choosing to speak again.

'We were always like afterthoughts to my parents. It was only a matter of time before we did the same,' Joel said flatly.

'What do you mean?'

He took a drink of the wine and the sweetness took the edge off the bitterness. 'They were junkies for the most part, although my father was partial to alcohol. The booze was what wrote him off in the end. Or the tree did, after he'd drunk too much and got in the car. Mum died of a drug overdose about a year later.'

Joel could feel Em staring at him, but kept his eyes directed towards the view. He felt tension in every part of his body, like he was a spring ready to release.

'If that was your situation, why were you allowed to live with them?' Em asked softly.

He turned back to face her. There was sympathy in her expression, but not the horror he had feared. He felt himself relax a bit. She was tougher than she looked. Nor was she the princess everyone referred to. Joel had always suspected it, but now he knew.

He found himself telling her more. Giving her more detail than he'd given anyone in the last decade. 'We bounced around a few foster homes from time to time, but Mum always played the system to get us back. Deep down, I think she loved us. She was just too fucked up to be able to be a real mother.'

Joel knew his tone of voice was flat, devoid of all emotion, but that was the only way he could talk about his childhood.

'And your father?'

'Was a mean son of a bitch. Even without the alcohol. I'm glad he's dead.'

Em released a breath. 'I'm—'

'Don't say it, Em. Sorry doesn't change anything. It just is. Or was. Thinking of it as "was", as something that happened in the past, is how I've gotten to where I am now.'

'And your sister? You mentioned that you're not close?'

'She's not my parents, but she's not well adjusted either. Stays away from drugs, but her addictions are booze and arse-hole guys.'

Em nodded at his wine glass. 'You're drinking sensibly now, so I guess that means you don't share that addiction.'

A part of Joel wanted to hug her for being ever practical and observant enough to notice details.

'I usually nurse the one beer or wine all night,' he admitted. 'I don't mind the taste. I just don't have a thirst for it. I never wanted to.'

Em nodded. 'You should be proud, then.'

The scoff of disbelief was out of Joel's mouth before he was able to stop it. 'Proud of attempting to be a well-adjusted adult? I don't think so. It should just be a given, but my parents never figured it out. Their addictions were too strong.'

'No, I meant proud of what you've achieved. Your career. Your business. I'm not surprised you avoid heavy drinking or drugs. I have a girlfriend who is the same. Her dad's an alcoholic, so she's never touched it.'

Joel wasn't sure what he'd been expecting when he'd raised the subject of his family, but it wasn't this. All right, that wasn't entirely true. He'd expected Em to show empathy and understanding. For all her bravado, she was more like her exterior than she would have people believe—sweet and caring—not that she'd ever admit to it.

But what Joel hadn't expected was the admiration. It had him standing up and making his way over to stand by the railing.

'I don't deserve your respect, Em,' he said after a while.

'Well, you've got it,' she replied simply.

Joel already knew his heart was fractured. He'd grown up with it being that way and learned a long time ago to live with the deep cracks that would never heal. He swore he felt another fault line starting now.

He didn't turn around. 'Sometimes what's on the outside doesn't reflect the inside.'

Em stood up and came to stand behind him. 'I know that, because I'm an example of it, Joel.'

He closed his eyes as her hands slid around his waist and she pressed herself against him, laying her cheek on his shoulder blade. The part of him that wanted her—no, *needed* her—hardened. But another part of him, the part that he kept hidden, sighed silently in response. Her embrace was sexy yet sweet. Strong yet soft. All those damn contradictions that had attracted him to her in the first place.

'Em,' he said, his voice low. 'I don't want you thinking that I'm something I'm not. I want this—you—but I'm not the sort of guy—'

'That I take home to my parents? I already know that you're a Big Bad Wolf. You've been quite open about that. Plus, you've met my dad and he's considering working with you, so you can't be that bad.'

Joel squeezed his eyes shut tighter. *Oh, Em. If only you knew.*

He felt her laugh against him, and he shifted to ease the pressure in his pants.

'Joel, all I know is that whoever you are, I want you. Can we go inside now?'

A better man, a more decent man, would have told Em

that it would be better for her to leave now. That she shouldn't have anything further to do with him. He knew he'd indulged his attraction to her long enough.

But Joel wasn't either of those men, and he wanted Em, too.

Chapter Sixteen

THE FOLLOWING MORNING, Joel almost thought his night with Em had been a dream. It certainly seemed that way when he woke up in an empty bed. Mind you, trying to fit two adult bodies in his king single was laughable at best, so maybe he really had dreamed it.

Then he smelled the bacon.

He shifted into a sitting position in bed, rubbing his eyes. Yes, that was definitely bacon. When he stood to grab a pair of shorts and a T-shirt he'd left on the armchair, he saw that Em's heels were still by the door.

Em was still here? The girl who was only ever casual with guys and had wanted him gone in the morning?

Joel took the stairs two at a time with a dopey grin on his face, following the scent of the frying meat. When he arrived in the kitchen less than a minute later, the smell confirmed his suspicions.

'You're still here,' he announced.

Em flipped a piece of bacon over in the pan using tongs. 'I'm still here. Is that a problem? You didn't leave when you stayed at my place. You can kick me out if you like, but only after I've eaten breakfast. I'm hungry.'

She wasn't looking at him, and Joel wasn't sure if it was deliberate or not. He intuitively understood that this was new territory for her—for both of them. It gave him a good opportunity to look at her properly.

She'd found an old T-shirt of his and it was the only thing she wore, obviously of the mind that her office dress was too formal for breakfast.

He cleared his throat. 'Are you wearing anything under that?'

Em met his eyes for the first time, and hers were almost shy. 'And if I'm not?'

He reached out for the bench to steady himself. 'Do you want breakfast or not?'

'Definitely breakfast first. Then I'm open to . . . other things.'

There was no way Joel was throwing her out now. Not that he would have in the first place. It was cloudy today, but she lit up the kitchen like a bright morning. It was the sunniest his place had ever looked.

'I could be convinced of other things,' he told her.

She threw back her head and laughed, the sound warming the small space.

'I bet you could,' she agreed, 'but a girl needs to eat after the things you did to me last night.'

'What about what you did to me?' he shot back.

Em grinned at him, her blue eyes innocent. 'Why, Joel Scott, what could a sweet girl like me possibly do to a wicked man like you?'

Her demure expression had him striding over and pulling her roughly into his arms. The tongs clattered to the floor as his lips closed over hers, drinking her in like she was all the sustenance he needed.

She moulded her body to his, and he growled in response, grabbing her by the hips and scooping her up onto the bench in one swift move. Em released a muffled cry, and with her facing him, he stepped in between her legs.

'You're not wearing any underwear,' he whispered.

His hand slid up her inner thigh, and the closer he got to the edge of the T-shirt, the wider her eyes became. She darted a glance over to the bacon still popping and spattering in the pan.

He leaned in so that his lips brushed her ear. 'You choose.' His fingers slipped under the T-shirt and when they stroked her, he found her already damp. 'Me or the bacon, honey. Which one is it?'

She licked her lips. 'Turn it off, please,' she replied, sounding breathless. 'We can heat it up again later.'

Joel reached over with his free hand and cut the heat, then he drew her closer and kissed her senseless. He didn't need to be asked twice.

MUCH LATER, when they'd eaten and showered—then showered a second time because getting dressed in each other's presence had proven dirty work—Em sat outside in the back courtyard cradling a cup of coffee and sunning herself. Joel loved watching the way her hair changed colour in the daylight. Today it almost looked as if it had strands of sunshine intermingled with the auburn.

Em sighed. 'I really should go. I have work to do.'

'On a Saturday?'

'A PhD doesn't care what day of the week it is.'

'Surely, from what you've told me, you're close to finished already?'

'So close,' Em agreed. 'That's why I've been procrastinating, because it's going to be so weird to have finally finished it after this long. I'm not quite sure what I'll do with myself, to be honest. And don't say get a job. That's obvious.'

'When's it due?' Joel asked, an unlikely but nonetheless very tempting idea forming in his mind.

Em waved a hand at him. 'Oh, not for another month. But you know me, I'm a high achiever.'

Joel hadn't actually known Em until a week ago, but somehow in that short space of time he'd come to know her well enough to appreciate the truth of that statement.

'If you're desperate to procrastinate, you could always help me paint,' he suggested.

Em shifted in her seat and lowered her sunglasses so she could see over the top. 'Seriously? You want me to help you paint? Or are you just in need of slave labour?'

'Both,' Joel admitted.

'Huh,' Em said, then flopped back onto the chair.

Joel didn't say anything, giving her the time she needed to think it through. 'Another coffee?' he offered, because even if she said no, he was putting off her saying goodbye.

'No, I'm good. If I stay, what will I paint in?'

'My old clothes will be fine. It will help me to keep my hands off you.' Unlikely, of course, but he'd at least try.

Em set her coffee down on the paving beside the chair and swung her legs around so that she could face him. 'Show me what we'd be working on today before I decide.'

Joel nodded and gestured with his thumb to head back inside. He set off before she could join him, her words affecting him oddly.

We. What we'd be working on today.

Aside from Nate always having his back, Joel was a lone wolf. There'd never been a "we". But right now, the idea of a "we" was . . . interesting. It sounded kind of nice, actually.

When Em joined him in the rear living area, Joel nodded at several cans of paint sitting in the corner.

'This room is basically good to go. It's in better condition than the rest of the house and I figure if get a coat of paint on the walls, I can move up here and stop living in the garage.'

Em shot him an amused look. 'And stop bunking in with your Porsche? She'll get lonely.'

'She's a big girl.'

Em walked over to the tins of paint and crouched down in front of them. 'What colour scheme are you going with in here?'

'Keeping it simple,' he told her. 'An off white for the walls, as well as the skirting boards and picture rails. The sample cards are there.'

Em picked them up and thumbed through them, then stood up and surveyed the walls. 'No,' she muttered.

Joel's eyebrows rose involuntarily. 'No?'

Em turned to face him, hands on her hips. 'No,' she repeated. 'You're aiming to restore this place rather than modernise it completely, is that correct?'

Joel tried not to let his amusement show. With a project in mind, Em appeared more determined than ever. 'That's correct.'

'Then off white is fine for the walls but you need something else for the skirting boards and picture rails.'

'I do?' Joel replied, still amused. 'I don't mean to be rude, but I've lived here for a while now and—'

Em shushed him with a wave of her hand. 'Oh, I know that, but sometimes it takes someone to bounce ideas off to come to the right decision. You'd know that. You're an architect. It's just that this is such a beautiful old house, and everyone does the whole "light and airy" look. It's become boring. It almost cancels out the character of these old houses.'

'It does?'

'It does,' she replied firmly. 'I mean, you don't want to go gaudy and multicoloured like they did in the old days. That was overkill. But a touch of colour to hint at the life this old beauty has lived would add something, I think.'

Keeping a straight face, Joel nodded. 'What do you propose?'

Em pressed her lips together and narrowed her eyes. She spun around, looking at the room as if the walls themselves held the answer.

'Of course! I've got it!' Em came over and dragged him out into the courtyard. Then she pointed at the windows. 'This is the final colour scheme, isn't it? I love it, by the way.'

'Yes, the exterior was one of the first things I had done.'

'Good,' Em said. 'Then you bring some of the outside in by painting the picture rails that classic blue-grey colour.'

Joel rocked back on his heels and surveyed his house. Damn. She was definitely on to something. He bumped her shoulder with his.

'I'll only go with your suggestion if you agree to paint the picture rail. It's too detailed.'

'Gah. You hate detail and you consider yourself a painter? How about this, then? I'm guessing you need to buy that colour as an interior paint, so why don't we swing by my apartment so I can grab some of my clothes? Then we'll head to the hardware store and pick up food on the way back. You know how these things always go. Once you get into the job, you never want to stop for food. And renovating makes me hungry.'

Joel wasn't observing Em with amusement anymore. He

was observing her with something approaching disbelief and wonder. 'What about your PhD?'

'It'll keep. And this is a much more enjoyable way to spend a Saturday.'

'You think painting is enjoyable?'

Em screwed up her nose. 'Good point. But the end product is always worth it, isn't it? Don't make me reconsider or you'll lose the offer of help.'

Joel didn't want her to reconsider. Truthfully, he didn't want her to go anywhere. He wanted her to stay right here with him. Whether it was painting, or cooking, or doing toe-curling things to her in the bedroom, he wanted Em here for as long she was willing to stay.

Which was an extremely bad idea, but right now Joel was too charmed by her to care.

Chapter Seventeen

A WEEK later on Sunday morning, Em arrived at the beach right on time for her exercise session with Jess and Kat.

'You look chipper,' Jess exclaimed.

'Chipper?' Kat asked Jess. 'You're the only person I know who uses a word like "chipper".'

Jess grinned, not insulted. 'Hey, if the shoe fits. Good weekend so far, Em?'

'Not bad,' Em agreed, doing her best to tone down her smile a bit. If it had warranted a "chipper" comment from Jess, then she was definitely acting too happy. Usually she was half asleep and less than motivated for their weekly exercise sessions.

'What gives?' Kat demanded, and Jess rolled her eyes.

'Really, Kat? It's a beautiful morning to be out exercising on the beach. Nothing has to give.'

Kat ignored Jess and put her hands on her hips. 'I'm guessing it has something to do with your mystery man, am I right? I've seen him here a few times this week.'

Of course you have. Kat never missed a damn thing.

'So?' Em replied.

'So I didn't think you'd decided whether you were going to see him again or not?'

'I decided to see him again,' Em said vaguely, and Kat shook her head.

'And?'

Rather than labour on the physical side of their relationship, Em chose to be honest. 'And I've been helping him with some painting.'

Kat gaped at her. 'You *what?*' It was unusual for Kat to lose her cool.

Em grinned. 'You heard me. I helped him paint his living room.'

'That sounds . . .' Jess began.

'Boring,' Kat finished for her, appearing as though she didn't believe Em.

Em sighed and got her phone from her back pocket, because experience told her that Kat liked proof. 'Here,' she said, and shoved the phone at Kat. 'Before and after photos. The picture railing colour was my idea.'

'Oh, it's beautiful, Em,' crooned Jess, looking at the images over Kat's shoulder. 'Where is it?'

'Over in Manly. It's a seriously gorgeous old colonial that he's fixing up. He's got so much work to do it's not funny, but it's going to be magnificent when it's finished.'

Kat's free hand shot up. 'Hold on for just a minute. Two weeks ago you had a one-night stand with this man and now you're helping him paint his property? That doesn't sound like a one-off thing to me.'

Well, when Kat said it like that . . .

Em's reply was to shrug. 'So? We both like old houses. He needed help. Can you believe he's doing it all himself?'

'And so you just went around there and painted his house with him and that was it?' Kat asked.

Em's shrug was a little stiffer this time. 'We ate some food together, too.'

'Kat,' Jess interjected. 'I'm not sure it's any of your business—'

'Did you sleep together again?' pressed Kat.

Jess shot Em a look of apology. It wasn't her fault that Kat was paid to be nosy for a living.

'Fine. We slept together,' admitted Em. At least now maybe Kat would let the subject drop.

'And?'

Jess eyed Kat. '*Kat.*'

'And it was nice, OK? We might even do it again on account of it being so nice, if you get what I mean.' In fact, Em had plans to head over to Joel's place again tonight once she'd spent a couple more hours working on her PhD.

'And the painting?' Kat asked.

'I won't rule out helping him again if he needs it. It was fun.'

Kat observed Em through narrowed eyes for a second longer, then started doing stretches.

'That's great, Em,' Jess said, ever supportive. 'It will be nice for you to have something else to focus on other than your university work.'

'Doesn't sound casual to me,' Kat muttered, still stretching.

'What did you say?' Em demanded.

Kat stopped stretching and turned to face Em. 'I said it doesn't sound casual to me.'

'Of course it's casual,' Em snapped, not certain what her friend was getting at. As chipper as Em was this morning, between her PhD, the painting, and Joel, she was actually pretty tired.

Kat appeared unperturbed. 'Multiple sleepovers and helping the man renovate his house is your definition of casual, is it?'

'I don't know. He's becoming a friend, I guess.'

Kat's dark eyebrows rose in disbelief and she collapsed onto the picnic table beside them, doubled over with laughter.

'What's so funny?' Jess asked.

Kat pointed at Em. 'She is.'

'Why?' asked Jess, which was what Em was thinking as well.

Kat caught her breath and patted her chest like that was the best laugh she'd had in a long time. Em still couldn't work out what was so funny.

'Think of it this way. If he's a friend that you're having sex with, what is it?'

'Friends with benefits?' suggested Jess.

But Kat's words had hit their mark, and Em collapsed unsteadily on the seat beside Kat.

Kat patted her shoulder. 'Sorry I'm coming across so rude. I just couldn't believe that you didn't see it, that's all.'

'Oh, I see it now.' Em was pretty sure she'd gone pale. 'Thanks. I think.'

'See what?' persisted Jess.

'If she's seeing mystery man for meals, helping him around his house, and sleeping with him, that doesn't really make him just a friend or the relationship casual, does it?'

'Oh. *Oh*,' said Jess, finally seeing Kat's point. 'No, it doesn't. Does it? Em?'

Em was too busy fanning herself with her hand, because she suddenly felt way too hot and they hadn't even started exercising yet.

'What are you going to do about it?' asked Jess gently.

'I don't know. Pretend it's normal?'

'Well, it kind of is. If he's your——'

'No! Don't say it!' cried Em.

'Boyfriend,' Jess finished. She reached over and squeezed Em's hand. 'If he's worth more than a one-night stand, he must be special.'

Joel was special all right. More special than Em had been willing to admit to herself before now. Trust Kat to bring it up.

'He's . . .' started Em, but she wasn't sure how to finish the sentence. Joel wasn't her boyfriend, but he wasn't a casual fling either.

'Like no one you've ever met. Isn't that what you said to us the other week?' Kat asked.

'Yes,' Em said morosely. 'What the hell am I going to do now?'

'Well, having a boyfriend isn't so bad,' Jess told her.

No, it wasn't, actually. If having a boyfriend involved all the things that she and Joel had been spending the last week doing, then it wasn't so bad at all. Except that neither of them wanted it, of course.

'I don't think he sees himself as boyfriend material,' Em clarified.

'Oh,' Jess said, slumping slightly beside her.

'Why not?' Kat asked.

'Oh, a number of things,' Em said vaguely. 'Like me, he's not into relationships, for one. And he's committed to his business.'

'Matt and I live and breathe our work and we're engaged,' Kat pointed out.

'Not to mention my father,' Em added. 'He can't find out about this either.'

They all fell silent.

'So you don't tell your father,' Kat said after a while. 'You keep having the relationship you're not having and see where it goes. You don't need to tell anyone else at this stage. We won't tell anyone.'

'No, we won't say a word if you don't want us to,' Jess affirmed.

'Thanks, guys. I'd appreciate that. I never set out for this to happen. It just kind of did,' Em replied, feeling a bit numb.

'If you're really worried about the relationship thing, you could call things off. Or give it some space for a while perhaps?' Kat suggested.

'I could . . .'

That would certainly be the sensible thing to do. She didn't want Joel getting the wrong idea, but then he hadn't been putting any pressure on Em. Things had been evolving naturally on both sides.

And the idea of not seeing Joel for a while? It made her heart clench. It had only been a couple of weeks, but Em couldn't imagine not having Joel in her life.

Holy shit. Her heart? Since when did her heart have anything to do with this?

Em groaned.

Kat put an arm around her and squeezed lightly. 'You don't have to figure it out now, trust me. Give it some time and you'll work it out.'

'Come on,' Jess said, standing up. 'Let's get moving. It will make you feel better, Em.'

Em followed her friends, lagging behind slightly.

'And hey, Em,' Jess called back to her as they started a light jog along the beach. 'If you do decide to keep the mystery man around, we'd love to meet him, of course.'

Kat held up her hands. 'I promise I'd be on my best behaviour. Mostly.'

Em shook her head, and they all laughed.

'Regardless, you should still have celebratory end-of-PhD

drinks at your apartment,' Jess suggested. 'That's what you've been planning, isn't it? It will be fun.'

Yeah, and invite Joel along like he's my boyfriend? Em thought, but didn't say it. She didn't think Joel would go for that. Especially if they wanted to keep things casual.

If that's what they still were. Em suddenly wasn't so sure anymore.

Chapter Eighteen

JOEL JUMPED when his phone rang. He'd been jumpy all morning. Every time someone messaged or called, he twitched like the goddamn phone was connected to one of his nerve endings. This time when he saw who was calling, he became short of breath, too.

Chris Georgiou.

This was it. D-Day. The day Georgiou Developments would announce the winner of the tender. This phone call was going to be either good or bad news. Chris would let him down easy or inform him that this was the start of their long-term working relationship. Joel honestly had no idea which one it would be.

The fact that he was involved with Em didn't make the waiting any easier. On one hand, it would probably be for the best if Georgiou chose the other tenderer. Less complicated. But damn, he still really, really wanted this contract because of the positive things it would mean for his business. A client like Georgiou would put them in the league of the big boys. It would catapult their reputation in the eyes of other major developers. It would take their firm from comfortably profitable to a period of growth and expansion.

'Answer the phone, you idiot,' Joel muttered to himself, then cleared his throat as he hit accept. 'Chris, hi.'

'Joel. I'm not going to beat around the bush. You know why I'm calling. You've got it. We're giving you the contract.'

A moment of silence followed while Joel digested Chris's words.

Holy shit. They won! They won the contract!

Joel jumped up from his desk and ran out of his office, the phone still pressed to his ear.

'Chris, thank you. That's amazing news. Speaking on behalf of the team, I know they're all going to be as thrilled as I am by this opportunity.'

Joel skidded to a halt at Nate's open office door. When Nate saw him, Joel gave him a thumbs up. Nate's blue eyes widened, and he jumped up from his desk then did a fist pump. Grinning, Joel returned to his office. There would be time to celebrate later.

'I know you're keen to work with us,' Chris said. 'I'm not going to lie. It wasn't an easy decision and your sustainable approach represents a diversion from our usual path. I trust you'll make it the right decision with time and that's why we selected you. Audrey will be in touch with the documentation later this week, including some key dates for the project.'

'Great. I'll tell Tina to look out for it. And I'm well aware that our approach is different to your norm, so with that in mind I'll say thank you again for the opportunity.'

'I didn't survive in this business by doing what was always done. You have to take calculated risks to remain competitive.'

'Agreed,' replied Joel. While he didn't necessarily like being referred to as a "calculated risk", he wasn't going to look a gift horse in the mouth.

'There is one other thing before I go,' Chris added, his voice sounding thoughtful on the other end of the line.

'Sure,' said Joel, wondering what it could be.

'How did Emily really go the other day?'

Joel swallowed and lowered himself into his desk chair. This was the part of the relationship that he hadn't been so keen on, but they'd already won the contract, so he just needed to keep things professional and polite.

'I didn't attend the meeting,' Joel told Chris. 'But from what I've heard, Sasha was very impressed.'

'Good, good. Do you think you'll get her back?'

Joel felt some tension creep back into his shoulders that had vanished with the news of their tender win. 'I'll be meeting with Sasha in the next few days to discuss next steps.' In truth, Joel had been putting it off.

'Can I offer some advice?'

Joel suspected Chris would whether he wanted to hear it or not. 'Certainly.'

'I know my daughter is an unusual combination. Overqualified and underqualified at the same time.'

Joel assumed Chris was referring to Em's formidable knowledge compared to her lack of business experience.

'I'd like you to give her a chance,' Chris finished.

The elation Joel had been feeling a moment ago disappeared. Was Chris saying what he thought he was saying? Was he implying that he wanted Joel to offer her the job?

'I thought we were giving her a chance,' Joel replied carefully.

'She just needs a foot in the door, if you know what I mean. I would have given it to her myself, but she won't have a bar of it.'

'You asked her to work at Georgiou?' Em had never given Joel the impression it was even an option.

'Not in so many words,' Chris said. 'I knew if I did, she'd have rejected the idea. She's determined like her old man and wants to make a go of things herself.'

Joel didn't doubt Em's determination, but he did doubt this idea of a job offer from Chris, despite what he said. Everything he knew about Em suggested her father had always sidelined her goals. Joel needed to tread carefully.

'With all due respect, Chris, I don't think Em needs a foot in the door. I think more than one door will be opened to her once she looks properly.'

'That may be so, but I'd prefer if it was your door if you get my meaning.'

Joel stilled. 'And why is that?' Joel was glad that Chris couldn't see the way he was sitting stiffly in his chair.

'Because once she figures out that the corporate world isn't for her and decides to settle down like her sister, her passion will wane. The position you have going is perfect. She can fill the hole in your business under that older lady you've got there, and when she moves on to do other things, you can just employ another junior.'

Joel's free hand clenched the arm of his chair. 'Actually, I don't see the role as a junior position.' He attempted to keep his voice neutral.

Joel wasn't sure what version of his daughter Chris was talking about, but it wasn't the one that Joel knew. That Em was driven and thirsty to create change. The concept of her giving up or settling down wasn't in Em's vocabulary. Hell, even the way she had taken to painting his living room the other week was enough to tell him that. Everything Em did was infused with passion and determination, and it was one of the things that Joel loved about her.

Loved her? What the hell was happening to him?

Joel was glad he was sitting down. His brain must have

momentarily imploded, because he almost missed Chris's response.

'How do you see the position exactly?' he asked.

Joel cleared his throat, ignoring the way that his heart was pounding, and it had nothing to do with this painfully uncomfortable conversation with Chris.

'I see the position as one that will grow over time. Sasha can mentor the person in this role, and eventually they'll be able to take on more responsibility.'

'Ah, I see.' Joel could imagine Chris tapping his stubby fingers on the desk in front of him, a habit Joel had witnessed at many of their meetings so far. 'My mistake. Maybe my Emily isn't the best fit for this role. I might start putting some feelers out myself—not that I'll tell her that. She wouldn't like her father getting involved, but unfortunately her father is too involved in this industry already.'

'I'd appreciate if you didn't do that for now. I think she's a great fit for the role.'

What the hell are you doing?

Joel's words were met with silence, and he wondered if Chris was thinking the same thing. Joel barrelled on before Chris could say anything else.

'Of course, I still need to meet with Sasha and discuss the details further, but we'll definitely be getting her back in to talk.'

'Well then,' said Chris, sounding surprised. 'I won't interfere. I'll leave it to you and your team to make the final decision. If you do offer her the job, I won't say that I'll be disappointed. It will be good to know that she lands somewhere with people that I respect.'

'I appreciate that.' Joel's mind was still whirling with what he'd just said.

'Excellent. And Joel? We never had this conversation, alright?'

'How do you mean?'

'If Emily finds out that I've been interfering, she won't speak to me for weeks. I don't need to give her another reason to lecture me.' He laughed loudly, obviously amused at his own joke.

'Of course,' Joel said, once again with a certainty he didn't feel. Then added, 'We really do appreciate the opportunity to work with Georgiou.'

'That's enough of the formalities, son. We're partners now. I'll be in touch.'

Joel sat staring at his phone after Chris cut the line.

Holy shit. What had just happened? They'd been given the contract. That was cause for massive celebration. But the discussion about Em and the job? That had left a sour taste in Joel's mouth. As soon as Chris had mentioned it, Joel had been ready to shut the conversation down—respectfully, of course. He wasn't about to offend a new client.

But then when Chris had started saying those things about Em—those things that simply didn't fit with Joel's under-standing of who she was—Joel had seen red. He'd damn well offer Em the job if it meant showing her father what she was capable of, and that she wasn't just some academic kicking around in the corporate world for entertainment. Em had real potential, and she certainly wasn't going to "settle down" and forget about her passion for sustainability. It was part of who she was. If Joel had his way, Em would be managing that entire section of the business alongside Sasha before too long.

'Shit,' he whispered, and stood up.

What was he thinking? They were sleeping together. But the more Joel thought about it, the more he liked the idea of Em working here. Sasha had seemed very confident in Em's abilities after their initial meeting. Joel was confident in her abilities, too.

So confident that you'd offer her the job?

Joel swore again. That was exactly what he was thinking. And he sincerely hoped it wouldn't all blow up in his face.

Chapter Nineteen

ON THURSDAY EVENING, Em was over at Joel's place again, painting. They'd moved on to the bedrooms upstairs after the floorboards had been polished earlier in the week.

'You know, I'm beginning to think that you're just using me for my painting skills,' Em commented, angling her paintbrush to cut in the edges while Joel rolled the walls.

'I'm not just using you for your painting skills . . .' He was concentrating and didn't turn around, but Em still blushed.

They both fell quiet again. The conversation had been limited since she'd arrived, which was unlike them. They often had periods of comfortable silence, but tonight it felt like neither of them wanted to talk.

Em wasn't sure what was on Joel's mind—her father's new project, perhaps?—but she was quiet for a number of reasons. She'd completed her PhD on the weekend, and ever since, she'd felt like she was at a loose end. She'd been researching and applying for jobs, but that didn't fill her days completely. After so many years of study, it felt strange not to have something to learn or research. Em secretly worried that maybe she wasn't cut out for the corporate world after all.

It wasn't the only thing on her mind this evening. When Em had been applying for those other jobs, she'd kept wondering if she should cross Joel's job off her list. She hadn't heard back from Sasha, and Em didn't want to press Joel for more information until he was ready. While she was ecstatic that his firm had won her father's contract, it made her extra aware of the family connection. The last thing she wanted was for Joel to offer her the job because of that—not that she really thought he would. Joel was too much of an independent thinker, and he knew Em would refuse if that were the case.

The other complicating factor was that Em was starting to think that she would really like the job. All the other jobs that she'd been applying for didn't excite her in the same way as the one at Scott & Morris. The other positions were in large corporations that would require her to apply only a fraction of her knowledge. In companies that large, there seemed to be so many people that it meant you were only responsible for one tiny slice of the pie. At Joel's firm, it was different. They had about thirty-odd staff, which meant it was small enough to allow her to use her skills across a variety of areas, but big enough to grow and mentor her.

'You're quiet tonight,' Joel said as he dipped the roller in the paint tray.

'So are you,' Em shot back, not quite ready to share her thoughts with him.

He smiled. 'Touché. Anything you want to talk about?'

'It's nothing major. It just feels so weird not to have my PhD to work on anymore.'

'A relief, surely?'

'Yes and no.'

'You should do something to mark the occasion. It's the end of an era for you. It deserves to be recognised.'

Em debated whether to tell Joel about the other subject that was on her mind at the moment. She'd rather not bring up the job as it was too much of a minefield, so she settled on discussing her thoughts about the party. Mainly because she didn't want him to feel left out.

'You know my neighbours that I'm friends with? They keep telling me I should have drinks or a party at my place to celebrate.'

'That sounds like a great idea. I'm assuming they're offering to join you?'

'That was the suggestion. I thought I'd keep it low-key and just make it good friends, not family.'

'Yeah, otherwise it will get out of hand. How many cousins did you say you had?'

'Too many,' Em replied.

They kept painting, and the question that had been on Em's mind all week remained on the tip of her tongue.

Would you like to join me?

Except it was the sort of question that you asked someone you were in a relationship with. It wasn't what you asked someone when you were casual.

Because painting Joel's house means we're casual?

'Em, I can hear you thinking from over here. No pressure to tell me, of course. Just know that you're thinking loudly.'

Em dropped the paintbrush onto the paint lid in frustration. 'Fine. If I tell you, you have to promise not to freak out.'

Joel lowered the roller. 'That sounds ominous. It takes a lot to make me freak out, just so you know.'

Em grimaced. 'Yeah, I kind of got that already. Anyway, I'll just say it. My girlfriends suggested I invite you along to my drinks night and I kind of want to.'

There. She'd said it.

Joel set the roller back in the paint tray and came over to stand directly in front of her. As usual, his expression was hard to read. But his mouth twitched, so that meant he wasn't over-reacting at least.

'You "kind of" want to invite me,' he repeated. 'Why kind of? I'm not sure whether to be flattered or insulted.'

'Well, I know it's sort of overstepping the mark.'

'And what mark is that exactly?'

Em waved a hand in between them. 'This mark. The casual one. If you come along, then people will assume that we're . . . Well, *you know.*'

'Actually, I'm not sure I do.' He was smiling properly now.

'It's not the sort of thing you do when you're casual, that's all.'

He nodded once, still smiling. 'Ah, I see. So it would be inappropriate?'

'Well, yeah, I think so. Don't you?'

'I think . . .' He reached over and tucked some hair behind her ear. It had become something of a habit recently, and Em liked it. 'I think that we don't want to be *inappropriate.*'

Then he leaned in and kissed her until that familiar slow burn flared in her core, and she desperately wished that the walls weren't wet so that she could steady herself against one.

When he eased back, he gave her a knockout grin. 'There's nothing proper about us, Em.'

She threw her hands up in the air. 'I know! That's exactly my point. If you come along, then they'll assume.'

'Assume?'

He was going to make her say it, wasn't he?

'Yes, they'll assume that we're in a *relationship.*'

'Not if you tell people that I'm just a friend.' Then he kissed her again.

Em waited until he'd finished kissing her again. She was only human, after all. 'You seem extremely relaxed about my predicament. I didn't want you to feel offended if I don't invite you.'

His thumb brushed her cheek. 'Firstly, I won't be offended. Of course I'd like to celebrate with you, but we can do our own thing if you'd like. Maybe go out to dinner sometime? How does that sound?'

'Nice,' Em admitted.

It actually sounded really nice. Too nice, in fact, because it was exactly the sort of thing people in relationships did. What was happening to her? When had the idea of being in a relationship become so . . . so . . . well, not so bad?

'You're thinking again,' Joel warned her, and Em cracked a smile.

'So you're OK either way then?' she asked.

'Perfectly.'

'Huh.'

Joel appeared to hide a grin and turned to retrieve the paint roller.

'Hang on a sec,' she said, as another thought occurred to her. 'You *want* to come to my drinks?'

Joel began rolling the area of wall that still needed doing. 'In case you haven't noticed, I generally enjoy doing anything that involves being with you.'

Em found herself blushing. That was actually kind of sweet. It was the kind of thing that someone said when . . .

'Oh my God,' she breathed.

Joel kept painting. 'You're only just figuring it out, aren't you?'

'You *knew*?'

'Well, when we've been spending every waking minute with each other and it hasn't been all about the sex—

although the sex is pretty damn good—then you start to wonder.'

'Can you please turn around?' Em asked, her hands shaking slightly.

Joel did as she requested, and for once she could read his expression. It was gentle and almost amused.

'You think that we're in a relationship?' she asked.

'I suspect as much,' he replied simply.

'And it doesn't bother you?'

He shrugged, like what they were talking about wasn't as serious as it was. 'It would bother me more if you weren't around so much.'

'Oh my God,' Em repeated, and lowered herself onto the old wooden stool sitting nearby. 'We're in a relationship.' It was a statement this time.

Joel put the roller down again and crouched in front of her. 'I was kind of hoping you wouldn't notice.'

'Why?'

'Well, this.'

Em cracked another smile.

'See, here's the thing,' Joel went on. 'I don't actually care one iota what this is or isn't. Casual or a relationship. Call it what you like. All I know is that we're good together, Em, and the more time that I spend with you the better it gets.'

Em's heart clenched. That was definitely the sort of thing someone in a relationship said. Below the shock, there was something else surfacing.

Joy.

'Don't look so scared, honey,' Joel said, reaching over to cradle her cheek in the palm of his hand. 'It's really not that bad.'

'But we don't *do* relationships,' Em insisted.

'No,' Joel corrected. 'We didn't do relationships with *other* people. You're the only person I've ever met that I've wanted to be with like this. I can't explain it. And I don't want to. Just promise me that you'll stop trying to label it, because it doesn't make any difference.' Em groaned, and Joel chuckled. 'My theory is that I'm going to enjoy it as long as it lasts,' he said softly.

He was still looking at her with that, with that . . . deep affection in his eyes.

Em threaded her fingers through his. 'You say it like you expect it to end one day.'

His eyes darkened. 'Some things in life are too good to be true.'

Em gaped at him. 'So, according to you, we're in a relationship, but it's not going to last? Well, that's kind of depressing!'

Joel stood abruptly and turned away from her. 'Sorry. I didn't mean for it to sound that way.'

'But you believe it?'

Until a minute ago, Em hadn't realised that they were in a relationship together. But now it felt critical to make him understand that it wasn't going to end.

Joel picked up the roller again and started painting.

'Joel?'

Em knew that he was doing that avoidance technique thing that he did occasionally. Usually when the subject of his past came up. Suddenly, Em felt an intense dislike for his parents. She suspected they had something to do with this disturbing turn in the topic of conversation.

'Joel,' Em repeated, her tone firm.

Joel sighed and kept painting. 'Guys like me don't end up with women like you.'

Em stood up. 'I'd say that's up to me to decide.'

'I know. And right now you're happy to choose me. But later? We'll see.'

Em stared at his back, angry and confused. She wished that he'd let down his guard more when it came to his past. But then, who was Em to push? She'd had a loving, safe upbringing. Who knew what sort of horrible memories Joel had of his childhood that still affected him to this day? So she'd leave it. For now. But her mind was made up about something else.

'I'd like you to come to my party,' she told him.

Joel stopped rolling, then after a brief pause started back up again. 'OK. I'd like to be there. What will you tell people?'

'I'll tell them that you're a friend like you suggested. How's that? My two neighbours are the only ones that know anything, and I'll threaten to un-invite them if they're not discreet.'

His shoulders shook with silent laughter. 'So I guess that means we're not telling your family?' he joked.

Em went over and put her arms around him, hugging him from behind. As always, his muscled back felt strong and steady.

'Unless you want wedding bells sounding, I think it's better if we continue to keep this under wraps. It's for our own protection.'

Joel twisted in her embrace to face her, putting the roller down. 'Actually, I agree, but not only for that reason. We'd like to get you back into the office again to discuss that position. It's best if we're not . . . you know.'

'In a relationship? Sleeping together?'

'All the above, I guess.'

'Would Nate be angry if he knew?'

Joel rubbed a hand across his hair. 'I don't think he'd be thrilled, no.'

Em winced. 'It would definitely look bad. Like you were giving me the position because we're sleeping together. You're not, are you?'

Joel nudged her gently. 'Of course not. I genuinely think you're a good candidate for the role.'

'Then we keep it professional,' Em said firmly.

Joel pulled her closer so that they were pressed against one another and raised his dark eyebrows at her. 'Professional, huh?'

Em squirmed against him, rubbing against the hard rise in his jeans. Her body flared with heat.

Damn it. How had things gotten so complicated? She wanted Joel, and she wanted this job, too. Deep down, Em worried that if she was truly professional, then she would make a choice between them. But right now, the obvious choice was to surrender to Joel, because when she was in his arms like this, he was the only thing that mattered.

Chapter Twenty

EM RARELY DIPPED into the money that her father gave her. While he still insisted on giving her a monthly allowance, Em generally only used what she needed. It meant that she'd built up a nice little nest egg over time from the funds she hadn't touched. On this occasion, she'd figured what the hell.

She'd made it. She'd done it. She'd completed her PhD, and it was time to celebrate.

So maybe it wasn't so bad having a father who insisted on spoiling you. Her penthouse apartment overlooking the Pacific Ocean was the perfect place to host a party, and she'd splurged and hired caterers to supply food and drinks. So far about forty guests had arrived with another twenty or so due to come and go during the night. Joel being one of them.

'Is he here yet?' Jess whispered in Em's ear so that she couldn't be heard above the music.

'Not yet. And don't forget—he's a friend and work colleague. That's all.'

Jess grinned, her shoulders rising in excitement. 'Because

you've got a new job! That's so amazing, Em. I'm so happy for you.'

It was kind of amazing. As of Monday, Em would start work at Scott & Morris as their newest employee. The next interview with Sasha had gone well, and following that she'd had a final interview that had included Joel, Nate and a couple of their other senior managers. They'd been impressed, and soon Em wouldn't be an academic anymore.

'I agree,' said Kat, standing on Em's other side. 'Just don't rush to move out, alright? We'd miss you too much. And who else would suffer those early morning weekend exercise sessions with me?'

'Suffer?' scoffed Jess. 'I thought you enjoyed them!'

Kat's fiancé, Matt, joined them, along with Jess's comedian boyfriend, Ant.

'What's this I hear about exercise?' Ant asked. 'Jess hasn't signed me up for another triathlon, has she?'

Jess shot Ant an insulted look. 'No. And you loved it.'

'Shh, we agreed that we're not telling anyone, didn't we? Otherwise this whole exercise thing might catch on.'

Everyone laughed, because Jess was the creator and face of the country's hottest fitness brand, and until recently Ant had hated exercise. Not after Jess had spent three months training him, though. Ant looked better than ever, in Em's opinion. Or maybe that was due to moving in with Jess. They were really cute together.

Realising her train of thought, Em took a big sip of her drink. Since when did she find couples cute? It was really hard not to find Jess and Ant cute, though. They both laughed so much when they were around each other.

Em surveyed Kat and her partner, Matt. They'd been together longer and were just as in love as Jess and Ant. Kat was leaning against Matt's chest, his arm draped around her shoulder, and they looked completely relaxed in each other's company. Like they knew they worked well together, which Em supposed they did.

Good grief. What was wrong with her? When had she started obsessing about other couples and noticing if they were happy or not? It wasn't like she wanted that for herself.

Which made her think of Joel. Em looked around, wondering if she'd missed his arrival. They'd agreed not to make a big deal about it. Em was secretly glad that her sister, Ana, hadn't been able to make it tonight. While it turned out that Joel knew a couple of her university colleagues attending the party, as they'd done some research with Joel's company, Em was glad that she didn't have to explain his presence to Ana.

'Lost something?' Ant asked Em, and Jess nudged him.

'She's just being a proper host and ensuring all of her guests are enjoying themselves,' Jess told him.

'Then she needs another drink, because this night is about you, Em,' Ant told her. 'Or should that be *doctor*?'

Em screwed up her nose. 'Technically, that's not correct. I only just submitted my PhD, so it will be a few more months before that happens.'

'It will give you time to get used to it,' Matt spoke up. He was a medical doctor working as an obstetrician at a big Sydney hospital.

'You deserve the title,' Kat added.

'Stop,' Em urged them. 'Unlike all of you, I'm yet to make a living out of my work.'

'So?' Kat said. 'It doesn't make what you've achieved any less valuable. More so, given you weren't out to make a buck when you did your research.'

'Really, the admiration is flattering, but unnecessary,' Em told them.

Ant leaned in closer to Em. 'My tip? Take the admiration any way you can get it.'

They all laughed. Em supposed Ant had a point. Tonight she was celebrating what she'd worked so hard to achieve. So when one of the waiters offered her another drink, Em took it.

JOEL WAS RUNNING LATE. He'd been caught up at work and then the Friday night traffic had been horrendous. He'd tried messaging Em twice, but she hadn't replied. Joel could only hope it was because she was too busy celebrating to notice his lateness.

Finding a parking spot out on the street proved difficult. He would have much rather parked the Porsche in one of the visitors' spots in the basement of Em's complex, but that would look too obvious. He didn't need people wondering why she was giving him special treatment.

He ended up parking way down the street in a spot much tighter than he would have liked. By the time he walked to Em's building, a thin sheen of sweat covered his forehead. He debated taking his suit jacket off, but couldn't be bothered carrying it or returning to his car when he was already late.

At the front entrance, he hit the button for the penthouse. Thirty seconds went by with no reply. Joel could hear the party from down here. Laughter and music floated across the night, before being drowned out each time the waves crashed onto the shore below.

Impatiently, Joel pressed the buzzer again. At least he wasn't being missed, he supposed. This time the door buzzed and the speaker on the security system activated. All he heard was laughter and music, much louder this time, so he shoved the door open with his shoulder and went inside.

By the time he arrived at the penthouse, Joel was irritated to find himself nervous. There was absolutely nothing to be apprehensive about. He assumed that he'd be older than a lot of the people attending tonight, and he wasn't looking to fit in, just to drop by to say congratulations to a friend on her recent PhD completion.

Some friend.

Joel pushed the thought out of his mind. For tonight, Em *was* just a friend. That was it. And a new colleague starting Monday.

Aside from the unexpected nerves, Joel had to admit that he was a bit curious about what Em's circle of friends would be like. On account of their casual nature, Joel had never had the chance to meet any of the friends Em saw regularly.

Arriving at the front door, Joel had to excuse himself and slip past two young women having an intense conversation. They both looked to be about Em's age—late twenties perhaps? They gave him a curious glance as he passed, then went back to their conversation.

Inside, the music was louder than he expected. Some dance-style song that he wasn't familiar with. He excused himself again as he made his way past more guests drinking and chatting in the hallway. He felt all of a sudden like the suit had been a bad choice, but he'd been running so late that he hadn't had the chance to go home and change.

He stepped into the heart of the penthouse, an expansive space that housed the living area and kitchen. Tonight it felt less like a home and more of a function space. Em had placed fairy lights at various vantage points around the room and dimmed the overhead lights. With the spectacular view over the ocean and the catering staff swarming around like worker ants, Joel almost didn't recognise it.

'Would you like a drink?' One of the waiters had sidled up to him unnoticed.

Joel surveyed the tray the waiter was holding and reflexively held up a hand. 'No, thanks. I'm driving.'

'I can get you a mineral water?' the waiter suggested.

'That would be great. Thanks.'

'I'll be right back.'

Joel stepped to one side, placing himself at the edge of the kitchen area. He couldn't go anywhere now until the guy came back with his drink, so he took the opportunity to discreetly survey the party.

As far as parties went, it wasn't anything like the fucked-up shit he'd made a habit of going to in his late teens. This was polished. The guests all wore fashionable clothing and were mainly drinking wine, champagne, or the odd beer for the guys. Joel would be surprised if there were drugs to be found anywhere. It wasn't Em's style. She was too much of a good girl.

Joel tapped his thumb against his trouser pocket. Actually, recent experience had taught him Em was a lot less of a good girl than he'd imagined—not that he was complaining. Joel still doubted her mischievousness stretched to illicit drugs, though.

'Here you go.' The waiter returned and Joel accepted the mineral water gratefully.

He was thirstier than he'd realised after the drive and walk up here. Despite that, he paused with the glass to his lips when he spotted Em. She was out on the balcony, and until a moment ago had been surrounded by a group of friends. Several of them had just stood back so that Em could pose for a photo.

Even from the kitchen, Joel could see that her flawless skin held a rosy glow and her eyes shone. She'd piled her auburn waves into a messy up-do and the cute dress she was wearing made him wish once more that he'd ditched the suit. It was hotter in here than he'd expected, probably on account of all the people. But now, having seen Em, it felt several degrees hotter.

The dress she wore was a deep blue with some sort of glittery or reflective quality to it. It was strapless and fitted to the waist, then flowed outwards into a cheeky short skirt that did nothing to help Joel's intensifying heat. It revealed perfect legs that seemed longer than he remembered.

Just as Joel was preparing to go over and say hi, a guy stepped in and gave Em a tight hug. Em threw her arms around him happily and they embraced. For too long.

Much too long.

What was going on? Who was this guy?

The guy in question eased back and then Em stood on tip toes and pressed a kiss to his cheek.

At least it was on the cheek.

But they still seemed overly familiar with one another. Joel couldn't place why exactly.

The guy stepped in beside her for a photo, and the way his arm slipped easily around Em's waist made Joel's jaw clench. Em leaned against him happily and they kept chatting.

Joel blew out a breath and put his now empty glass on a tray a waiter offered. With nothing to do with his hands, he shoved them into his pockets.

So coming tonight wasn't such a great idea after all. Something told Joel when he went over there, he wouldn't get the same enthusiastic welcome on account of them having to pretend to be "just friends". Although maybe Em was this comfortable with everyone. That guy was just a friend, surely? What did he know?

With their casual arrangement/relationship/friends with benefits deal—Joel had given up trying to define it—he only saw one side of Em. Sure, it was the extremely sexy side. And the capable side when it came to her career and work. But it still wasn't who she was in her entirety.

Joel was starting to wonder if maybe he didn't know Em very well at all.

Chapter Twenty-One

'YOU MUST BE JOEL.'

Joel had been so busy watching Em outside that he hadn't seen the woman approach. When he turned to face her, he stiffened in recognition.

'Kat Chalmers,' he said.

The television news journalist was just as striking in person as she was on the screen, and a hell of a lot more intense than he'd anticipated. Em had hinted at Kat's fierce nature, and meeting her dark brown eyes, Joel didn't doubt it for a second.

'Have you seen Em yet?' Kat asked.

Her voice was low, but he could somehow make it out perfectly despite the noise. It was like she had some sort of magical ability to hold a completely private conversation in public.

'Not yet,' he replied, also keeping his voice low, and returning his focus to Em, who was outside laughing.

'Just so you're aware, everyone has been plying her with drinks, so she's a bit tipsy,' Kat informed him.

Joel swallowed and it felt forced. He guessed it was to be

expected given the celebratory circumstances. Normal even. Unfortunately for Joel, nothing in his life that had ever involved alcohol had been particularly normal. Em hadn't mentioned Joel's past to Kat, had she? Was that why she was warning him?

He returned his gaze to Kat. The amused expression on her dark features suggested a friend sharing in another friend's fun while watching out for her, that was all.

'You came straight from work.' Someone in Kat's profession didn't so much ask questions as determine answers.

'Yes, and now I feel overdressed, but I ran out of time.'

'It's nice to see one of Em's men polished for a change.'

One of Em's men? The stiffness Joel had experienced in his shoulders earlier when he'd seen Em with that guy—who was still much too close for Joel's liking—returned. He fisted his hands in his pockets.

'I think I'm unusual,' Joel said, keeping his voice neutral.

Kat turned to face him, her head tilted to one side. 'Oh, you most certainly are, and just between us, it's a welcome change. She's smart as a whip, but not when it comes to guys.'

Joel's mouth twisted into a wry grin. 'I'm concerned that means either I'm the arsehole or the guys she's seen before were.'

The only thing Em had ever alluded to about the previous men in her life was that they were casual, nothing more.

Kat's laughter was soft and rich. 'Don't worry. It's neither. I was actually giving you a compliment and implying that you're educated and smart like she is. The others weren't exactly Rhodes scholars. And now I know that you don't accept compliments easily.'

Joel's eyebrows rose. Yep, he was impressed. Kat Chalmers was smart as a whip herself, and her ability to assess people was impressive, if not a little unsettling.

Kat nodded over at Em. 'That guy she's with is bugging you.'

Joel hid a smirk. Her powers of observation were disturbing, but he couldn't help liking her. 'He's . . . how shall I say? Overly friendly.'

'I believe he was a friend with benefits way back. Now just a friend.'

Joel blinked. If that bit of information was supposed to make him feel better, it didn't. Mr. Hands On had done more than hug and kiss Em? Joel suddenly regretted skipping lunch as his stomach cramped uncomfortably.

'So is that what you are? Friends with benefits?' Kat asked.

She was nosy, but secretly Joel liked that she was being protective of Em. Someone needed to be, with Mr. Hands On all over her.

'I don't know what we are,' Joel said quite honestly. Kat was clever enough to figure out if he was lying, anyway.

'Hmm, interesting. I told her you were in a relationship.'

Joel coughed. 'And how did that go?'

'She said that you don't do relationships.' Kat slid him a penetrating glance.

Joel hid a smile. Man, she was good. She'd managed to answer without really answering the question.

'She's right. I don't do relationships.'

'Why not?'

Joel shrugged. 'I'm not that way inclined, I guess.' Vague. Joel was always good at being vague.

'Mmm,' Kat said. 'It's funny. Neither did I, on account of my father being a lying, cheating bastard and leaving me to pick up the pieces and help manage my mother's mental illness. It changes your view on happily ever after. But then I met my fiancé.'

'Congratulations,' Joel said, meaning it. Although it felt a bit like he was being tossed and turned in the waves outside the window with the constantly changing direction of this conversation.

'Thanks,' Kat replied. 'So what screwed up your view on relationships?'

Joel gave her a sideways look. She was gazing out the window serenely, seemingly uninterested in his reply, but Joel wasn't fooled. That was a challenge if he'd ever heard one. She'd just outlined her painful family history for him, now she was waiting for him to do the same.

Well, screw it. Normally Joel would gloss over it, but Kat's directness deserved some reward in his opinion. Joel had a feeling she could take it, at any rate.

'My parents were both junkies, and my dad had a predilection for mixing his drugs with alcohol. It turned a mean son of a bitch into an evil motherfucker who beat up on everyone to make up for his inadequacies.'

Joel swallowed, wondering if he'd said too much and spoken too harshly. When Kat met his eyes, Joel registered understanding, not pity. She seemed to be waiting for Joel to continue.

He released a tight breath. 'Usually it was my mother that he would hit first, but when the mood struck him, he'd turn his hand to me and my sister. He liked picking on me because I was tougher, and he had more to prove. That, and I'd do and say anything to stop him from touching my sister.'

Kat nodded like Joel hadn't just shared the vilest parts of his childhood. 'So you can fight?' she asked.

Joel released an unexpected laugh. 'I can now, yeah.'

'Good. I'd like to think you got a few punches in.'

'I tried.'

'Where's your family now?'

'My parents are both dead. Last time I checked my sister was in Western Australia going from one loser to the next.'

'I'm sorry.'

Joel had a feeling the sympathy was for his sister and not his parents.

'Does Em know?' Kat asked.

'Some.'

Kat nodded again. 'I'm thinking you sugar coated it more for her.'

'I didn't want to scare her.'

'She's tougher than she looks.'

Joel smiled. 'I know.'

They fell silent.

'Well, this has been fun,' Kat said after a while. 'And I do mean that.' She reached over and brushed a hand across Joel's suit jacket arm. 'It's nice to meet a man of character. Stick around, hey?'

She didn't smile at him before she left, but her eyes conveyed respect. The feeling was mutual. As for sticking around, Joel wasn't sure if she meant at the party or in Em's life in general.

Chapter Twenty-Two

EM WAS LEAVING tipsy behind and edging towards happy drunk when Joel stepped out onto the balcony. She didn't see him at first. It was her friends who alerted her to his presence.

'Who's that?' asked Agatha, one of her university friends.

Em swallowed nervously. Oh boy. Joel was looking fine tonight. Then again, he always looked fine. Whether he wore ratty painting clothes or a suit, he always looked amazing, although Em was particularly partial to the suit.

'Em?' Jess also stood close by and shot her a pull-it-together look.

Em gave her friends a confident smile. 'That's my new boss.'

'Oh,' Agatha breathed. 'How tough for you.'

'Agatha,' Em admonished. 'Get your mind out of the gutter. He's my *boss*.'

They both giggled, but for different reasons. Fortunately, they'd spent many university happy hours discussing guys as well as their areas of study, so Agatha was unlikely to suspect anything.

'He's looking at you funny,' Rob said into her ear.

That made Em realise that Rob still had his arm around her. She must be drunker than she'd thought, because she'd sort of forgotten he was there. It had always been like that between them. Easy. Relaxed. And since Rob had recently broken up with his long-term girlfriend, he was in need of sympathy.

Em nudged him gently and slipped out of his grasp. 'That's because I told him I don't have a partner and you're all over me.'

Rob looked offended. 'I'm not all over you. I'm no different from normal. And why is your boss asking about your relationship status?'

Em huffed, annoyed at herself for her slip. 'It came up at some point. It's usual to learn more about your employees when you're interviewing them. I don't think it's strange.'

'I don't think it's strange at all,' Jess chimed in, to Em's relief.

Em waved Joel over, keen to end the conversation with Rob.

'Hey,' Joel said, arriving in front of Em.

It was one word, but to Em it felt like a secret caress. Like the first night that she'd met him, his softly spoken, deep voice always hit her straight in the belly.

'Hi, Joel. Thanks so much for coming. Although now I'm wondering if it was a good idea after all,' she said with a confident smile.

Joel's expression stayed the same, but Em thought she saw a flicker of surprise in his eyes.

'I mean, seeing your future employee in a bit too much of a celebratory mood might not be career advancing,' she joked, and the others laughed.

His mouth quirked. 'I think we'll allow it on this occasion. A PhD is something to be celebrated.'

'I'll say! Hi, I'm Agatha.' Her friend leaned across Em to offer him her hand and an overly generous view of her cleavage, in Em's opinion.

Ugh.

'Nice to meet you,' Joel replied smoothly, keeping his gaze on Agatha's face. 'Let me guess. A university friend?'

'Same undergraduate degree and then we went on to do Masters together. I didn't attempt the PhD though. I'm enjoying earning money instead,' Agatha finished with a wink at Em.

Joel's gaze fell on Jess. 'You must be Jess. Hi.'

Jess beamed at Joel and they shook hands.

'Hi, I'm Rob.' Her ex-boyfriend leaned in from Em's other side and offered Joel his hand.

Em was secretly glad that Joel didn't know about Rob's former boyfriend status. Really, the situation shouldn't have made her uncomfortable. She and Rob had called things off years ago.

Em noticed Joel's eyes narrow slightly, but he took the hand on offer. 'Nice to meet you.'

'So will Em be working for you directly?' Rob asked.

Joel's eyes stayed narrowed. Not that anyone else would have picked it up. It was something that he did when he was thinking intensely, and Em had only come to realise it recently.

'Em will be working with one of our other managers, Sasha,' Joel replied.

'Nice. It's a big company, then?'

'Mid-size at the moment.'

'Big enough to provide opportunities for progression?' Rob asked with curiosity.

'Rob!' Em smacked him lightly on the stomach with the

back of her hand. 'You're sounding like a recruiter repre-
senting me.'

'That's OK. And yes, we like to provide opportunities for
progression when we can,' Joel told them, his dark eyes serious.

'Except it's early days,' Em interjected again, when Rob
opened his mouth to say something more. 'How about I just
start the job first and see how I go?'

Rob scowled slightly. 'I'm just looking out for you.'

'By interviewing my soon-to-be boss?' She poked him on
the chest gently. 'Back off, McRob.'

Rob shot her an unimpressed look at the use of his nick-
name. It was a mash-up of his first name and surname.
Everyone had used it at university, but he'd never really
liked it.

Joel was still regarding them, his dark eyes giving nothing
away.

Rob's scowl turned into a smirk. 'As you wish, Princess
Georgiou.'

Agatha's eyes rounded in glee and she rubbed her hands
together. 'Ooh, here we go. The battle will be commencing
before too much longer if this keeps up. Take your seats,
everyone.'

Jess shot Em a questioning look, and Em shrugged.

'It's an old university joke,' she explained. 'When we lived
in that falling down share house and they all found out how
much my father was worth, they'd occasionally treat me like a
princess to annoy me.'

'They'd do chores for her, like they were her slaves,'
Agatha told Jess.

'I've never seen someone get so annoyed when I took the
rubbish out,' Rob scoffed.

'That's because it was my turn,' Em shot back. 'And what
about hanging out my washing? You used to love driving me

crazy with that one. Personally, I just think you liked to get your hands on my underwear.'

Em snapped her mouth shut. *Whoops.* She was definitely leaving tipsy behind. She darted a glance at Joel. His eyes were darker than usual.

Rob leaned in, putting an arm around her shoulders and squeezed. 'Anything for Princess Georgiou. And I wasn't the one with the raunchy underwear. You might look sweet, but it doesn't mean you're virtuous. I learned that first-hand.'

Em's heart flipped. It was just a joke, but Joel's eyes had hardened to dark coals. Before she could speak, he cleared his throat.

'Well, I'll leave you to it,' he announced. 'Nice to meet you all. Congratulations again, Em. We'll see you Monday.'

Without another word, Joel turned and stepped back inside the apartment.

Em's heart recovered from its backflip, but now it was thumping painfully hard in her chest.

'Joel, wait!' she called, and went to follow him.

Rob grabbed her arm. 'Stay here.'

Em shook him off. 'He's my boss. I should see him out.'

Agatha's smiled smugly. 'Suck up.'

She ignored the joke and hurried inside, glancing back in time to see Jess's worried expression.

It wasn't just Em. Thanks to Rob and his big mouth, Jess had noticed that Joel was annoyed, too. She needed to go after him.

Chapter Twenty-Three

'JOEL, WAIT!'

Joel heard Em's voice over the noise of the party, but kept moving. He scrunched his eyes shut for a second, trying to clear the image of Rob with his arm around Em from his mind.

Jealous. He was jealous. Joel didn't do jealous. It wasn't his style. He'd never been jealous over a woman in his entire life.

That's because you've never cared for a woman like this before.

The reality of the situation slammed into his chest and Joel stumbled, but he managed to keep walking.

'Hey, man! Watch out.'

Joel raised a hand in apology after he accidentally bumped the arm of a guy standing in the hall holding a beer. The amber liquid sloshed over the edge of the glass, but Joel didn't stop to help him clean it up.

'Joel, wait up!' Em called.

He'd just reached the front door when he felt a hand on his shoulder. Her surprisingly strong grip stopped him in his tracks.

'For God's sake, Joel,' Em said. She hooked her arm through his elbow and tugged him into her bedroom.

'What are you doing?' he asked.

She slammed the door behind them.

He went to step around her and reach for the doorknob, but she stepped in front of him.

'We can't be alone in here,' he told her.

'My house, my rules,' she tossed back. 'What the hell was that?'

'What?'

'That.' She gestured with her thumb. 'Back there. You went all serious and broody.'

'No, I didn't. I was just keeping things professional.'

Em stepped in closer and his gaze drifted to the door behind her. 'Look at me,' she demanded. 'What's going on?'

He shoved a hand over his hair. 'Nothing is going on. I came to the party like we agreed. Now I'm leaving.'

'Why?'

'Why?' He dropped his hand.

'Yes, Joel. Why are you leaving?'

Suddenly the burning need to escape disappeared. Em was standing close. Real close. His hand twitched to touch her, but he held back.

'Because this is your night to be with your friends,' he lied.

'Something was wrong back there. Was it Rob? He's just a friend. He's harmless.'

How did she do that? It wasn't the first time, and Joel had no clue how she managed to see past every one of his defences.

'It's fine,' he told her.

She reached up and stroked his cheek. 'Didn't seem fine, that's all.'

He closed his eyes. Her friends were outside. He needed to

go. But he hooked an arm around her waist instead and pulled her to him. Her eyebrows shot up in surprise and he could feel her heartbeat pounding against his chest.

That was all the invitation he needed to crush his lips to hers.

Fine. He was fine now.

Now that her soft lips were on his, her warm hands were stroking his neck, her taut body was arching against him.

She shuddered when his hands skimmed the side of her legs and drifted beneath her skirt.

'Anyone seen Em?' a voice just outside the door said.

Then the door handle jiggled and turned. They jumped apart as the door was thrust open and Rob entered.

'Hey, Em. There you are.' Rob shot Joel a confused look. 'I thought you'd left.'

'Just about to,' Joel replied, but he didn't move.

Rob ignored him and went over to Em.

'We were just finalising a few things for Monday morning,' Em said. Her face was still flushed, but it was hot in here, so Rob was unlikely to notice.

He stepped in and rubbed his palm across Em's bare arm. Joel flinched.

'We were wondering where you were,' Rob said. 'Come on. You should be celebrating, not worrying about work.'

His hand slipped down to the small of her back to guide Em towards the door. Rob's thumb played with the material of her dress as they walked.

It was the thumb that did it.

Joel stepped in front of the door.

Rob shot him an unimpressed look. 'Hey man, I thought you said you were going?'

Joel directed his attention to Em. 'You know he likes you, right?'

Em's eyes widened and Rob frowned.

'Of course he likes me,' she replied, sounding confused. 'We've been friends for years.'

'No. I mean, he more than likes you.'

Rob's expression turned angry. 'And what the hell does it have to do with you? You're her *boss*.'

This time Joel directed his attention towards Rob. 'I'm also a guy. And I can see when another guy is lurking.'

'Lurking?' Rob growled. 'What the fuck, man? Who the hell do you think you are?'

'Rob.' Em reached over and brushed his arm. 'Forget it, OK?' She threw Joel a warning look that said *back off*. 'Joel was just leaving.'

The hell he was.

Joel stayed where he was. 'He wants to sleep with you again, Em.'

Rob stiffened and Em gaped at him.

'How do you know about that?' she whispered.

'Kat told me.'

While Em digested this information, Rob stepped in front of Joel.

'If anyone is lurking, it's you. You hardly know, Em. You heard her. It's time to leave.'

Joel felt the temper that had been simmering spark and flare. 'So you can keep touching her?'

Rob tried to shove Joel back out the door, but Joel's anger was burning full force now. He shifted his weight and caught Rob unawares, planting his forearm under the guy's chin and pinning him to the wall behind them in one swift move.

'Joel!' Em cried.

Joel didn't move. 'Tell Em what you're really thinking about her.'

'Joel, please,' Em whispered, tugging on his suit jacket, her expression desperate.

Rob didn't speak. His green eyes were filled with hatred, but Joel recognised the edge of panic in them. Both of Rob's hands were free, but they flapped around uselessly because he was too busy straining to breathe. Preppy guys like him didn't know the first thing about self-defence.

'So what were you thinking exactly?' Joel asked again, like they were having a normal conversation and Rob wasn't currently pinned against the wall.

'I was thinking what a complete arsehole you are,' Rob wheezed, then looked over at Em. 'Em, you can't be serious about working for this guy.'

Joel applied more force to the arm that was holding Rob, and Rob made a choking noise.

'*Joel!*'

'No, that wasn't it. Try again,' Joel suggested, then eased the pressure so that Rob could answer.

'So what if I want to touch her! I've slept with her before. I can sleep with her again if I want.'

Em let out a shocked gasp.

Satisfied, Joel stepped back. Rob's hand went to his throat, rubbing it while he glared at Joel. Em rushed over to Rob and flashed Joel an icy glare.

'Don't say I didn't warn you,' Joel threw over his shoulder as he left. Then added, 'See you Monday.'

Chapter Twenty-Four

EM DIDN'T SPEAK to Joel for the rest of the weekend, and by Monday her first-day-of-work nerves were almost unbearable. Not because of the job—she was genuinely excited about her new role. Only now she was wondering if taking the position had been a good decision after all. It had been a questionable enough choice when she was involved with Joel, but now that they were . . .

That was the problem. She had no clue what they were. Em hadn't called Joel, and he hadn't gotten in touch with her either. Was he angry? Apologetic? Embarrassed? Or feeling justified?

If anything, his outburst on the weekend proved to Em how little she knew him. She was beginning to think that his cool, professional demeanour hid a lot more than she realised.

Upon her arrival Monday morning, Em was greeted by Sasha. To Em's relief, her desk was located nowhere near Joel's office, and by lunchtime she still hadn't seen him. It was possible he wasn't even here today at all. His absence allowed Em to relax enough to chat to her co-workers and start to settle into her new environment. By five o'clock, Em was feeling a lot better about her decision to take the job. From the little she'd seen so far, she was going to enjoy it. There would be opportunities to share her knowledge as well as develop her skills further.

'Emily. Can I see you in my office for a minute please?'

Emily.

All the positive thoughts about the job vanished in an instant at the sound of Joel's deep voice.

How did he do that? Sneak up on people like that? Em hadn't even heard him approach. Slowly, she pivoted her chair to face him.

His dark eyes were unreadable. 'It won't take long.' He turned on his heel and walked off in the direction of his office.

Em released a breath.

'Don't stress,' Damian told Em from his cubicle opposite. 'I'm sure it's nothing major. Joel's serious vibe is a constant around here. You get used to it.'

Em forced herself to smile. Damian was a few years younger than her, and one of the junior architects. It was hard not to like him with his bright orange hair and mischievous blue eyes.

'He's probably just checking in, I guess,' Em said, standing.

She made her way to Joel's office, trying to look relaxed. Whatever it was about, it had better be work-related. Em didn't have any intention of discussing the events of last week-end. That would have to keep until they were in private.

When she arrived at his office, he nodded at her. 'Close the door.'

Em narrowed her eyes at him, but did what he asked. She didn't sit down and hovered between the door and the visitor chair. She couldn't care less if he interpreted it as her being uncomfortable, because frankly, she was. That was what happened when you manhandled one of her friends.

Joel remained seated. 'How's your first day been?'

'Fine.'

His eyebrows rose.

'Alright, good. It's been good,' Em admitted.

Joel nodded. 'I'm glad.'

Funny. He didn't look glad. He was still completely unreadable and serious. And damn, it annoyed her that she still found him so sexy.

'Anything else?' Em asked.

'I think it's best if you focus on your job for the time being,' he said.

'I thought that's what I was here to do,' Em replied carefully.

'You are. What I mean is that I don't think we should see each other outside of work anymore. It's a bad idea.'

Em blinked. Right. Apparently Joel had decided that they were talking about this. She opened her mouth to say that she didn't think now was the time or place to discuss it, but he spoke over her.

'You need to concentrate on what you're here for. And that's not me. I'll do my best to stay out of your way.'

Em closed her mouth. Was he breaking up with her? Except that would imply they'd been in a relationship when Em still wasn't sure what it was they'd had. It certainly hadn't been as casual as she'd first anticipated, that was for sure. But it wasn't like they'd committed to anything either.

'I'm capable of getting my work done when you're around, you know,' she told him.

'I know. But things are getting complicated. I think it's best if they stay simple.'

'You were the one that got all hands-on with Rob,' Em pointed out.

Joel's dark eyes flickered with annoyance. 'He deserved it.'

'According to you. And what if I'd wanted to sleep with him?' As soon as Em said it, she regretted it. She was being petty and trying to get a rise out of him, but God knew how hard that was—unless, of course, you were Rob.

His eyes remained dark, but his expression was neutral. 'I was just making you aware of the situation.'

'Was that what it was? You could have hurt him.'

'I barely touched him.'

Em fell silent. Afterwards, Rob had carried on and on, actually annoying Em with his need for sympathy by the end of the night. Em suspected Joel had been telling the truth about Rob's intentions. At the time she'd sensed anger in him, but not rage. He'd been too calm for that.

'I am sorry, though,' Joel added after a moment. 'It wasn't how I wanted the night to go. My . . . protective tendencies run deep.'

He was referring to his sister, Em was sure of it. The knowledge made her stomach twist with a mixture of uncertainty and grief.

'I won't say it was OK, because it wasn't,' she said. 'But thank you for saying sorry.'

Joel nodded. 'I think it's better to end things now.' He grimaced. 'I don't always play well with others.'

Em couldn't help herself and grinned. 'You played well with me.'

He appeared momentarily stricken. 'For a while, Em. Let's not wait until things fall apart.'

Em continued to stare at him. Part of her felt numb about his announcement, not yet able to process it. She genuinely wasn't sure what she should be feeling. If she got upset, that would mean that things between them had been more serious than she'd intended. Another part of her felt sad, but not for her. For him. His certainty that things were bound to end was just plain depressing. It wasn't the first time he'd spoken like that. It was no wonder he'd never bothered with relationships. When you constantly expected them to end, what was the point?

'I think you're right,' Em said softly. 'I need to concentrate on my job.'

They stared at each other a moment longer.

Finally, Joel pushed away from his desk and stood up. 'Go home, Em. Go celebrate your first day of work.'

Em nodded and said goodnight. As she walked back to her desk, she couldn't help feeling that her first day wasn't worth celebrating without Joel to toast to her success.

Em pushed the thought from her mind. She'd never thought she'd needed a man before. She sure as hell wasn't going to start now.

Being with Joel had been fun while it had lasted. He was actually doing her a favour. She had a job to do, and she planned to excel at it.

Chapter Twenty-Five

'WHAT? No! That's really sad, Em.'

Em managed an offhand shrug. It was Sunday morning, and she was down at the beach again with Jess and Kat. It was almost a week since Joel had suggested that they end things, and Em still wasn't sad. How could she be sad when they hadn't officially been in a relationship?

'It's OK, Jess. I'm fine. But I thought I should tell you guys, because you knew what was going on between us.'

Jess stepped in and rubbed Em's arm lightly. 'Still. Are you OK?'

'I'm fine,' Em repeated. 'Plus, my new job is really great and keeps me busy.'

'It was the party, wasn't it?' Kat asked, crossing her arms.

'It was him that suggested we end things, actually,' Em told Kat. 'But yeah, his behaviour at the party didn't impress me very much.'

'But would you have ended things because of it?' Jess asked.

'Honestly? I'm not sure. I didn't really get a chance to discuss it with him properly.'

'Protective mechanism,' concluded Kat.

'Pushing Rob around or ending things?' Em wondered aloud.

'Both,' Kat said. 'He's not an easy guy to get close to.'

'But he let Em get close to him,' Jess pointed out.

'Really,' Em said. 'We don't have to analyse this. There's nothing to analyse. Things were fun while they lasted. Now that he's my boss, I agree with him that it's better to keep things professional.'

Jess gave her a sidelong look. 'So you don't miss sleeping with him?'

Em winced. 'It's easier when you don't bring it up. But come on, I missed Armando, too.'

Jess waved a hand in the air dismissively. 'Joel is better than Armando.'

Em's eyebrows rose. 'You know this how?'

Jess's eyes turned dreamy. 'Armando was like a holiday romance. Sweet and sexy while it lasted. Joel got under your skin.'

'No. He didn't. You're only saying that because I hung around at his house. Secretly I was in love with his house.'

Kat snorted. 'You keep on telling yourself that. I give you one month.'

'What do you mean?'

'One month before seeing Joel every day drives you crazy enough to do something stupid.'

Em sighed. 'Look, I know I have a tendency to enjoy men, but I do have some self-control.'

'Fine,' Kat said. 'I give him one month. His actions at the party spoke volumes if you ask me.'

'You mean his behaviour indicates how he hasn't got a good handle on his emotions,' Em corrected.

'On the contrary. I think Joel behaved himself quite well, given Rob's wandering hands. He was looking out for you. I say one month.'

Em rolled her eyes at her friend while secretly her heart flipped at the idea that Joel had lost his cool because he was trying to protect her. It was so archaic to be excited by it. She was a modern woman, not some lady in distress.

'Hmm. I think I agree with Kat,' Jess mused.

'Not you too!' Em exclaimed.

'Well, it was kind of romantic,' Jess told Em.

'Romantic? It was poor behaviour, that's all there is to it. Rob didn't deserve to be pushed around.'

'Rob was being really touchy feely,' Jess pointed out. 'Don't tell me you didn't notice.'

Em shrugged. 'That's just Rob.'

'In other words, he's wanted to sleep with you for a long time,' Kat concluded.

Em frowned. 'No . . .'

'Yes!' Jess cried. 'I swear if he'd stroked your arm one more time out on the balcony, I was considering accidentally spilling my wine on him just to make him stop. It was creepy, Em.'

Huh. For all Em's involvement with men, she'd never once considered Rob creepy because of their ongoing friendship. But Joel had called him a lurker. Another thought occurred to Em.

'Did Joel see us out on the balcony?'

'I was talking to him inside at one stage,' Kat answered. 'He saw enough. Seriously, Em. Unless you are planning on sleeping with Rob again, tell him to keep his hands to himself.'

Em nodded. She suddenly felt naïve. She'd invited Joel along to her party as a friend, and then he'd been forced to watch another "friend" be overly personal with her. Now Em felt annoyed with herself.

She sighed again. It didn't make any difference now. Things with her and Joel were over either way.

'Thanks for pointing out Rob's behaviour. I was a bit tipsy and I guess I'm just so used to our closeness that I didn't see it. But Joel and I are done, and I won't change my mind.'

'He could try to change it for you,' Jess said hopefully.

Em smiled in spite of herself. 'You're a romantic. I'm a realist. And when you've got two people who don't want to be in a relationship, it doesn't equal romance.'

Kat nudged her. 'Romance isn't the same thing as love, in case you're wondering.'

'We weren't in love,' Em said firmly.

'Love doesn't care if you do or don't want to be in a relationship,' Kat told her.

'Being in love with Matt has turned you into a romantic,' Em accused her.

Kat grinned. 'Hardly.'

Jess touched Em's arm. 'Maybe if you both gave it a chance, it could be love?'

'Aren't you supposed to be making us exercise or something?' Em complained.

Jess shot Em a look and sighed. 'Fine. Let's warm up, ladies.'

They fell into their usual stretching routine while Em's mind wandered.

What she'd felt for Joel definitely hadn't been love. Love was what her sister and parents had. A sort of comfortable co-dependence in which they admitted they couldn't live without the other. She and Joel had never been dependent on each other. Em could most certainly live without him. Wasn't that what she was doing?

And she wasn't sad about it. More like empty. When she thought about Joel now, Em felt an emptiness that she couldn't put her finger on. And possibly a slight ache. She'd never experienced anything like that with the other men she'd been involved with.

Em had absolutely no idea what it meant. She figured that it was probably better that she didn't try to figure it out either.

'EMILY, honey. I've got someone new that I'd like you to meet.'

Em resisted a loud groan. So much for her father forgetting about his matchmaking attempts after she'd made the effort to get to know Joel. She'd hoped it would get her off the hook for at least six months or more.

'Hi, Dad,' Em said into the phone. 'Let me guess. This person will be at Aunt Helen's anniversary celebration?'

Em was striding down the street towards the bus stop on her way home. She'd stayed later than intended at the office, and it was becoming something of a habit. It's not like Sasha expected her to. Usually it was because Em got so immersed in what she was doing that she was happy to stay. That, and she didn't have a certain someone to distract her after hours.

She could have lined up a date, she supposed. But honestly, Em just couldn't be bothered. While the empty feeling still lingered and could probably be filled with meeting someone new, Em didn't have the motivation for whatever reason. Probably because she was so absorbed in her new job. She was usually that tired when she got home, she'd be in bed by nine.

'Em? Are you still there?'

'Sorry, Dad. Just thinking about work.'

'You're enjoying it then?'

'Definitely.'

'And how's Joel treating you?'

Em hesitated, but only for a second. 'Joel's great, although I rarely see him. I work closely with Sasha and a few others.'

'Good, good. I thought perhaps there was a spark between you two, but then my average has never been good, has it? Plus, now he's your boss, so it was probably for the best.'

Her dad chuckled. A sensible person would have come to the same conclusion and decided that there was no point trying to line up more potential beaus for her, but not her father.

He pressed on, like a freight train on a deadline. 'Gavin's a great guy. I think you'll like him. A year or two younger than you, but he's super smart and going places.'

'And if I say no?'

'I'll introduce you two, anyway.' Another chuckle.

Em rolled her eyes as she walked. 'Sure, I can say hi, I guess,' she said noncommittally. There would be a lot of people at the anniversary celebration, many of who would be decades older, so Em wasn't about to turn her nose up at someone from her generation.

'That's my girl. Your mother says to wear that dress you wore to Tia's engagement party. I assume you know what she's talking about?'

'Yes,' Em said, trying not to roll her eyes a second time because the footpath was uneven and she didn't want trip.

'Excellent. See you Saturday, sweetheart.'

'Bye, Dad.'

Em tossed her phone in her handbag and dashed towards the bus stop to catch the next bus.

Dating advice from her father and fashion advice from her mother. Normally she'd get annoyed at her family's over-involvement in her life, but this time Em found herself reflecting on it differently. As irritating as it was, they were just trying to help because they cared.

An image of Joel came into her head. He'd never had parents that cared enough to get involved. Or perhaps even parents that cared full stop.

Em grimaced at the thought as her high heels clicked along the footpath.

Em wondered what it would be like to go through life without the love of your family. Hers were like her backbone. Occasionally there'd be a few aches and pains, but Em couldn't imagine not having their support.

Perhaps it was time that she grew up a bit and graciously endured her father's well-meaning attempts to introduce her to men. In the past, she would have turned up with a partner of her own, unannounced, but Em didn't have the heart for it this time. She'd simply say hi to this Gavin guy, have a polite conversation with him, and that would be the end of it. Easy. No angst. No drama.

What could possibly go wrong?

Chapter Twenty-Six

'QUICK, over here before anyone sees us,' Em whispered and tugged on her newfound friend's arm.

Gavin grinned, and they slipped out of the kitchen unnoticed.

They made their way around the front of the house and sat on the low brick fence, nursing their drinks.

'I swear if one more old lady pats my cheek this evening, I'm going to run crying from the party,' Gavin told her.

Em smiled at him. Her dad was right. Gavin was young, but he was a hell of a lot of fun. Blond and blue eyed, his frequently mischievous expressions hinted at a reformed naughty boy.

'For me it's the never-ending questions about my single status,' Em lamented. 'Honestly, I'm not even thirty, but I'm considered an old maid.'

'Honey, they're just jealous. They were probably married with five kids by your age.'

Em winced. 'Gosh, I'd never thought of it that way. Wow.'

'Exactly. And just in case you hadn't already figured it out, the fact that I'm gay doesn't stop my family from setting me up with women. You're quite the catch, by the way. I'm just not into you like that, so you know.'

Em gave him a sideways look. So her suspicions had been right, but it had only occurred to her after Gavin had opened up and starting chatting to her freely.

'I did suspect, but not at first,' Em told him.

'I've had years of perfecting my straightness.' Gavin didn't sound distressed by this fact.

'It's not right that you should have to pretend to be something that you're not,' Em said, alarmed.

Then again, if Em's tastes had leaned towards the same sex, she wasn't sure how her family would take it either. She'd like to think they'd come around, but she guessed it wouldn't be without some drama.

Gavin waved a hand in the air. 'Oh, don't worry. My sister knows, and so do my parents. They're fine with it. We've all agreed it's best not to rock the older generations' worlds at this point in time. But if I find someone long-term, I'm totally going to be open about it, and so will my folks.'

'That's good. I'm glad. So there's never been anyone long-term?' Em asked with interest. Gavin was maybe twenty-five or twenty-six and extremely charming, so she found it hard to believe he hadn't found someone serious by now.

'There was one. He broke my heart. It's pretty recent, so I don't want to talk about it. You?'

'No one, really. I've never felt the pull towards a long-term relationship.'

Gavin's eyebrows shot up. 'Seriously? No wonder your family introduced us. They must be desperate by now as I'm not exactly your type.'

Em bumped her shoulder to his. 'You're a lovely type.'

'Honey, we look more like sisters than lovers. The only

reason the oldies haven't come to the conclusion I'm gay is their failing eyesight and my deep baritone.'

'Gavin, you're gorgeous. So what if you're not the typical alpha male? Not all women go for that. Or men.'

'Ha. True, I suppose. I see you with someone more manly, though.'

'Manly enough to take on another guy, you mean?' Em said wryly. The words slipped out before she could think better of it.

Gavin's blue eyes lit up, and he set his drink on the fence, then rubbed his hands together. 'Ooh, I sense a story here. Do tell.'

Em pondered it for all of a second, then gave him a quick run down, finishing with, 'But it's over now and it's for the best.'

Gavin picked up his drink again, taking a sip and looking thoughtful. 'If only a man would fight for me.'

Em grimaced. 'It's not as romantic as it sounds. It kind of worried me, to be honest.'

'Come on, don't tell me that it didn't give you a thrill?'

She shook her head. 'For maybe a split second, and then I realised how little I know about him.'

Gavin cocked an eyebrow. 'So why didn't you find out more?'

'He never gave me a chance to.'

'Interesting.'

'Not really. More like frustrating.' Em downed the rest of her drink in one mouthful.

'Doesn't sound like it's over to me,' Gavin commented.

'Oh, it's definitely over. He's my boss now.'

'*Nooo!*'

Em cracked a smile. 'It's kind of messed up, isn't it?'

'I wonder what he'd do if you found a new man? Someone who wasn't just a casual thing?'

Em shrugged. 'Nothing. We were never serious, and he ended it.'

'Then why don't you have a new man?'

'Busy.'

'Liar.'

Em ran her finger along the edge of the glass. 'I haven't told anyone this, but I do kind of miss him.'

'Sucks, doesn't it? I miss my guy, too.' Gavin extended his hand in Em's direction, his palm open.

Em took it, touched by the unexpected sympathy. 'I need to move on, but I just don't feel like meeting anyone new right now.'

'That's OK. I currently have an opening in my life. I'll be your man in the meantime, how does that sound? I'm available for family functions and events, but I draw the line at dress-up parties. It's too tempting to go in drag. For your information, I look awesome in a dress, so it would totally give the game away.'

Em laughed, feeling lighter than she had in days. 'That sounds really nice, actually. The man part, not the drag part, although I'm sure you'd look amazing. Let's be friends, hey?'

'Sounds good to me. And I meant what I said. If you need a plus one, I'm your guy. When you bat for the other team it takes all the weirdness out of asking, trust me. You know you're safe.'

Safe. That was what Em needed right now. Not some brooding, hard-to-read, sexy architect who said he wanted her around one minute, then broke things off the next.

'Deal,' Em told him.

Gavin raised his glass. 'I think we need to drink to that,

don't you? Ready to brave the aunty brigade? I'll risk it for another wine if you will.'

Em stood, still holding Gavin's hand. For once, her father's suggestion hadn't been so bad. Totally off the mark, mind you, not realising that Gavin was gay, but they'd certainly clicked.

Em headed inside with Gavin, buoyed by the certainty that she'd gained a new friend.

JOEL PACED HIS OFFICE. He'd been doing a lot of that in the last month. Ever since he'd broken things off with Em. Just the knowledge that she was within walking distance made his skin itch. He'd gotten into the habit of pacing his office to work off the nervous energy. It never helped much, but at least it stopped him from marching downstairs and telling Em what he really thought.

Which was that he still thought about her all the time.

That his house seemed empty without her, even though she'd only spent a short amount of time there.

That the feelings he had for her scared him.

That everything about her scared him. Her eyes, her skin, her intelligence, her determination. All of it.

And that even though he was scared, it didn't stop him wanting her even more.

'Stop it,' Joel told himself gruffly.

These feelings and thoughts weren't helping. He'd done the right thing. The only thing that he could have done in the circumstances, which was to stay away from her. There were no happy endings in Joel's life. There never had been and there never would be. The most he could hope for was to be a responsible member of society who ran a business. That was the most he'd ever let himself aim for.

The most that he deserved.

Joel looked up when Nate knocked on the door. 'Coming?'

'Yeah,' Joel said. 'I'll just shut my computer down.'

Nate stayed waiting in the doorway, leaning against it. 'Everything alright? You haven't seemed yourself lately.'

Joel didn't look up. 'All good. Just trying to keep the new client happy.'

Nate scoffed. It turned out Chris Georgiou was as demanding as a client as he was during the tender process. Joel shouldn't have been surprised—he supposed the signs had been there from the beginning.

'Still happy he's a client?' Nate asked.

'I can handle it,' Joel replied, and picked up his phone. Demanding or not, Joel wanted Chris's business for what it would mean for their firm long term.

'Is Chris coming tonight?' Nate queried.

'Not sure. He said he'd try, but I haven't heard anything.'

If it hadn't been for the possibility of Chris attending their monthly Friday night work drinks, Joel probably would have made an excuse and not gone. The word around the office was that Em had a new man and that he would be coming tonight. He knew this because Damian, who had a not-so-secret crush on Em, had told him.

On one hand, Joel wasn't surprised. Em was a gorgeous woman. On the other hand, he couldn't help feeling like Damian.

She's making a statement, you idiot.

As in, she could do better than some hot-headed, possessive arsehole.

Joel had thought about trying to explain to Em why he'd reacted to Rob that way. But when all was said and done, Em deserved better, so what was the point?

'Man, are you sure you're alright?' Nate asked. 'You don't usually vague out on me like this.'

'Huh?' Joel shook himself and realised he was still standing by his desk holding his phone, staring off into space. 'Shit. Sorry. Not enough sleep, I guess. I'll try to catch up this weekend.'

Nate patted him on the back as Joel joined him. 'You do that. But first, let's head downstairs for a drink.'

Chapter Twenty-Seven

'THIS WAS A BAD IDEA,' Em told Gavin when she saw Joel enter the foyer.

Gavin reached out and caught her hand. 'I beg to differ. Inviting me is never a bad idea.' When he saw the direction of Em's gaze, he added, 'Is that him?'

'Yeah.' Em looked away and studied her drink.

'Oh boy. Nice. Very nice.'

'Don't get any ideas. I don't think he swings both ways,' Em told him dryly. On second thought, it was probably a good thing having Gavin here. She could do with the distraction.

'I can try to turn him. It might be fun.'

Em smiled despite the nerves twisting her stomach. 'Stop.'

'I'm going to put my arm around your waist now,' Gavin whispered.

'And I'll pretend to like it,' Em whispered back.

'You love me, remember?'

'Closest thing to a serious relationship I'll ever have,' Em joked.

She wasn't sure why she'd invited Gavin. It wasn't necessary that he was here, and no one expected her to have a boyfriend, let alone show him off. It also wasn't like Em hadn't seen Joel around the office in the last month either. Whenever they'd crossed paths the contact had been professional and polite. Em didn't have anything to prove, except maybe to herself.

'Honey, do you always think so loudly? Take another swig of your drink.'

Em smiled again and did as he'd suggested.

'Stop overthinking,' Gavin continued. 'I'm simply a prop to highlight that you've gotten on with your life. That's all.'

'You're more than a prop, and you know it. Plus, a prop implies that I'm only pretending to be over him.'

'Why, you *are* pretending, darling. I wouldn't be over that gorgeous hunk of man if he'd been in my bed either.'

Em choked on her wine and Gavin rubbed her back.

'But you will be eventually,' Gavin promised. 'Especially with me around to lead you astray. Uh oh. Here he comes.'

Oh God. This had been a bad idea. Joel would surely see through the ruse in a second. Em was determined and clever and many other things, but she'd never been a good liar.

'Hi, Joel,' she managed when he arrived in front of them.

He nodded.

Gavin thrust his hand in Joel's direction. 'I'm Gavin.'

'Nice to meet you,' Joel replied, and shook Gavin's hand.

'Likewise.' Gavin held on to Joel's hand a little longer than necessary.

Yep, real smooth. Clearly Joel was irresistible to both women and men.

'So, a month already,' Joel said. 'Has it gone quick?'

Em wondered if that was a trick question. The work side of things had gone quickly, while the missing Joel side of things had dragged.

Gavin shot Joel a confident smile. 'She's barely had time to breathe. You've been keeping her too busy, and so have I.'

Em leaned against Gavin, indicating that he should ease off the innuendo.

'What Gavin means to say is that I'm enjoying the job.'

'And me. She's enjoying me, too,' Gavin added, smiling brightly.

Em stepped on his toe and Gavin winced.

'Glad things are going well for you, Em. And for you both. Anyway, I have somewhere I need to be. Enjoy the drinks.'

Gavin gaped as Joel retreated. Em dropped Gavin's hand.

'Well, he's like an impenetrable wall,' Gavin said when he was out of earshot.

'Not always. But come to think of it, that's normal lately.' Em released a breath. 'Come on. There's a few more people I'd like you to meet. You up for it?'

'Of course. Lead the way.'

JOEL'S PHONE hadn't stopped buzzing in his pocket during the short time he'd been down in the foyer. He knew without looking it would be his sister, Mia.

Joel also knew it would be easier to ignore it, but that's not how their relationship worked. Mia was the one to ignore him until she needed something. And now she obviously needed something.

Joel slipped inside his office and closed the door. He walked over and propped himself against the edge of the desk, so that he could scroll through the messages. The general gist was always the same.

I need help.

I can't take it anymore.

He (insert the name of any number of useless guys here) isn't treating me right. Why don't men ever treat me right?

Joel sighed and scrubbed a hand across his face. The answer was complicated and simple at the same time. The men Mia got involved with never treated her right, because she didn't treat herself right. But of course the real truth was the complicated part. That his sister had no self-esteem was hardly surprising after the upbringing they'd had. While his mother had occasionally shown Joel some scrap of affection, she'd only ever viewed Mia with wariness, like she was a competitor for their father's attention. Add in their mean, useless, abusive father and Mia's self-esteem had never stood a chance.

Hell, it had taken years for Joel to build up his self-esteem to a point where he could function in society and try to run a business. It had only been because of his determination not to be anything remotely like his father that he'd not succumbed to the same addictions as his parents.

Joel called Mia's number and waited.

'Oh, thank God you called. I need to get out.'

Despite having heard it all before, Joel's stomach twisted at the tortured note in his sister's voice. She sounded sober for a change.

'You know there's not a lot I can do from here, unless you want me to fly over there to be with you.'

'No, that's a bad idea. I don't want you getting involved.'

Joel flinched. It wasn't the first time he'd heard that, and it wouldn't be the last. It still stung, though.

'What would you have me do, then?'

'I just need some money to tide me over until I can get back on my feet again,' Mia whispered into the phone.

Joel imagined her hiding in a bathroom or a bedroom from the nasty son of a bitch she was involved with. Joel closed his eyes.

'How much?' he asked flatly.

It wasn't the money that hurt. He could afford it. It was the fact he'd heard this all before, and he'd likely hear it again, which was why he didn't ask to know any of the details.

'Just a few grand should get me through,' Mia promised, but her promises were always empty.

'I'll do it now,' Joel replied.

'Thank you. I knew I could rely on you.'

Joel swallowed a bitter laugh, but he needn't have worried. The line was already dead. His sister's address might change frequently, but her bank account details never did. With another sigh, he opened the banking app on his phone and made the transfer.

Hell, what a day. As if seeing that Em had moved on wasn't hard enough, throw his messed-up sister into the mix and he was ready to go home. Fast. His feet itched to get behind the wheel of the Porsche. Then he could ease his foot down on the accelerator and forget about how he continually failed the women in his life.

He grabbed his jacket from where he'd tossed it on the back of the visitor's chair and set off towards the lifts.

THE BATHROOM DOOR shut behind Em as she rushed back up the hall.

Until a minute ago, Em had needed to pee. Badly. Gavin had kept insisting that she drink. After the second glass of wine on an empty stomach, she'd chosen water, because getting tipsy at work wasn't on her list of career goals.

Em had held it as long as she'd been able to, as she hadn't wanted to leave Gavin alone during the company drinks. Not that he wasn't able to hold a conversation. Quite the opposite.

She'd been more worried about Joel making a reappearance and approaching Gavin alone. It was a completely paranoid thought, because Joel had said that he'd had somewhere to be. Except Em had seen Joel head off in the direction of his office rather than the exit. She figured it was better to be safe than sorry and not leave Gavin by himself for too long.

Her heels weren't helping her reach the foyer quickly and nor was her pencil pleat skirt, but it didn't stop her from attempting to stride down the hallway. Which turned out to be a bad idea.

Her heels skidded on the glossy floor tiles and Em felt her feet go out from under her.

Swallowing a gasp, she reached out for something—anything—to steady herself on at the same time as Joel rounded the corner.

'Whoa.'

Em's heart thundered in her chest and leapt into her throat as Joel's strong arms caught her easily. Her feet skittered uselessly on the stupid tiles, unable to find purchase, so Joel held her fast.

'What's the hurry?' he asked.

The low bass note of Joel's quiet voice did nothing to improve the state of her heart.

'Toilet,' she managed, finally able to stand upright.

Joel's hands hovered just above her arms. 'The toilet is back that way.'

'I mean I've already been,' Em corrected, feeling more stupid.

Joel's eyes narrowed like he didn't quite believe her. Or at least understand her, which wasn't surprising seeing as she'd been practically running to get back to the work drinks.

Em gestured in that direction. 'Gavin . . .' she added lamely.

Joel nodded once, slowly. 'Is an interesting guy.'

Em crossed her arms in front of herself. 'What's that supposed to mean?'

Joel shrugged and dropped his arms to his sides. He remained standing close. 'What I said. He's interesting.'

'Too interesting for me?' Em demanded.

She wasn't sure why she was making a point of it, but whether Em was or wasn't actually dating Gavin, she felt protective of him. While they'd only known each other for a short time, Em had grown fond of his company and his friendship.

Joel shrugged again. 'It strikes me that if you had a type, he probably wouldn't be it.'

Em felt her temper flare. 'Oh, so because he's not all masculine and hot-headed like you, he's not suitable for me?'

A muscle in Joel's jaw twitched, then he raised his hands, palms open. 'You're aware he's not just into girls, aren't you?'

This time Em was the one to narrow her eyes. 'Just because he's slightly effeminate doesn't mean he likes guys.'

'Oh?' Joel raised an eyebrow and nodded in the direction of the foyer.

Em followed his gaze and felt her face redden. Gavin was chatting happily to Damian and leaning in close. Much too close. Combined with the subtle arm touches and the way Gavin was giving Damian his undivided attention, Gavin wasn't making a secret of his admiration for Damian.

'He checked out my arse earlier, too,' Joel told her.

Em ignored the hot flush burning her cheeks. 'So what? He's bisexual,' Em lied. 'I'm comfortable with that.'

Joel regarded her thoughtfully. 'But you're not comfortable with me.'

Em blinked at the sudden change of conversation. 'I don't

see what that's got to do with anything, and what on earth gave you that idea anyway?'

'Possibly the fact that I've barely seen you the entire month you've worked for me.'

Em uncrossed her arms and smoothed the front of her skirt. 'I've been busy. I haven't been avoiding you.'

There was that raised eyebrow again. 'So every time I've come into the break room to grab a coffee and you've been there, you haven't walked out within seconds because of me?'

Em glanced towards the foyer where Gavin was still chatting—flirting—with Damian, who was one hundred per cent straight and seemingly clueless as to his appeal.

'Em? You're doing it again.'

'What?'

'Avoiding me.'

Em huffed. 'What would you have me do? It's weird otherwise.'

'Because I'm your boss.'

'Yes, because you're my boss,' Em whispered, darting her gaze around the hallway to make sure they were alone.

Joel sighed and thrust a hand over his cropped hair, suddenly looking tired. 'It would have been weirder if we were still together.'

'Yes, well you didn't give me a choice in the matter, did you?'

Em hadn't realised how angry she was until the words spilled out. All the weeks of feeling not exactly sad, but empty, made more sense now that she was standing face-to-face with Joel.

She'd missed him.

She'd missed him so much that it hurt. And he was right. Every time she'd seen him, she'd actively avoided him, because the only thing worse than missing him was having him nearby and not being hers.

Joel frowned. 'It was the best choice, Em. Come on, you don't want to risk your reputation in a new job over me.'

'You didn't give me a choice,' Em repeated.

Joel's frown deepened. 'Are you saying that you would have chosen differently? I'm not going to deny the spark between us.' He swallowed and licked his lips, looking as though he wanted to reach out and touch her.

Em cocked her head to one side. 'It's more than a spark, Joel, and you know it. I was prepared to be in a relationship because of that spark.'

Joel stiffened and stepped back, putting some space between them. He was silent for a long moment, probably because Em uttering the "R" word had shocked him as much as it had shocked her.

She wasn't going to take it back. Joel *was* the only person she'd ever wanted to be in a relationship with. Hell, she still didn't want to be in a relationship exactly, but where Joel was concerned, she'd make an exception.

He cleared his throat. 'The fact remains that I'm your boss.'

'We could have kept things quiet initially, then after a while told people that we are seeing each other. Plenty of couples end up in relationships because they've met at work.'

Joel looked away. 'What about your father?'

'What about him? He introduced us, remember?'

'Before I was your boss.'

'Oh, for fuck's sake, Joel. Why don't you just come out and say it? I scare you. *This* scares you.'

Em snapped her mouth shut. She'd practically been yelling. They stared at each other, waiting to see if anyone had heard her outburst, but the chatter in the foyer didn't stop.

Joel shook his head. 'You don't know what you're talking about.'

Em was still angry and maybe it was wrong, but it felt good to release some of that anger. Instead of raising her voice again, this time she stepped forward. She pushed against his chest with her palm, shuffling him backwards into one of the meeting rooms behind them so that they could talk in private.

Inside, she closed the door and glared at him.

'No, I guess you're right. I don't know what I'm talking about. Do you know why that is? Because you were happy to pass the time with me and screw around with me, but you never let me get to know you.'

Joel backed away to stand closer to the meeting table. 'We were casual—'

'I painted your house.'

'You offered to.'

'I invited you to my party,' Em went on.

Joel's eyes went from unreadable to a smouldering black. 'As your friend.'

Em's heart skipped a beat. 'Did that bother you?'

Joel shook his head like he was trying to clear it. 'Forget about it.'

Em advanced on him so that she was standing right in front of him, her toes almost touching his shoes. 'Kind of hard to forget about it when you push my friends around.'

'Your *friend* wanted to get in your pants.'

'So you highlighted. So what? Are you going to punch every single guy that gets a hard on in my presence, or is that not what that was about?'

Joel reached back and clutched the edge of the table, his knuckles turning white. 'Let's just call it an involuntary reaction.'

'Kind of extreme.'

'And exactly why us—this—is a bad idea,' he ground out.

'Coward.'

Joel closed his eyes. 'Em . . .'

'What are you so scared of? For God's sake, I'm standing here telling you that I miss you and I want you, and you back away.' She sighed and gave him a wry smile. 'And you're right, I'm not Gavin's type.'

Joel remained silent, and Em's mind kept whirling.

When another thought occurred to her, she couldn't ignore it. The idea had her backing away, much like he had. 'Oh, wow. I'm stupid, aren't I? There's someone else, isn't there?'

Joel's dark eyelashes fluttered as he blinked several times.

He didn't reply, Em let out a disgusted laugh. She had to admit it made sense. His distance. His unwillingness to let her really get to know him.

'You know what? Forget I said anything. You're right. We're over. I might do casual, but I don't do dirty little secrets.'

Em turned on her heel. Just as she reached the door, Joel spoke.

'There's no one else.'

Em's hand hovered near the handle, and this time she was the scared one. She was too scared to speak in case she said something wrong and Joel closed up again.

'Em?' he said to her back. 'There's never been anyone else.'

She turned to face him, her skin still prickling with fear. 'Then why?' She didn't add "push me away", but the meaning was clear.

His dark eyes held her to the spot, and she couldn't move even if she'd wanted to.

'Because there's no one else like you.'

Then he stepped forwards, grabbed her hands, and pulled her to him.

Chapter Twenty-Eight

JOEL HAD LOST HIS MIND.

That was the only reason to explain what he was doing. The truth was, he'd been avoiding her, too. Because, yeah, it goddamn hurt every time he was close to her. Every time he breathed in that familiar scent of jasmine mixed with the seaside. Every time he caught her looking at him with those deep blue eyes that reminded him of a calm ocean pool on a windless day. Every time she spoke. Every time she laughed.

Every time she was near him it was enough to drive him mad. To make him lose his resolve.

Screw resolve.

He pulled her into his arms so roughly that she bounced off his chest, and he caught her and wrapped his arms around her waist, lowering his lips to hers.

Em let out a strangled whimper, but she didn't resist. Hell, she practically melted against him, offering up her mouth and her body freely, so that he had no idea why it had been so important until a second ago not to touch her.

They kissed deeply, like they'd just crossed a parched

desert and discovered water. They held each other like a storm raged outside and the only way to stay safe was to be together.

But it still wasn't enough.

With Em it would never be enough.

'Joel,' Em gasped between kisses. 'I need you.'

He was already hard, but now he hurt.

'Can't,' he whispered. 'No protection.'

'I'm on the pill.' She shoved a hand down the front of his pants, her fingers wrapping around the length of him.

He groaned, unable to think properly.

She unbuckled his belt and undid the zip on his trousers, releasing him so that his need was undeniable.

'Joel,' she begged, and it was the pleading note in her voice that did it. Like she needed him as much as he needed her.

Still not thinking, only feeling, he pushed her skirt up to her waist roughly and slid her panties down to her knees. When his palm rubbed against her sweet spot and she shuddered, he shuddered too because she was so wet, so ready for him.

'Turn around,' he growled.

She did as he requested and he stepped behind her, positioning her so she was in between him and the table.

'Bend over,' he told her.

He cupped her gorgeous peachy arse and pushed inside her, feeling her shudder. He had to grip her hips to stay standing or else he'd have buckled at the knees.

Fuck. She was so sweet. So strong. So willing. So demanding. So everything.

And that was why he couldn't be gentle. Not with this need. Not with this wanting pulsing inside of him, insisting that he make her his.

He thrust into her, again and again. With each thrust she

met him, arching her back to take him deeper, and it was so damn good that he felt close to tears.

He reached around and cupped her breast through her shirt. Teased the nipple through the fabric. With hands shaking, she undid the buttons of her shirt for him so that he could slip a hand underneath her bra and cup her in his palm.

She panted and squirmed against him. He knew that meant she wanted more. All of him.

Had he ever given her all of him, he wondered.

Now he would. It wasn't a conscious decision. Just the deep knowledge that he would give her everything.

He released her hip and slipped his hand down the front of her skirt, his finger finding her sweet spot easily. He circled it languidly, at odds with their frantic lovemaking.

She moaned softly, and it was a request. To own her. To fill her up.

She was right. He hadn't given her a choice. Because there was no choice when it came to Em.

She was his and he was hers.

And with that thought, his release was swift as she contracted around him, tremors rocking her body as they held on to each other.

When they were still, he drew her to him, holding her tight.

Never wanting to let her go.

EM REMAINED STILL in Joel's arms. Sated. Relieved. Savouring the moment of closeness between them.

God, she'd missed him so much. The feel of him inside her. Having him hold her close.

She knew she'd been pushy before. Demanding, even. But

she didn't care, because if it meant he was finally letting his feelings show again, it was worth it.

Em also could have been wrong, but she swore she'd sensed a change in him. A kind of release. Or, at the very least, acceptance.

At the sound of voices coming along the corridor, she stiffened and looked around in alarm.

Oh my God. They were in the office and she was splayed across a meeting table.

How could she have forgotten where they were?

Somehow Em had forgotten everything when Joel had started kissing her. Where she was. Who she was. The only thing that had mattered was Joel.

Joel swore under his breath and helped her to stand.

They stepped apart and Joel immediately pulled up his pants.

Em looked around in a panic for her panties, which had slipped off. She'd just discovered them near the foot of a chair and grabbed them when the door handle to the meeting room turned.

Holy shit.

Em balled up her panties in her hand and tugged down her skirt, but it was too late. The door was already opening and her shirt was still undone.

All the blood drained from Em's face when she saw three people staring at them from the hallway, taking in her state of undress.

Gavin's blue eyes rounded in surprise. Nate's grey eyes cool and hard. And her father's wide with horror.

'Dad,' Em gasped.

Chapter Twenty-Nine

'LOOK ON THE BRIGHT SIDE,' Gavin told them from the back seat. 'You were both fully clothed. It could have been a lot worse.'

Em darted a glance guiltily at her handbag sitting in the footwell of the Porsche. That was where she'd stuffed her panties when she'd had to hide them earlier. Em supposed she had to be thankful for her knee-length skirt.

Joel's hands kneaded the steering wheel as he drove. He'd been doing a lot of that since they'd gotten in the car.

'I'm not sure that it could have been much worse,' Em admitted softly.

On a scale of one to ten, being caught in an obviously dishevelled state in a work boardroom with your boss was a ten on the career limiting charts.

'I beg to differ,' Gavin said from the back seat. His chirpy voice was completely at odds with Em's devastation about what had just happened. 'You got the guy.'

Joel snorted quietly. 'Is that what this is? I'm not sure I'm the prize that Em thinks I am.'

'Stop saying that,' Em said. 'It was a poor choice of loca-tion, but Gavin's right.'

They all fell silent, the low hum of the Porsche's engine cancelling out the need for conversation, each lost in their own thoughts.

Ten minutes later, Gavin announced, 'This is me.'

Joel pulled over in front of Gavin's terrace, and Em got out of the car to allow Gavin to climb out of the back seat.

'I'm going to hug her goodbye now,' Gavin called out to Joel.

Em saw Joel's mouth quirk, but he didn't say anything.

Gavin pulled Em in for a tight hug. When he released her, he looked into her eyes.

'You'll be OK. This will all be OK, trust me. As far as drama goes, this has got nothing on some of my friends. I'm here if you need me. Just call, alright?'

'Alright.' Em gave him another quick hug. 'And thank you.'

Gavin waved a hand in the air as he headed towards his front door. 'Nothing to thank me for, gorgeous.' He mimicked holding a phone to his ear. 'Call me.'

Em returned the wave and lowered herself back into the passenger seat.

'I like him,' Joel said as they pulled away.

'I think he likes you too, for the record.'

Joel smiled, but his hands were still gripping the steering wheel tightly. 'Where to?'

Em played with the hem of her skirt with her fingertips. 'Home, I guess.'

She had no idea what came next, if she was honest. With Joel, with her job, with her dad.

'Did you manage to speak to Nate?' Em asked.

After they'd been discovered in the boardroom, Nate had guided a sputtering Chris away while Gavin had suggested Em go tidy herself up. Then they'd met Joel in the car park basement for a lift home. Talking to her father at that exact moment hadn't seemed like a good idea.

'Nate stayed with your father. I thought it was best to keep my distance.'

Em nodded.

'I'll talk to him tomorrow,' Joel added.

Tomorrow was Saturday, but Em guessed Joel and Nate's close business relationship extended to all hours of the week. She closed her eyes, hoping desperately that she hadn't caused a rift between the two of them because of this.

'Hey.' Joel reached over and squeezed her hand. 'It ain't all bad. I got the girl.'

Em choked out a laugh. 'Oh, God. I'm going to have to resign.'

Joel removed his hand. 'You'll do no such thing. Just let me talk to Nate.'

Em wanted to argue, but she was too tired. How had everything gone so right—and so wrong—in such a short space of time?

'Do you want to come back to my place tonight?' Joel asked her softly.

'Yes,' Em breathed, wanting it very much. She had no hope of sleeping tonight, anyway. At least she could lie awake in Joel's arms pretending everything was OK.

The sound of two phones pinging at the same time chorused over the engine noise. Joel frowned and Em bent over to fish hers out of her bag.

'Oh my God,' she murmured when she saw the message.

Joel swore as he read his phone sitting in the cradle on the dash.

'You first,' he said, his voice sounding strained.

'It's my father,' Em told him, her hand shaking as she

lowered the phone onto her lap. 'He's told me that I've disgraced myself and that I need to move out of the penthouse by the end of the weekend. Whether I have a job to support myself or a place to live is no concern of his.'

Joel swore again.

Em blinked away tears. She'd just discovered the hard way that there was actually a limit to her father's endless involvement in her life.

'Apparently when Dad introduced me to you, he had a more traditional idea of the sort of relationship we might have —one that doesn't involve sleeping with my boss at the office and risking my professional reputation.' She inhaled a much-needed breath. 'What was your message?' Em asked weakly.

'It was Nate. Chris wants me off the project.'

Em put a hand to her mouth, covering a sob, and then closed her eyes. She rested the back of her head on the head-rest. It felt like it was spinning out of control, much like her life currently was.

She felt Joel's hand rest on her thigh. 'Em, we'll get through this.'

Despite the fact it felt like her heart was breaking, Em didn't miss the "we'll" part of his sentence, and it eased some of her pain.

'You can come and live with me,' Joel told her.

Em's head shot forward and her eyes blinked open. 'What? No. I can ask Jess or Kat if I can stay in their spare room until I find my own place.'

Em knew both of her friends would be there for her. She would only have to ask. Although it would be weird and probably a bit uncomfortable sharing an apartment with a couple —Em knew she'd feel like she would be invading their personal space. It didn't matter though. It would only be for a week or so until she found somewhere to rent.

'Your place is at my place,' Joel said quietly, but firmly.

Em twisted to face him. 'What are you saying?'

'Move in with me, Em. I want you with me no matter what happens from here on in.'

Em flopped back against the seat to face the road. A continuous stream of lights flashed past and the headlights from the oncoming cars hurt her eyes.

'Em?'

'I . . .' She didn't know what to say, but she tried to put her jumbled thoughts into words anyway. 'It seems sudden, that's all. Until tonight we were both avoiding each other.'

'No, Em. We were running away from each other because this scared us.' He reached over again and held her hand. 'But you were braver than me to call me out on it. I don't want to let you go again. I can't promise what comes next will be easy, but I want you with me. Besides, I need you to help me finish painting the damn house. What do you say?'

Em looked down at her hand in his. Hers delicate. His large and strong. Hers pale. His tanned. She wasn't sure why they worked, but they did. And maybe it was time they stopped fighting it.

'Alright,' she said. 'But only if I get to have a say on the colour scheme.'

'I wouldn't expect anything less. Come on. Let's pick up some things from your apartment and we'll return for the rest on the weekend.'

Em nodded. She had no idea what the future held, but she knew one thing. She'd found someone that she wanted to share it with.

Chapter Thirty

JOEL DIDN'T ALLOW himself to think about the momentous life decision that he'd made on Friday night. He was too busy helping Em move out of her apartment and getting her set up at his place. Then, when that was done, there had been chores to do like food shopping and buying more paint in preparation for the next round of renovations.

A picture of domestic bliss.

Joel shoved the cynical thought aside as he strode towards his office. The last thing he needed was old demons rearing their ugly heads thanks to his shitty childhood. So he would do what he'd learned to do in the past—ignore them.

She doesn't know who you really are. What you are.

That thought was harder to push away, because at times it felt like Joel led a double life. Who he was then and who he was now. It was the now that he chose to concentrate on though, like he always did.

And right now, it was Monday. He'd given Em a lift into work, but they'd been careful to part ways in the car park so it would appear as if they'd arrived separately. He knew Em was feeling nervous about returning to the office today, and Joel was going to do everything in his power to make things right for her.

Starting with talking to Nate.

He'd tried calling his business partner three times on the weekend, but each time it had gone to voicemail. Joel wasn't entirely surprised. Nate was the sort of guy who liked space and time, so Joel had given it to him. He knew it meant that Nate was angry with him. So be it. Joel wasn't afraid of a little anger directed his way, but he was worried about their relationship.

Joel didn't knock when he reached Nate's door and walked straight in.

Nate ignored him and remained focused on his computer screen.

Joel crossed his arms in front of his chest. 'Time to clear the air. You're pissed at me. I get it. I'm pissed at myself, for what it's worth.'

Nate pushed away from the desk with a sigh and sat facing Joel. 'Pissed doesn't really cover it.'

Joel sighed too. 'Yeah, I know.' He dropped into the chair opposite Nate's desk. 'Em wanted to resign. I told her not to. If anyone is going to take the blame for this, it's me.'

Nate's eyebrows rose. 'That's very gentlemanly of you.'

Joel glared at him. He knew his friend and business partner well. That was a dig at his expense. It pissed Joel off more, but he knew he deserved it. The only option now was complete honesty.

'I fucked up. You know I don't make a habit of sleeping with our employees. That's not my style. Em's different. We had a thing going before she took the job here. Turns out the thing was more serious than I thought. I've asked her to move in with me.'

Nate's eyebrows shot upwards. 'Holy shit. The bachelor does have a heart.'

Joel grimaced. 'Apparently. That's why when she started here, I told her it was over. I was trying to do the right thing and keep things professional.'

Nate released a startled laugh. 'Is that what you call Friday night?'

Joel looked down at his hands. 'Like I said, I'm sorry. It won't happen again.'

'I think maybe it might from what you're telling me, but not on work premises.'

Joel raised his eyes at the amused tone in Nate's voice. His friend's grey eyes were sparkling.

'What?' Joel asked.

'You know what.'

Joel stood and paced the office. 'This isn't easy for me, you know. Asking her to move in with me wasn't something I planned. It just kind of happened.'

'Like the boardroom.'

Joel glared at Nate. 'She's got me all twisted up in knots and I can't describe it, other than to say that having her live with me feels right.'

Nate grinned. 'That's what we call love, my friend.'

Joel collapsed into the seat, his legs feeling shaky. 'I don't know about that. But can we not fire her?'

Nate's smile faded. 'I wasn't going to fire her. I was considering the longevity of our partnership after a few beers, though.'

Joel didn't say anything, because what else was there to say?

Nate blew out a long breath. 'For the record, it would take more than that. And that's not a challenge.'

'Trust me. Challenge not accepted. I'm sorry I jeopardised

the Georgiou contract. I deserve it, but I can't believe I won't be working on it anymore.'

'Your absence from the team will leave a gaping hole. We won that contract because of you. But we pick ourselves up, dust ourselves off, and move on.'

'Shit. It still bites. Em's distraught about it.'

'Has she spoken to Chris? He kept opening and closing his mouth like a startled trout afterwards. He only settled down once I'd given him a shot of whiskey.'

Joel winced. Seeing your daughter in that way was likely to make any father speechless.

'No, she hasn't spoken to him. He told her in no uncertain terms that she can't live in the apartment anymore. I don't think they'll be talking for a while.'

Nate absorbed this information with a restless finger tap on the desk. 'I'm sorry to hear that. Well, her job is safe here provided you two can control yourselves. She's done amazing work so far.'

'I know.' Joel was only too aware of how close they'd come to risking everything. 'Do we keep our relationship quiet?'

'If it's a relationship, no. You do what normal people do. Tell people what you told me. That you knew each other before she started here. Things developed. Feelings changed. Yadda yadda. My bet is the women will love it. The guys, not so much. They like Em more than they like you, you brooding son of a bitch.'

Joel shot Nate a dark look.

Nate raised his hands in response. 'She's a smart, beautiful woman. You're prickly.'

'Fine. We'll be honest, but only if Em's comfortable with that.'

Nate's grin returned.

'What?' Joel shot back.

'Shit. You're under the thumb already. You must love her.'

Joel pointed a finger at his business partner. 'Call it whatever you want. All I know is that she's mine.'

Nate's amused laughter followed Joel all the way back to his office.

'IT'S NOT the same without you in the apartment complex,' Jess told Em a few weeks later after they'd finished their workout session at the beach.

Em lay down in the sand, letting the morning sun warm her face. 'I miss you guys, too. Although living at Joel's is kind of nice.'

Kat sat beside her and took a swig from her water bottle. 'True love got you in the end, huh?'

Em ignored her friend's knowing smile. 'I wouldn't call it true love. But it will please you both to know that we're calling it a relationship.'

'I'm proud of you!' Jess held up a hand for a high-five and Em slapped her palm in amusement.

'Me too. I'm trying not to overthink it. At the moment, the arrangement—'

'Relationship,' Jess corrected, and Kat laughed.

'Relationship,' Em continued, 'feels right. That's good enough for me.'

'Well, when you're ready, you should have us over to this gorgeous house of his that you keep talking about,' Kat suggested.

'That's a great idea,' Em agreed. 'The living area is almost finished. It would be fun to have you over for a dinner party once it's done.'

'We're in,' Jess told her.

'Have you spoken to your father yet?' Kat asked, and Jess shot her a warning look.

'It's alright,' Em said with a sigh. 'No, I haven't. Only Mum.'

'How's she?' Kat asked.

'Fine, actually. She didn't have the shock of seeing me and Joel caught in a compromising position. She's really excited that I've finally got a relationship happening, go figure.'

'But not your father?' Jess asked.

'No. The irony is not lost on me. I finally find a guy I want to be with, and my dad doesn't want to know about it.'

'He'll come around eventually,' Kat said.

'Are you sure about that?' Em said. 'He's probably arranging a detective to spy on us. He's a very stubborn man.'

'If that's true, that's going beyond stubborn. More like controlling.'

Em sighed. 'He means well.'

Jess reached over and rubbed Em's arm reassuringly. 'It almost sounds like you miss him, which surprises me a bit after all your complaints about his meddling over the years.'

'It's screwed up, isn't it? He drives me crazy, but yeah, I guess I do miss him. Sort of.'

Kat grunted. 'That's family for you. I love my mum unconditionally, but it doesn't mean that she doesn't drive me mad.'

'Ant's dad is exactly like that, too,' Jess added.

They fell silent for a while, basking in the sunshine and the after-effects of their exercise session.

'You could try to contact your father again,' Jess said. 'You might have to turn up in person, though, if he's as stubborn as you say he is.'

Em inhaled a big gulp of salt air. 'Yeah, I think you're right. I will. It can't hurt, right?'

'Just don't mention the boardroom again,' Kat advised. 'The less said about that, the better.'

Jess giggled and Em managed a smile. The tightness in her stomach had eased a bit. Maybe things weren't perfect right now, but it sure made a hell of a lot of difference knowing that she had friends she could laugh about things with.

And tomorrow she'd take their advice and turn up at her father's office unannounced. Whether he liked it or not.

Chapter Thirty-One

FIRST THING MONDAY MORNING, Em strode into her father's office.

'Em! You don't have an appointment,' Tina, her father's PA exclaimed. 'Now isn't a good time. Perhaps you can come back—'

Em ignored Tina and marched straight past her towards Chris's office. When she arrived at the closed door, she briskly knocked twice then went inside.

Chris Georgiou was on the phone, sitting with his back to Em, overlooking his impressive top floor view of the city. When Em had been a child and he'd brought her to work for a visit, she had always been in awe of her father's expansive office. Back then it had seemed like he was the master of all that he commanded.

Well, not anymore. At least not of her.

'Dad. We need to talk.'

Her father stopped talking and swivelled the chair around to face his daughter. His brown eyes regarded her coolly.

'Now isn't a good time.'

'Yes. It is,' Em replied, and waited.

Not taking his eyes off Em, Chris politely ended the conversation with the caller on the other end of the phone.

'Go on,' he said.

'I'm not asking for your blessing. I've moved in with Joel. We're in a relationship. He's important to me. I remain employed at Scott & Morris with Nate's approval. I'd prefer not to have this cause a rift in the family, but I'm not giving Joel up over this.'

Chris waited a beat before replying. 'I know all of this. It's not news to me.'

Em blinked. It was on the tip of her tongue to make an angry retort about her father's nosiness. The joke that she'd made to her friends about her father hiring a detective probably wasn't too far from the truth, but Em honestly didn't want to know at this point. She didn't need another thing to be angry with him about.

'Then why have you chosen not to talk to me?' she demanded instead, still secretly hurt that her father had thrown her out of the apartment.

'I was waiting for you. And I needed to make my own enquiries. Your life is yours to live, Em, but I think you should know that I'm not comfortable with Joel Scott.'

'You were the one who introduced us,' Em pointed out, careful not to mention the boardroom incident.

Chris stood up from behind his desk. Now that she was an adult, Em always found her father's short stature slightly disconcerting. He'd seemed like a king or a giant when she'd been a kid. Now, not so much.

Chris came around the desk and leaned on the edge. 'I've done some investigation into Joel's background.' He held up a hand at Em's cry of disgust. 'Just hear me out, will you? Scott isn't his real surname.'

Em glared at her father. 'I'm not entirely surprised. From what he's told me, he had an awful childhood. Maybe he was trying to put it in the past.'

Chris considered this piece of information with interest. 'What else has he told you?'

'Enough,' Em replied, feeling protective of Joel. 'Enough to know that his parents weren't good people and that he should be proud of what he's become in spite of his messed-up childhood.'

'Interesting,' Chris mused.

'Why is that so interesting? Is this your way of saying that he's not worthy of me because he doesn't come from a good family? None of us get to choose our family, you know.'

The last comment was aimed at her father. She couldn't help it. As much as she wanted to clear the air with him, he still drove her crazy with his control freak ways.

Chris thrummed his thumb against his trouser leg. 'I haven't been able to find out anything further apart from the fact that Scott isn't his real name.'

'Then leave it,' Em said firmly. 'Joel's past is his business.'

'It doesn't bother you that he might be hiding something?'

Em threw up her hands in exasperation. 'What's to hide? His parents were messed up, but they're both dead now. I haven't met his sister, but from what he's suggested, she's messed up too and lives in Western Australia. He doesn't have a great relationship with her. He's worked hard to get where he is despite his tough upbringing, so just leave it, Dad. Let Joel live his life. And for that matter, let me live mine, too. I hope in time he'll be welcome in our family. In the meantime, you know where to find me.'

Em stalked out of her father's office.

Well, that had gone well.

A MONTH LATER, Em stood with Joel admiring their finished living room.

'It's amazing, Joel.'

'I know.'

Em nudged him in the side. 'Very humble.'

Joel leaned in and brushed his lips against hers. 'It's even better than I imagined thanks to your input.'

Em flushed, genuinely flattered. Although the ultimate vision for the space had been Joel's, he'd welcomed all of Em's thoughts on the interior design, including the rather fancy fireplace surround that was now a showpiece.

She leaned against his side, content. More content than she'd ever thought she could be when it came to a man. 'I love how this house has come alive with the work that you've done. It's like it was waiting patiently all along for someone like you.'

'If I didn't know you better, I'd almost accuse you of sounding romantic.'

Em grinned. 'Me? Never. But I might just fall in love with this house if you're not careful.'

An odd expression flickered over Joel's face, then he looked away. 'Some houses are easy to fall in love with.'

'Oh, I don't know. I think it took someone like you who has a certain skill and vision to make it come alive. You definitely should get a photographer to come in and take some shots. I think it deserves it.'

'I'm not planning on selling it,' Joel said.

'Over my dead body. I just think it would be nice to catalogue the transformation, the way your firm does with its finished projects. We could even create a photo montage of before and after shots and arrange them on the hallway wall.'

Joel smiled, his olive skin creasing around the corners of

his eyes. Em still loved it when he did that. His smiles were rare, but always worth the wait.

'That's a hell of an idea. Ideas like that are the reason I keep you around.'

Em cocked her head to one side and gave him a wink. 'Not the only reason, I hope?'

Joel's eyes darkened and he hooked an arm around her waist. 'Definitely not the only reason.'

They shared a long, deep kiss. The sort of kiss that left you feeling slightly drugged, in a good way.

When the doorbell rang, they reluctantly pulled apart.

'Damn,' Joel muttered. 'Who invited them?'

'We did,' Em retorted, and slapped him lightly on the backside, then went to open the front door.

Secretly, Em was super excited about having her friends over for dinner tonight. It would be the first time they'd shown the renovation off and had guests over. A year ago, if someone had told her that she would be giddy about hosting a dinner party with her boyfriend, Em would have scoffed in disbelief.

Now she felt slightly ashamed of that point of view. Relationships certainly weren't for everyone, but it had been rather naïve and closed-minded of her to view others in relationships negatively.

She'd thought of relationships as a sort of unhealthy co-dependency. While it was possible there were relationships like that, it wasn't how she would describe her relationship, or those of her friends.

Em didn't need Joel. But she definitely loved having him around.

Love.

It was something that Em found herself pondering from time to time these days. Like in the evening when she was curled up on the sofa with Joel, chatting about their days or watching a movie. Was she in love? The fact was, Em didn't really know, because she'd never been in love before. One thing she did know for sure was that she loved having Joel in her life.

Em opened the door and her face lit up with a big smile. 'Welcome! You've all come together.'

Kat, Matt, Jess and Ant smiled back at her from the front porch.

'I drove everyone here,' Jess informed Em. 'As the only one who doesn't drink, I'm official chauffeur.'

Ant gave her a lopsided grin. 'Best looking chauffeur I've ever had.'

'Only chauffeur you've ever had,' Kat said, rolling her eyes, and everyone laughed.

'Come in,' Em told them and stepped aside.

Em didn't miss how her friends' eyes widened when they came into the now open-plan living and dining area. The ceilings towered above them with strategically placed beams made of reclaimed timber.

When Jess saw the fireplace, she gasped. 'Oh, Em, it's beautiful.'

Joel cleared his throat. 'What makes you think Em had anything to do with it?'

Ant walked over and slapped Joel on the shoulder. 'Mate, it's not really your style.'

Joel's lips quirked. 'Oh, I don't know. The silver leaf finish was always part of my vision.'

'Liar,' Kat told him. 'It's stunning, and you're a smart man listening to your better half.'

Joel's gaze clouded, and Em shot him a dazzling smile. She hated the way that sadness would surface in his eyes at the oddest times. Usually when things were going well. It didn't make a lot of sense, and Em knew that it had something to do with his upbringing, so she never made a big deal about it. Better to concentrate on the positive.

Em strode over to him and planted a loud kiss on his cheek. 'Can you pour our guests some wine while I check on the dinner?'

Joel squeezed her hand before she slipped away to the kitchen. Whatever ghosts haunted Joel, Em wouldn't allow them to intrude on their night. They had too much to be proud of, and good company to enjoy.

TWO HOURS LATER, Kat groaned. 'I don't often say this, Jess, but I'm looking forward to our exercise session tomorrow.'

'I'll take that as a compliment about our cooking,' Em told them.

'Definitely,' Matt agreed. 'As the only chef in our house, you've outdone yourselves.'

'Hey,' protested Kat. 'I cook toast.'

'And not much else,' Matt replied fondly.

Kat shrugged. 'You're more domestic than I figured you would be, Georgiou.'

Em grinned. 'One of my best-kept secrets. Just don't let the word get out.'

Matt and Kat shared a look, then Matt cleared his throat. 'Speaking of secrets . . .'

Kat rolled her eyes. 'Quit with the suspense, already. We're pregnant, alright? We haven't announced it publicly yet, but we wanted you all to know before it hits the media.'

'Or I open my big mouth on-air,' Ant added, and Jess giggled.

Em stared at her friends. 'A baby? Oh, wow.' She jumped

up and raced around the table to give Kat a tight hug. 'Congratulations!' Then she directed a curious glance at Jess. 'You knew already?'

Kat grimaced. 'I threw up during one of our morning beach walks earlier this week. It wasn't pretty, and Jess figured it out when I stupidly insisted it wasn't anything I'd eaten.'

Jess grinned while Joel reached over the table to shake Matt's hand.

First her sister, and now her friends. For whatever reason, Em couldn't imagine having a baby. But Kat and Matt were both in their thirties and obviously more ready than Em was—or perhaps ever would be.

Kat smiled sympathetically, reading Em's thoughts. 'You'll get used to the idea. I'm still getting used to it myself, to be honest. But Matt here isn't getting any younger . . .'

They all laughed.

Now that she looked closely, Kat was glowing. To Em, a baby seemed like the biggest commitment you could make. Bigger than moving in or . . .

'You're not married,' Em said without thinking, then winced. 'Sorry. Ignore me. Years of conditioning by my father. Have ten kids and stay unmarried, for all I care.'

Kat held up her left hand and wiggled her fingers. Em's mouth dropped open.

'When?' Jess demanded, before Em could say anything.

'Oh, you know, the other week, I think it was.' She gave Matt a coy sidelong glance.

'It was the twenty-first,' he said. 'And don't worry. A big party is in the works.'

'But no wedding,' Kat said firmly. 'As you know, I'm not into the fanfare.'

Em nodded, filled with respect for her friend. She appreciated that Kat and Matt were doing things their way. Kat had a failed engagement to a previous boyfriend and had watched her parents' marriage fall apart, so it was a big deal when she'd accepted Matt's proposal. And an indication of just how much she loved him.

'Good for you,' Em said. 'The media won't be impressed, but that's their problem.'

'Don't worry,' Ant said. 'When my time comes with Jess, I'll be sure to go all out with a big Cinderella dress.'

Jess choked on her drink. 'Oh, please, no.'

Em's eyebrows shot upward. 'Is there something you're not telling us?'

'About my sexual orientation?' Ant asked. 'No, I'm good with women. I meant Jess can have the big Cinderella dress, not me.'

'Like Em said, is there something you're not telling us?' Kat demanded, not missing a beat.

Jess flushed. 'No, we're not engaged. Ant's just being silly.'

'We're not engaged *yet*,' Ant added, and Jess blushed brighter. 'I have every intention of holding on to this lovely woman, in case you're wondering. But I need to come up with a really memorable way of asking her.'

Kat sniggered. 'Watch out, Jess.'

Jess grinned. 'I'm sure he'll strike when I least expect it.'

They all jumped when the front doorbell rang, and Jess directed a panicked look at Ant.

He held up his hands. 'Don't look at me. That was merely a coincidence.'

Joel stood up. 'I'll go see who it is.'

With Joel gone, they continued to chat about Kat and Matt's baby news. When Joel didn't reappear, Em stopped listening to the conversation, which was when she registered an angry male voice.

Em stood abruptly.

It was her father.

What on earth was he doing here?

By the time Em had rushed to the front door, Chris was already pushing past Joel into the front hallway. Em skidded to a stop in shock. There was no doubt that Joel was strong enough to stop her father, but Joel stood pale-faced, gripping the edge of the front door so tightly that his knuckles were white. Her father bustled towards Em like a rotund terrier on the hunt.

'Emily. There you are.' His hand closed around her arm. 'You need to come home. Now.'

Em didn't move when Chris tugged on her arm. 'I am home. What are you talking about?'

'No, our home. You can't stay here.'

Em stared at her father in disbelief. 'Dad, you're not making any sense.'

'It doesn't matter. I'll explain when we get back to our place.'

Chris pulled on her arm again, and Em shook him off, taking a step back.

'Dad! You can't just barge in here and tell me what to do. I'm a grown woman.'

Chris pushed a hand through his thinning dark hair sprinkled with grey. 'I know that. But this is for your own safety.'

'I'm not a child!'

At the sound of Em's raised voice, her friends rushed into the hallway.

'Is everything alright, Em?' Matt asked casually, but his tall stature, and firm, deep voice showed that Em had their support.

Chris blinked when he saw the group of guests. 'I suggest that your friends leave now, too.'

Kat stepped forward. 'Mr. Georgiou, what is this all about?'

Chris swallowed like he'd tasted something awful and jabbed a thumb behind him towards Joel. 'Him. It's about him. But I don't think I should explain here.'

'Why don't you just say it?' Joel's voice was soft, and Em detected a note of weariness in it. 'Or are you afraid of me?'

Chris stiffened, but ignored Joel. 'Emily. Please. Grab your purse and let's go.'

'Dad. That's enough. You owe all of us an explanation,' Em told her father.

Chris cast a glance backwards in Joel's direction, and Em caught a hint of fear. What on earth was going on?

'Dad?' she said more quietly this time. Her dad was genuinely worried, and she wanted to know why.

Chris closed his eyes briefly and when he opened them again his expression was stricken. 'You were right, Emily. Joel does want to forget about his past, but not for the reasons you might think.'

'Just say it,' Joel ground out, still gripping the door tightly. He wasn't looking at any of them and was staring at the wall intently.

Chris cleared his throat. 'Emily, as I told you earlier, Scott isn't his last name. It's Cooper.' Chris cast another nervous glance over his shoulder. 'And Joel Cooper was responsible for killing someone.'

Chapter Thirty-Two

JESS GASPED, and there was a shocked silence.

Em couldn't move. She couldn't breathe. All she could do was look past her father's shoulder to where Joel stood facing the wall, her eyes rounded in a sort of silent plea.

Look at me. It can't be true.

But everything in Joel's body language told her otherwise. The way his jaw was tense and his hand fisted against his leg. He still wasn't looking at them. Why wasn't he looking at them?

Because it's true.

'Emily.' Her father touched her arm lightly. 'I'm so sorry, honey. I didn't know. Not until today. We should go.'

Kat shook her head, like she was shaking away the shock. 'Now, hang on just a minute. You can't just come in here and accuse someone of something like that. Joel?'

They all fell silent again. After a long moment, Joel dropped his chin to his chest and squeezed his eyes shut.

Haunted. He was always so haunted. That's what had struck

Em since getting to know Joel. But she'd just assumed that it was because of his childhood, not because of . . .

'Do you want to tell them or will I?' Joel said, his voice louder and firmer than it had been.

When Chris didn't answer, Joel sighed.

'I was sixteen.' Joel's words lacked any emotion, and it almost didn't sound like him. 'I came home to find the piece of shit my sister was dating trying to rape her, so I pulled him off her. He went crazy. I found out later that he was drunk and on drugs. He tried to kill me, but I ended up killing him first.'

He said it like it was that simple. His life or someone else's.

Ant held Jess to his side, her blue eyes impossibly wide, while Matt stood behind Kat appearing watchful, but not showing any emotion.

'Were you charged?' Kat asked.

Em appreciated Kat's courage to ask what they'd all been thinking, but then she was a journalist.

Joel opened his eyes and blinked as if he didn't know where he was. 'Yes, but I was a minor, and it was ruled self-defence in Children's Court.'

'I found several newspaper reports,' Chris told them. 'It's all there in black and white. It would be on Joel's police record if he authorised a National Police Check. It's probably why he prefers being self-employed.'

A flicker of disgust contorted Joel's face, but then he looked away. 'Well, when you come from scum, everyone assumes the worst.'

Em put a hand to her mouth, caught between horror and grief.

Kat was still studying Joel intensely with no fear, just curiosity. 'Does your business partner know?'

'No.'

'I've already told him,' Chris said at the same time, and Em released a startled cry.

Joel dropped his head into his hands.

Kat pushed past everyone, the only one currently brave enough to go to Joel, but Joel raised his hand. 'Leave it. If it's taught me anything it's that you can't forget it. You can never forget it. That's why I tried to spare others from knowing.'

'No,' Chris shot back, 'you're a liar, that's what you are. Don't try to sugar coat it. You just didn't want people to know who you are. *What* you are.'

No, Em thought silently. None of this made sense. Her father liked Joel. He'd chosen Joel and trusted him enough to work with him. Except now he'd learned something so serious, so shocking about Joel, and his precious daughter was involved. Despite the fact it was clearly a horrible accident on Joel's part, Em knew any esteem or respect her father held for Joel until this point would be cancelled out by the primal need he had to protect his daughter.

'What does your sister think?' Kat pressed, ignoring Chris. 'Surely she understands that you saved her?'

For the first time since Chris had walked through the door, Joel looked over at them. He met Kat's gaze, and his eyes were so dark, so empty, that Em's heart clenched.

'She was so drunk at the time that she doesn't remember. It's probably better that way.' He pushed away from the wall and grabbed his jacket, which was hanging on the coat rack opposite. 'Let me do you a favour. I'll leave instead. You can see yourselves out when you're ready.'

He stalked past them and Em suddenly sprung to life, catching his shoulder in a desperate attempt to stop him from leaving.

Joel shook her off roughly and kept walking. Em stared after him in dismay. She wanted to run after him, to go to him, but she discovered that her body wouldn't move. She felt frozen in time.

She wasn't the only one. No one else moved. No one said anything, until about half a minute later the sound of the Porsche roaring to life in the basement garage cut through the silence. The engine growled as it reversed onto the street, then it didn't so much as growl but snarl as it accelerated away.

When it was quiet, Em discovered that she was shaking. She looked down at her hands like they didn't belong to her. They trembled, but not in a good way, not the way they did when Joel touched her . . .

'Oh my God,' she whispered.

She stumbled down the hall to the living area and collapsed on the nearest armchair.

Joel had touched her. Everywhere. Those same hands that had held her and made her moan in pleasure . . . had killed a man.

Em put her head in her hands.

It doesn't matter. It doesn't matter. It doesn't matter, her mind chanted.

This was Joel. Stoic, confident Joel, who just got on with things.

But of course it mattered. It mattered very much. Em knew Joel was caring and kind, so he wouldn't hurt someone intentionally or easily. But what mattered was that he hadn't told her. It mattered that he'd lied to her. She could understand why he'd lied to everyone else. Even to her father. But she was his partner and surely she deserved to know the truth about him. And what about Nate? As Joel's business partner, Nate trusted Joel, yet he didn't know either.

Joel was living a double life.

The realisation sounded dramatic, but it was true to some extent. Despite trying to move on from the darkness in his past, he'd carried it with him. By never telling his truth, he'd allowed that darkness to fester.

But what would Em have done if Joel had told her the truth? What would Nate have done? Would they even have a business now if he had?

The Big Bad Wolf.

That was what he'd been all along. She knew now that he'd tried to warn her. He'd even put an end to things because of it. But Em had still wanted him.

Did she still want Joel now?

She honestly had no idea. Em was too numb to feel anything properly. And she wasn't sure if she'd ever be able to feel anything again after this.

EM HAD WANTED to stay and wait for Joel, but her father had insisted that she come home with him. When she'd protested, her friends had told her gently that she probably needed space to think and to recover from the news before talking to Joel again.

There was no point talking to him while she was still in shock, Kat had reasoned. Rest and regroup, then talk to him.

At the time, it had sounded like good advice—wise advice —so Em had relented. In reality, the familiarity of her childhood bedroom and bed had been comforting. Even if it was just one night of pretending that everything was like it used to be, it gave Em a brief reprieve from facing what she knew was to come.

She needed to talk to Joel. To ask him to let her in fully, so that she could process everything. So that she could make her mind up about things.

Or was it her heart that had to decide? In some ways, her

heart was an unreliable judge. It just wanted the old Joel back. The Joel she knew. Not this mysterious, broken Joel who had withheld vital information about himself from her.

Em sent Joel a text.

I'll be home in the morning before lunch. We can talk then.

She'd deliberated over finishing the message with a kiss, but then had left it off. Joel deserved love like everyone— possibly more love than anyone after what he'd lived through —but she didn't want to promise anything before she'd had time to think through everything.

He didn't answer the message, but Em could see that he'd received it. The worst part was thinking about what he was putting himself through. She knew now that his self-deprecation was fuelled by self-hatred. And he probably hated himself even more now.

Despite all the rampant thoughts making her head spin, Em slept soundly that night because she was so exhausted.

The first thing she did when she woke up was check her phone. The only message was from Kat.

I won't ask how you are. Call me if you want to talk x

Em found herself hitting "call" before she knew what she was doing.

'Hey,' Kat said, like she'd been expecting the call.

'Hey.' Em played with the edge of the bedsheet. Funny. It had seemed imperative that she call, but now she wasn't sure what to say.

'Did you sleep?' Kat asked.

'Yes. More than I thought I would.'

'Good. Where's your head at?'

'Confused.'

'And your heart?'

Em released a shaky breath. 'It hurts.'

'Understandable. For what it's worth, I don't think he meant to hurt you.'

Em huffed. 'Just the guy he killed, hey?' She winced. 'Oh my God. Forget I said that, will you? My thoughts are all screwed up right now.'

'I bet they are. Imagine what his are like then.'

Tortured, Em thought, but didn't say it. 'Part of me doesn't want to feel sorry for him because he lied to us.'

'I'm used to seeing both sides of a story. Whichever way you look at it, his side is pretty grim, Em. It's pretty goddamn grim.'

'I know. But that's just the thing, I *don't* know. I wasn't there. I didn't live his shitty childhood. I could never imagine what it was like, yet here I am, still judging him.'

'Because he killed someone.'

'Yeah.'

They fell silent.

'Forget about what you think, for a moment,' Kat suggested after a while. 'How about what you feel?'

'Hurt. Betrayed,' Em admitted. 'But sorry for him. No, not just sorry. Devastated. That he's had to live with it. Had to deal with it. Alone, from what I can gather. Can you imagine killing someone unintentionally because you were trying to protect your sister?'

'No. I can't,' Kat replied simply. 'Well, actually, when I try to, it hurts my brain.'

'Imagine living with that every day of your life,' Em whispered.

'It doesn't bear thinking about, does it?' Kat said.

'No.' Em paused. 'I think I still love him.'

'Still? I didn't realise that you loved him in the first place.'

Em let out a quiet sob. 'Stupid me didn't either, until now.'

'Love often messes with your head. It's probably messing with his head right now, too.'

Em frowned, although Kat couldn't see her. It made no sense that her heart leapt at Kat's last comment. 'You think Joel loves me?'

'It doesn't matter what I think,' Kat pointed out. 'But yeah, I don't think he ever would have let you get so close if he didn't feel strongly about you. That man is used to building walls around himself.'

'Do you think he ever would have told me?' Em asked softly.

Kat sighed. 'That's not a question I can answer. You'll have to talk to him.'

'You're right,' Em said decisively. 'I need to talk to him. I'd better go.'

Chapter Thirty-Three

JOEL MADE sure he was gone before Em returned to the house. He left the Porsche behind and took the beat-up old utility that he held on to for renovation work. It was the more practical choice given his destination.

Besides, what was more discomfort in the scheme of things? His time with Em had been a brief reprieve from the life he'd come to expect—one where hurt featured large. It seemed to follow his family like a bad smell.

Or a curse.

Was that what he was? Cursed?

It was what it felt like. Despite Joel's desire to be nothing like his parents—and in particular, nothing like his dad—his own damn fists had brought him down to the same level as his violent, hideous father.

One punch was all it had taken.

A single blow to the back of the head to take a young man down. That one punch had decided the man's fate as well as Joel's. It had almost put him behind bars, too.

Joel had been fighting for his life—and for his sister's. Joel had ended up with broken ribs, a broken nose, a fractured hand. Joel had landed the punch when the guy had turned his back to try to harm Mia. To hit her. Possibly still try to rape her. The guy had been so out of his mind on whatever he was on it had been impossible to tell what his next move would be.

All Joel had known was that he had to stop him.

So he had.

In that moment, when Joel realised the guy wasn't getting up, he'd had the strangest thought.

That he was lucky to be alive. Not just from this fight. But from all the others.

How many punches had he received at the hands of his father? Too many to count. Suddenly it seemed like a goddamn miracle that Joel had survived his sixteen years up until that point.

One punch too hard, or just in the right spot, and Joel may never have gotten up.

Instead, this guy was lying on the ground, knocked dead, and Joel was still alive.

It made no sense.

Another strange thought—why couldn't it have been his father?

So not only was Joel guilty of killing someone, he also wished that he had killed another.

That's why Joel still felt, to this day, that he deserved to be punished. When he'd walked free after the trial, he'd been in shock. He'd already geared himself up for a gaol term. After all, it was what he deserved. He'd killed a man. Surely there had to be a consequence for that.

When there hadn't been, he'd tried to punish himself. He dropped out of school. He never took drugs and rarely drank alcohol, but he surrounded himself with people who did. Because it was what he deserved.

Joel had spent the rest of his teens in a dark, dark place, because that was where he was supposed to be. He'd virtually been homeless at one point, relying on the charity of friends to give him a bed for the night.

He hadn't cared. What was the point in caring?

Then his little sister had found him. Crying. Their mum had died. Mia didn't know what to do. She was scared.

Somehow, Joel had pulled himself together, because when all was said and done, he was a sucker for a woman in distress. He took the first job he was offered—a labourer's hand on a building site. No one there cared about who he was. Only that he was strong enough for the grunt work that needed to be done.

By the time Mia finished high school, Joel had been offered an apprenticeship. The men at work didn't know anything about his past. They didn't think to ask. He was just Joel—solid, reliable and hard working.

After he finished his apprenticeship, Joel decided that he wanted to go to university. It wasn't easy balancing part-time study with work, but in the end, he got there. In truth, the struggle had seemed easy compared to his childhood.

Then during his first job out of university, he'd met Nate. By then the old Joel was someone else, someone not worth mentioning, especially seeing as he'd moved to the other side of the country.

And now he was going back.

Joel was driving all the way to Western Australia. Almost four thousand kilometres. He could have caught a plane, but he wanted to feel every single kilometre pass by. To remind him that all the distance and time he'd put between him and the sixteen-year-old kid he once was didn't make a pinch of shit's difference.

Joel would always be Joel Cooper, no matter what his driver's licence said.

And for that matter, he'd always be a murderer.

Nothing could ever change that.

EM LET herself into Joel's house. She knew immediately that he wasn't there, because it was quiet.

Joel wasn't a noisy man, but there was something about his presence that filled a space. Quietly, but irrefutably. Like the absence of the moon on a cloudless night. Without it, the world was dark.

'Joel, where are you?' Em whispered.

She set her keys down carefully on the antique hall table they had chosen together not that long ago, and went in search of him.

Every room was the same. Empty. But with undeniable signs of their connection. The wall colour they'd argued about. The picture they'd bought.

This place wasn't just his. It was theirs.

'Joel,' Em said louder this time and with a note of pleading to it.

Upstairs, she found it. Signs that he'd been home.

The bed was unmade and the wardrobe door had been left open. Inside, clothes were missing.

Em felt a sharp stab of foreboding and looked around desperately. There. On her bedside table. A note.

With hands shaking, she picked it up and lowered herself to sit on the edge of the bed.

Dear Em,

I'm sorry. No amount of saying sorry will ever be enough. For you. For what's come before. Sometimes action is the only way.

I'm selling the house. Feel free to take whatever you want once it's sold. It's as much yours as it is mine.

Know this. You're better off without me. Honestly. The irony is that for a brief moment in time, I was better with you by my side. I see now that it was selfish of me.

Don't try to contact me. Stay strong. You're the most amazing woman. You deserve to be happy. I can never offer you that.

I mean it, Em. Don't contact me.

Joel.

Em balled the note up in her hand and threw it at the wall with a pained cry, tears streaming down her face.

It was bullshit. This was bullshit.

They *had* been happy. The two of them together, living in this house. Everywhere she looked, even now, there were signs of their happiness.

It was like he didn't believe he could be happy. That was the problem. He felt he didn't deserve happiness. Or her.

'Oh, Joel,' Em said, not bothering to wipe away the tears staining her cheeks.

He was broken. There was no question.

He'd lived a tragic life for his first two decades. But that didn't mean that he was unlovable. That his past set the course for the rest of his life. He'd proven that with his business and this house. In so many different ways.

Yet he still didn't believe it.

To himself, Joel would always be that scared, angry boy. His father's son.

Like Em would always be Daddy's girl.

Em jumped up. 'That's bullshit!' she cried.

Em wasn't Daddy's girl, not anymore. She was so much more than that. She'd proved that to herself by following her passion, in obtaining her PhD. Her father might still think of her as Daddy's girl, but it didn't matter what he thought anymore.

Just like it didn't matter what anyone else thought of Joel.

It struck Em that Joel had imprisoned himself all these years despite not being sentenced to gaol. He'd placed invisible walls around himself due to his own negative view of himself. That was why he'd never had a serious relationship.

'You're not the Big Bad Wolf, Joel,' Em said to herself, now pacing the room as her thoughts came rapidly, like errant tumbleweeds caught in the wind. 'Not at all.'

Em stopped and looked out the window with its serene view of the harbour. Where was he now? And where was he going? What was he going to do?

Em gripped the window ledge as a fresh realisation settled on her. 'I know who you are, Joel. You're the lone wolf. That's who you are.'

Chapter Thirty-Four

ONE MONTH later

'Em, I'm here.' Kat's voice came through loud and clear on the other end of the phone.

'Any sign of Joel?' Em asked.

'None. There's a good crowd here. I think you might have your work cut out for you. I suspect that your buyer's agent will call you in a sec, so I'd better get off the line so that you can win this thing.'

This "thing" was Joel's house, which about to be auctioned. Em was a few blocks away, sitting in Kat's car. Kat had offered to watch the auction for her. Not that it was necessary, because her agent was there. But Em couldn't exactly grill her agent afterwards with questions about whether the vendor had been there and what he looked like. It would seem strange.

Stranger than this already was, at least.

A minute later, her agent, Cameron, rang.

'Alright, we're good to go,' he announced. 'There's strong interest. Are you still happy with your budget?'

Em liked the tall older man who she'd engaged to help her buy Joel's house. He was confident without being arrogant, and she couldn't imagine him ever wearing anything other than a suit.

'Until we reach my limit,' Em answered, 'and then you can ask me again.'

Cameron chuckled. 'You know that's not what I recommend.'

'I know. But like I told you. This house is mine.'

Em meant it. She'd spent every waking minute thinking about this auction during the last month. She'd even had Cameron make a pre-auction offer, but Joel was stubborn. He might have disappeared from her life like a puff of smoke, but he knew that his house would sell well in a competitive market.

'You're insane, girlfriend!'

Em jumped at Gavin's teasing voice from the back seat. She was so absorbed in her pre-auction jitters that she'd forgotten Gavin and her sister, Ana, were here for moral support.

Em covered the mouthpiece with her hand. 'I'm perfectly sane, thank you very much. But I'm about to be a lot poorer.'

'No, honey. You won't be poor,' Gavin replied. 'You'll be in debt. For the rest of your life, thanks to a man who no longer exists. But you have my full support,' he finished with a grin.

Em grinned back. 'You're just thankful that you've found a friend who's as crazy as you are.'

'Don't I know it.' Gavin reached forward and squeezed Em's hand in a show of solidarity.

Ana rolled her eyes. 'At least you're not related to the crazy.'

Her sister looked comical perched on the tiny back seat of Kat's car nursing her extremely pregnant belly. When Em had tried to talk her out of coming, Ana had insisted. She'd claimed it would be the most excitement she'd have for months after she had the baby, which would be any day now.

Em had discussed her crazy idea endlessly with all of her friends during the preceding weeks. Kat. Jess. Gavin. Plus her sister.

Then there was her father.

Em had been determined to do this on her own and buy the house by herself. She'd saved up a nice nest egg thanks to not spending her father's money over the years, but that still hadn't been enough. Em's salary didn't quite make the criteria for the loan, so she'd started considering other options like having another investor.

Thanks to her sister, that investor was now her father.

Em had fought the idea for almost two weeks, mainly out of frustration with her sister and the idea of being beholden to her father again. Now that Em had a full-time job, he was all for her investment plans. That was until he'd learned which house Em wanted to buy, then he'd hit the roof.

Ana had come to the rescue. She'd thrown around words like "good investment" and "one-of-a-kind" property. In the end, when Chris had seen how determined Em was, he'd come forward with extra cash.

That and the fact that Joel was nowhere in sight.

'What happens if he comes back?' Chris had asked suspiciously before signing the loan documents.

Of course, Em was hoping that was exactly what Joel would do when he saw whose name was on the settlement contract, but she just shrugged. It was an extreme way to try to get the attention of your ex-boyfriend, but then Em never did things by halves.

It was a long shot, and one that Ana had termed "extremely romantic" more than once. The fact that Em was in love with someone who had once been accused of murder didn't seem to register on her sister's radar.

'Pfft,' she'd said, waving a hand dismissively when Em had told her the entire, ugly story. 'Self-defence. I'd kill to protect this baby. And probably you too, I suppose.'

'But what about Dad?' Em had asked.

'Let me deal with him,' Ana told her.

Ana did have a particular knack for wrapping their father around her little finger, but even Em thought in this case that it might be a stretch. She'd worry about that later, though. First she had to buy the house.

'Em!' Ana called out from the back seat. 'Your agent is saying something.'

'Shit,' Em swore, removing her hand from the phone so that she could speak again.

'Language, Aunty Em,' Ana hissed at her, and Em turned back to the front of the car, ignoring her sister. Her niece or nephew wasn't even born yet and her sister was unbearable.

'OK, Em,' Cameron said. 'The auction is starting now. I won't say anything further unless I need to confirm your bid— in other words, that you want to go over that budget you set.'

'Thanks, Cameron.'

Em put the phone on speakerphone and laid it on her lap so that the others could listen. The auctioneer's voice was so loud that they could all hear it. Em put a finger to her mouth to indicate that they should stay quiet.

Em listened restlessly as the auctioneer listed the wonderful qualities of Joel's house. She knew all of that, and she didn't need everyone else knowing it, too. They heard words like "architectural brilliance", "sustainably designed" and "flawless renovation".

Hurry up, already.

Em didn't have to wait much longer.

The auction started at a cracking pace, with someone—
Em had no idea who because she couldn't see anything—
starting with a strong bid. It could have been Cameron for all
she knew, but Em doubted it, as he'd already explained his
strategy. He was unlikely to make the first bid unless there was
little interest, and there was plenty of interest in this case.

The bids kept going up at an alarming rate, and then they
heard Cameron say quietly into the phone, 'Permission to
proceed?'

Crap. This was Em's cue. Did she break her budget or
stop now?

There's no way I'm stopping.

'Another twenty, but not in that increment,' Em told him
firmly, her heart fluttering nervously in her chest.

Less than thirty seconds later, Cameron spoke again. 'Our
turn?' Which meant he'd bid to her limit.

'Another twenty,' Em told him, and her sister gasped from
the back seat.

Em had no idea where this extra money was coming from.
Her father, most likely. Em didn't stop to think about it.

'I'll need more,' Cam told her after a beat.

'Shit,' Em said.

'Your call,' he replied.

'How close?' Em asked. She knew he couldn't say much or
he'd give the game away, but they'd planned for this.

'How much?' he asked.

That meant that they were close. Real close. If he'd said,
"What's your figure?" that would have meant they'd need a lot
more.

'Another ten if you need it,' Em told him, and this time
Gavin squeaked.

They held their breaths as the bids went up more slowly in

lots of thousands. Then it went up by two thousand, and the agent was calling it. The house was sold.

But to who?

Going once, going twice . . .

Just hurry up and go already!

Going three times. Sold!

'It's yours, Em. Congratulations,' Cameron announced.

Em gaped at the phone on her lap and released the breath that she'd been holding.

'It's mine?' she said in disbelief.

'All yours. We just need to sign the papers.'

Gavin and Ana erupted into squeals of delight while Em sat perfectly still in the front seat. She was vaguely aware that she was in shock.

Holy shit. She'd just bought a house.

Joel's house.

It was her house now.

And Joel was nowhere to be seen.

Chapter Thirty-Five

JOEL FINISHED STRAPPING the cover over the full load in the back of his utility. It contained the luggage he'd left Sydney with, together with the entirety of his sister's worldly belongings. Which didn't amount to much.

He registered the familiar pang of guilt that had plagued him ever since arriving in Western Australia and locating his sister. Visiting her was something he should have done years ago. Instead, he'd left her to fend for herself, which meant she was destined to repeat the same mistakes again and again, just like their mother.

And now she was pregnant.

Mia wandered out of the motel they'd been staying in together for the last few weeks. By Joel's standards, it was pleasant but simple—he hadn't wanted to break the bank while they figured out what came next. Yet Mia thought it was luxurious. That only made the guilt twist harder in Joel's belly, and made him stop and wonder just how bad her living arrangements had been in years past. While Joel had been busy building himself a new life, a different life to that of his parents, Mia had been stuck in a never-ending cycle of poverty and addiction.

Joel schooled his features into a neutral expression as his sister came out of the motel room. He'd taken her to get a haircut last week, and it was styled in a short bob, the same dark colour as his. They also shared the same eye colour—the eye colour of their mother and not their father, thankfully. She looked good. Vital. Alive. It wasn't just because she was pregnant. It was also because she hadn't touched any alcohol in almost four months. As soon as she'd found out that she was pregnant, she'd stopped.

Mia finished sipping the McDonald's thickshake he'd gotten for her earlier and grinned. She looked young. Younger than her twenty-eight years, which was surprising given the hard life she'd had so far. Maybe it was something to do with the baby, after all. She was more positive than he could remember since learning that she was going to be a mother.

She let out a polite burp and giggled. 'Ugh. Sorry. But that was awesome. I tell you, this kid wants dairy. And hot chips.'

Joel allowed himself a smile. 'That sounds like a fair deal to me.'

'Not really. I'll be the size of a house by the time I'm full term at this rate.'

'You're tiny, Mia. Keep drinking the thickshakes.'

Her lips quirked. 'If you insist.' She appeared to hesitate when she saw the utility that was packed and ready to go. 'Are you sure about this?'

'One hundred per cent. I should have done this years ago.'

She cocked her head to the side. 'What? Come to the rescue?'

'That's not what I'm doing.'

'It's kind of what you do.' She hesitated again. 'And I'm kind of glad, too.'

Joel's stomach clenched. Guilt. There was always so much guilt when it came to his family. Well, he was finally going to do something about it. He turned to face his sister.

'Are you sure about this?'

The hesitation was replaced with determination. 'I'm sure I don't want to be anywhere near this child's father—not that he wants anything to do with us, anyway. And I'm sure I want to try to be a good mum.'

'Then get in. We've got a long drive ahead of us,' Joel told her.

'With lots of toilet stops. Don't say I didn't warn you.'

'I can take it.'

After one last tug on the strap holding the load down, Joel got into the driver's seat. His phone vibrated just as he was putting it in the hands-free cradle.

He frowned when he saw the email preview. It was from his agent. The title of the message read "Sold" along with the sale price.

Joel glanced at his watch. It was done. The house had sold. He knew it would, even without looking at the message. There had been plenty of interest. The price was almost irrelevant as Joel wasn't in any rush to buy again. His main objective was getting his sister set up.

'So the Central Coast, then?' Mia said, tapping her knee nervously with her fingers.

'You'll like it there. It's only an hour north of Sydney, but the pace is much more laid back.'

'More affordable, too,' she added.

'Definitely,' Joel agreed.

That was one of the reasons he'd settled on that location for Mia. Joel still didn't know exactly where he was going to end up. Nate kept messaging him, telling him to call, but Joel had been largely uncontactable except for where work was concerned.

Now he was off the Georgiou contract, Joel's workload was almost non-existent. He'd been sure to check his emails twice a day and make it look like he was still working, only "out of the office".

He needed to speak to Nate in person to arrange what needed to be done so that he could extract himself from the business. Joel had no idea if Nate would argue or not. Either way, it didn't matter, because his mind was made up. He'd rent a place for Mia and stay with her until he was certain that she was managing, then he'd worry about himself. Between the money from the sale of the house and hopefully picking up some consulting work, he was confident that he could get by.

'Aren't you going to read it?' Mia asked.

Joel jerked out of his reverie. The engine was running and his hand was hovering near his phone. He dropped it to the steering wheel.

'No. Later. It's nothing important.'

That was a lie, but he didn't have the urge to explain his messed up personal life to his little sister. Like the fact that he'd just sold the house he'd poured his heart and soul into. Or that he'd left behind a woman he was certain also owned a fair chunk of that same heart and soul.

Instead, he released the car's handbrake and steered the ute in the direction of the highway for the long journey back east.

SIX WEEKS later

Anything yet?

Em read Jess's text message and then typed a quick reply.

Nothing yet.

Her friends and sister had been checking in like this regularly. She was surprised that they hadn't given up. Em almost had.

Six weeks. It had been *six weeks* since she'd bought Joel's house, and nothing. No recognition whatsoever that her name was on the contract.

Don't contact me.

Well, she hadn't. Em had bought his house instead. It was a different thing entirely.

'A certifiably crazy thing,' Em muttered to herself as she dropped the bags of groceries onto Joel's kitchen bench.

Her kitchen bench.

Settlement had taken place earlier that day and Em was officially moving in. Or back in, anyway. The house was just as she'd left it. Gorgeous and utterly too spacious for a single woman to live in alone. Still, it was hers. And for now, she planned to live here, even if doing so reminded her of Joel everywhere she turned.

Perhaps she could rent out the downstairs garage. Or eventually the entire damn house? Just because it was hers, didn't mean she had to live in it.

Em closed the fridge and sighed. 'I'm too stubborn not to —for now at least.'

She'd give Joel a bit longer. Surely knowing that she'd bought his house was cause for some sort of reaction. Or not. Maybe Em had completely misunderstood him. She thought that in his case, actions spoke louder than words. He'd said as much in his goodbye letter—that sorry was never going to be enough.

Em actually agreed. Sorry was a word. But things like Joel's business and this house spoke volumes. They demonstrated who the real Joel was. Not who he had once been, many years ago. Except that's who Joel thought he was destined to be for the rest of his life.

Em put her hands on her hips and looked around the kitchen. 'There's nothing else for it. I'm opening a bottle of wine and toasting my new house. And wherever you are, Joel, I'll raise a glass to you, too.'

JOEL WAS CURRENTLY STARING at a message on his phone and rubbing his temples. His head was throbbing. It was yet another message from Nate, and this one he couldn't ignore.

I'm not asking anymore. I'm telling you. It's been 3 months. Wherever you are, come into the damn office next week so we can straighten things out. Name a time.

He didn't have any more justifiable excuses, and he was being a coward. He was less than an hour away from the office. He'd set his sister up comfortably in her new two-bedroom villa, with him taking the second bedroom temporarily until he figured out what next.

Well, it looked like this was what came next. Joel would have to go and see Nate. He couldn't care less about his part ownership in the business. Joel would hand it over willingly on whatever terms Nate wanted. His friend deserved that much from him.

What he did care about was the look on his oldest friend and partner's face when they met. The disappointment. The horror—but probably less of that seeing as it had been a few months. It would more likely be a sort of awkward wariness. Joel could handle that from strangers. But from Nate? To lose the trust and respect that he valued so much was going to be a huge loss.

Mia came into the living area where Joel was sitting at the dining table and placed a mug of steaming coffee in front of him. 'Everything OK?'

'Just work. Something I need to go and sort out.'

'Sounds serious.' She put her own mug down and lowered herself into the chair opposite. Her pregnant belly was well and truly on show now. She grinned at him. 'I just got an email from the college. My application has been accepted.'

Despite the pain caused by Nate's message, Joel smiled. 'That's awesome, Mia. Truly.'

'They even agreed to let me defer the last subject for six months or so until after the baby is born. I couldn't believe it.'

'I can. You'll be great at this.'

"This" was a certificate course in early childhood teaching. Joel and Mia had been talking a lot since they'd been living together, and at one point, Mia had told Joel that she liked the idea of working with children. Joel liked the idea of it, too. When Mia was sober, she was warm and caring. She'd also been naturally bright at school, so Joel had no doubt that she would complete the course with flying colours. Then, when her baby was old enough, she could look for part-time work in a childcare centre nearby.

'I've never felt like this before, you know,' she admitted.

'What's that?'

'Hopeful. Like I've got something to look forward to.'

'You do,' said Joel, eyeing her stomach.

She laughed and rubbed her belly. 'You mean plenty of sleepless nights? But yeah, I do, don't I?'

'Can I ask you a question?'

Mia's hands stilled. 'Sure.'

'Do you miss the drink?'

Mia considered her brother's question. 'No. Not like I thought I would. It was always there, you know? With the guys

I lived with, there was always too much alcohol on hand. I told myself that I was doing the right thing by keeping away from the drugs. The alcohol seemed safer. Stupid, right?'

Given their father's long-term alcoholism it was naïve of Mia to think that, but then alcoholism didn't make sense. It just craved more of the same.

'Living here, with you,' Mia went on, 'made me realise that I'd always surrounded myself with it. Which is dumb given our history. Now it's not in my face, it's easier to catch myself when I find myself thinking about it.'

'Is that often?' Joel asked carefully.

Mia had been true to her word—she hadn't touched a drop since she'd been pregnant, as far as Joel was aware. But that could change in the months ahead if she felt lonely or depressed. Motherhood was tiring and hard work.

'It gets less often the longer I go without it. And now I find myself thinking of it differently. I find myself saying, "See? You don't need it. Look how good things are without it." I think I'll be fine, Joel. I can't say for sure that I know I will. But I'll tell you this much. I'm going to try as hard as I can. For this baby. For you. And me. I don't think I've ever tried this hard for me before. Does that sound odd?'

'Not at all. Just remember to tell yourself that you're worth it.'

'Thank you.' She reached over and squeezed his hand. 'So are you, Joel.'

Joel removed his hand and stood abruptly. 'You don't need to worry about me, Mia.'

'I don't need to, but I do. You seem sad. Sadder than I've ever known you. When we were younger there were times when you were angry. Times when you were unreachable. Probably because you were numb. And I get that. But now you seem sad. I wish I could help you.'

'You already are by being here,' Joel assured her.

'I'm here if you ever want to talk.'

Joel gave her a reassuring smile. 'No point. It's all in the past.'

Mia returned the smile, but her eyes held worry. 'That's what I'm concerned about. Too much of your life has been spent in the past. It's time both of us started looking to the future.'

Chapter Thirty-Six

JOEL IGNORED the raised eyebrows when he walked through the open-plan office on the way to see Nate. Several of the staff noticeably stared while a few raised their hands in greeting.

Joel returned the gesture. He knew Nate wouldn't have told the staff the real reason for his recent absence—Nate was too diplomatic for that. He wondered what Nate *had* told them. Most of the looks directed his way appeared friendly and curious. That was a good thing, surely.

When Em saw him, her blue eyes went wide, their colour just as intense as he remembered.

His chest tightened painfully, but he forced himself to ignore her and marched towards Nate's office without looking back. The sooner this was over, the better. When he arrived, he knocked once and entered.

Nate was standing, waiting for him. 'Close the door.'

Joel turned his back and did as requested, steeling himself for what was to come.

When Joel faced Nate again, he gestured to the chair. Joel shook his head.

'Fair enough,' Nate said, and crossed his arms. 'What the fuck, man? What the absolute fuck?'

Joel didn't say anything, but held his gaze.

Nate rounded the side of his desk and came to stand in front of Joel. 'That's it? You've got nothing? Three months, and you've got nothing?'

Nate's eyes were a steely grey and understandably angry. That was OK. Joel could deal with anger. It was better than fear or hatred, but he was sure it would come.

'I didn't think you'd want me here,' Joel told his oldest friend flatly.

Nate threw his hands up in the air—a surprisingly animated gesture for someone who was usually so calm. 'So you just thought that you'd make your mind up for me, is that it?'

Nate waited and Joel remained still, not saying anything. What was there to say, really?

'Joel, I deserve an answer, both as your business partner and as your friend.' Nate's voice was dangerously low. He wasn't the sort of man to yell, so Joel knew that he was supremely pissed right now.

'I was trying to make it easier on everyone,' Joel told him.

Nate's eyebrows rose in disbelief. 'Easy? You think this has been easy? Lying to the staff? Not knowing where the hell you've been? Not being able to talk to you? Nothing about this has been easy, mate.'

'I'm sorry,' Joel said, meaning it, but hating himself for needing to say it.

Sorry. Sorry. Sorry. No amount of sorry would ever be enough.

'No, you're not sorry. Do you know what you are? You're a coward,' Nate accused, only inches from Joel's face.

Joel blinked. Em had called him the same thing.

'You heard me.' Nate punctuated his sentence by pointing towards the rest of the office. Fortunately the walls were opaque glass, so no one else could see them. 'And what about that woman down there? Are you going to say that you're sorry to her as well?'

Joel looked down at his feet. 'I already have.'

'Not. Good. Enough.' Nate swiped a hand across his face and turned to pace the room. 'Why the fuck didn't you tell me?'

'What? Do you think I should have just casually dropped it into conversation sometime?' Joel snapped bitterly. '"Oh, by the way. You know how we're going into business together? There's something that you should know. I once killed a guy." Yeah. It doesn't quite fit, if you ask me.'

'Before then!'

Joel jolted at Nate's raised voice, and Nate released a breath.

'Before then,' he repeated at a normal level this time. 'We've known each other a long time, Joel.'

'Yeah, and I can tell you one thing. We would have known each other a hell of a lot less of a long time if I'd told you in the beginning. You wouldn't have wanted to know me.'

Nate walked over and got right in Joel's face. 'That's bullshit.'

'Quit pretending. We'd never have been mates, let alone business partners if I'd told you.'

Nate shoved him gently on the shoulder. 'You're fucked up.'

Joel swallowed a cynical laugh. 'I could have told you that.'

'No, seriously. You're fucked up. You're so busy deciding

how everyone else is going to judge you that you can't see yourself for what you are.'

Joel swallowed again, but this time it was with a solid lump in his throat. 'And what's that?'

A murderer? A lying piece of shit?

'You're a survivor, Joel. A fucking survivor.'

Nate's voice cracked, and Joel stared in shock at his friend, who seemed more sad than angry now.

Nate went on. 'Don't you think that I didn't notice how you didn't like talking about yourself when we first got to know each other? Then slowly, as you learned to trust me, a few things would come out here and there. Your piece of shit father. Your tragic mother. Your sorry story of a sister. You hated talking about it. I thought it was because you were embarrassed about it. Then I realised that wasn't it at all. You put yourself in the same category as them—broken.'

Joel frowned, but didn't say anything. He didn't know what to say.

'That was part of the reason I decided to go into business with you, did you know that?' Nate told him.

'What?'

'You heard me. You're a damn good architect—that was non-negotiable. But I wanted to show you that I had your back. I always got the sense you were in short supply of that growing up.'

'That's a stupid reason to go into business with someone,' Joel managed.

'No, it isn't. Not when you can see their potential. And you never let me down. Not once. Until now. I deserved your honesty from the beginning. I deserve it now.'

Joel rubbed the back of his neck with his hand. Sorry was on the tip of his tongue again, but he held it.

Nate tilted his head, regarding Joel. 'So what's your plan now?'

Joel forced himself to hold Nate's gaze. 'I was going to rescind my ownership in the business. Or give you time to find a new partner, whatever works best for you.'

'Coward.'

Joel winced. 'It's the truth. That's what you wanted to hear.'

'What I want is for you to show some courage.'

'What has courage got to do with any of this?'

'Everything.' Nate's voice was quiet and measured. 'It has everything to do with it. Are you going to live your entire life lying to people? And when and if they do finally find out, you'll just keep walking away before they even have a chance to make their own minds up about you?'

'I was trying to make it easier on everyone.'

'No, mate. You're refusing to let anyone in, that's what you're doing, and it's no way to live your life.'

Joel released a tight breath. 'It may not be, but it's better than people knowing.'

'Why? Why is it so bad? I'm not suggesting that you tell everyone. But you should give those closest to you the chance to know you, warts and all.'

'Warts and all?' Joel scoffed. '*Warts and all?* I fucking killed someone, Nate! I'm a murderer. No one wants to get close to that.'

Nate shoved Joel—hard. Joel stumbled back. The visitor chair stopped him from falling, and Joel braced himself against it.

'You weren't listening to me, were you?' Nate said. 'You're not a murderer. You're a survivor.'

'Stop saying that,' Joel ground out.

'Why? Because it's true?'

'It's not true, and you know it.'

'A court of law ruled it self-defence. I call that surviving.'

Joel closed his eyes. 'It doesn't matter what a court of law said. It still won't change the fact that someone died because of me.'

'Someone who tried to rape your sister and kill you. Joel, you were surviving. That's what you were doing. That's how you spent your entire fucked up childhood. Stop punishing yourself.'

Joel squeezed his eyes shut tighter. 'I can't.'

Joel felt Nate place his hands on Joel's shoulders. 'You need to. It's time, mate.'

This time the word "mate" was said with all the affection it deserved, and Joel's eyes fluttered open. Now there wasn't sadness or anger in Nate's eyes, but genuine love.

'You don't hate me,' Joel said. It was a statement.

Nate offered him a lopsided grin. 'You piss me off from time to time, but no, I don't hate you. You need to forgive yourself.'

'I'm not sure I ever can,' Joel admitted.

'It doesn't mean you approve of what happened. It just means that you've acknowledged it and are letting yourself move on.'

Joel stared at Nate. 'That's very . . . Dr. Phil of you.'

Nate grinned properly this time. 'I've got a point, don't I? Stop letting the past hold you to ransom. You can't change it. You can decide how you live now, though.'

'Jesus.' Joel rubbed a hand over his hair. 'You don't hate me.'

'No. And for the record, I don't want to get in a fight with you, but I'm not scared of you either.'

'Not even a little bit?'

Nate's grin was replaced with a frown. 'I'm scared you're

going to try to go through with handing over your part of the business. Then I'll have to get our legal team on to you so they can find a loophole and make you stay.'

Joel lowered himself into the chair. 'Right.'

'Right? That's all you've got to say?'

Joel shook his head. 'Give me some time to process.'

'Not too much time. There's a woman downstairs with a broken heart and a rather large mortgage, thanks to you.'

Joel looked up at Nate. 'I'm sorry?'

'The mortgage. On your house. All this other crap aside, you don't deserve her.'

'A mortgage on my house? What are you talking about?'

Nate frowned. 'You know that she bought your house, don't you? I don't see how you could have missed it.'

Joel swore and grabbed his phone out of his pocket. While Nate watched on, he scrolled desperately through his emails.

Where was it? There. The email the agent had sent through after the sale of the house. Joel supposed it was incredibly unprofessional of him, but he hadn't even bothered to view the settlement document. He had solicitors for that, and he'd been preoccupied. He'd simply downloaded the file and saved it for his records.

He could also admit that it would hurt to look at the proof that he'd let that house go, so he'd chosen not to.

Now he opened the attachment and waited impatiently while it loaded.

He swore again. There it was in black and white.

Emily Annabelle Georgiou.

She'd bought his house. The house he'd loved. The house he'd made into a home—thanks to her. That felt like home.

He'd asked her not to contact him, but she'd bought his fucking house.

The woman he loved bought the house he loved.

He had no words. None. But he did know what he had to do now.

Joel stood quickly, forcing Nate to take a step back.

'Whoa. You seriously didn't know?' Nate asked.

'I had no idea. I'm an idiot.'

'I can agree to that.'

'Don't say a word to her,' Joel ordered Nate.

'A word about what?'

'That I know. Let her continue to think I'm a clueless idiot, for now. I'll sneak out the back exit so that she doesn't see me. I'm going to fix this. I'm going to fix all of this.'

Joel pushed the phone back into his pocket and strode towards the door.

'Where are you going?' Nate asked.

'To take your advice. I hope.'

'Makes for a nice change.'

Joel turned back just before he opened the door. 'By the way, I don't want to let go of my part of the business. You're stuck with me after all.'

'Better the devil you know, I say.'

Joel coughed, but managed a smile. 'So long as you're OK with it.'

'More than OK. Go get your girl. But don't keep her waiting too long. She's already waited long enough.'

Chapter Thirty-Seven

JOEL WASTED no time making the trip across town to Chris Georgiou's office.

He had absolutely no idea what he was going to say to Em's father when he arrived, but Joel didn't allow himself to overthink it. He was too busy thinking about something else.

She bought my house. She bought my damn house.

Our house.

When the last words settled into his consciousness, Joel became choked up.

Our house.

Plenty of things had never made sense in Joel's life. His screwed-up parents. That one punch that had changed the course of everything that followed.

But "our house" made sense to Joel. His and Em's. Together.

He'd never had a house that he'd considered a home his entire life. Even when he'd bought this one, he'd figured he'd do it up, enjoy it for a while, then move on. Except with every wall he'd painted, with every change he'd made, that house had started to become part of him.

And then along had come Em.

You're not what I expected.

You're better than I expected.

Yeah, so maybe Nate was right. Joel did lack courage. He'd lacked the courage to tell Em how he really felt about her. To the point where he'd run from her because he couldn't bear the thought of her running from him. But he'd never given her a chance to decide for herself.

Well, that was about to change. He'd take a risk—potentially the biggest risk of his adult life—and tell her how he felt. Then if she still wanted him to walk away, at least he'd tried.

Walking into Chris Georgiou's office was the first step on that journey. It was almost as scary as facing Em.

'Can I help you?' Chris's executive assistant addressed him when he arrived on the top floor.

'Is Chris in?'

'He's busy right now.'

'I need to see him.' Joel strode purposefully over to the closed office door.

The impeccably presented older woman jumped up. 'You can't just go in there!'

'It's urgent,' Joel told her, and pushed open the door.

Chris was sitting at his desk concentrating on his computer. His eyes widened when he saw Joel.

'It's you . . .' he sputtered.

Ordinarily, Joel would have completed the sentence in his head in any number of ways.

You liar.

You arsehole.

You murderer.

But Joel was past doing that now, he realised, and it filled him with a sense of hope.

'Why didn't you come to me first?' Joel demanded. 'And give me a chance to explain?'

With eyes still wide, Chris stood slowly, looking as though he'd seen a ghost. He smoothed his trousers with the front of his palms. 'I don't see how you could ever explain something like that.'

'You could have given me the chance to tell my side of the story.' Joel walked over to Chris, so that only the desk was between them. 'Your reaction is the reason I've always kept the truth to myself.'

Chris's eyes narrowed. 'Why are you here?'

'Because I want to ask for your daughter's hand in marriage.'

Chris's mouth dropped open and his face turned bright red.

Joel held up a hand. 'I know you'll need some time—'

'Time?' Chris bellowed. 'Absolutely not! Under no circumstances will I ever allow you to marry my daughter.'

Joel nodded. 'I thought as much. But I wanted to give you the respect of asking you first. I'll still be asking her. And you should know that she has a mind of her own.'

Joel turned to walk away. This had gone about as well as he'd expected, but at least it was done now.

'Stop right there!'

Joel turned back and watched Chris bustle over to him. The man was so angry he was practically frothing at the mouth. Joel felt sad rather than scared. After all, no one could ever be as terrifying as his own father, and Joel understood that Chris's anger was due to his love for his daughter.

'I appreciate that I'm not the man that you envisaged for Em, and I'm sorry about that,' Joel told him. 'It doesn't change the fact that I love her. If she says no, I promise you won't see me again.'

Chris stopped right in front of him. 'No. You will not ask her. I forbid it.'

Two emotions warred for Joel's attention. First of all, hope, because if Chris didn't want Joel to ask Em that much, perhaps it meant there was a chance. The other emotion was admiration.

'I used to wish I had a dad like you, do you know that?' Joel said softly. 'Someone who cared enough to set boundaries. My father had an odd take on boundaries. He used to beat the shit out of my mother. Then, as I got older, he saw me as a challenge. Mainly because I did everything I could to stop him from laying a hand on my sister.'

Chris blinked and his mouth turned downwards into a stunned frown.

'Yeah, that's right. Not only were my parents drug addicts, my dad was an abusive alcoholic. I just got lucky, I guess. I can understand why you wouldn't want someone like me in your family, but for what it's worth I've never touched drugs and I never developed the taste for alcohol. My sister wasn't so lucky. I'm helping her to stay dry for the first time in her life on account of my nephew, who is due to arrive in a few months.'

Joel backed away, feeling like he'd said too much. He was supposed to be winning over Em's father, not turning him off completely. Joel had kind of given up after he'd heard the "I forbid it".

'Joel?'

Joel's back was to the door. He should just go. He couldn't imagine that anything that Chris was about to say would improve the situation, but he had to at least try for Em. And deep down, Joel had always respected Chris Georgiou.

'That night. Was it an accident?' Chris asked.

Joel sighed. He supposed that he could understand the question. Joel may not take drugs or ever drink to get drunk, but how was Chris to know if Joel was like his father where violence was concerned?

'My sister's boyfriend was out of his mind. I didn't have time to think, I was just trying to protect her.'

Chris nodded once.

'When I did have time to think later,' Joel went on, not sure why he was still speaking, 'I realised that in that moment I hadn't seen my sister's boyfriend, I'd seen my father. That was because a few months before that, Dad was so drunk one night that he tried to rape my sister, Mia.'

Chris recoiled and took a step back.

'I stopped him,' Joel said quietly. 'That's why my sister moved in with the loser boyfriend. So she'd be safe.' Joel scoffed bitterly. 'She called me that night, saying her boyfriend's behaviour was scaring her, but she didn't know where to go. Certainly not back home.'

Chris cleared his throat. 'I'm . . . I'm sorry.'

'So am I. I'm not sorry that I stopped her boyfriend. He wasn't the most decent guy, but he didn't deserve to die. For a long time I was convinced that I was guilty, because I wished it had been my dad. It's not something that I'm proud of.'

A long stretch of silence followed.

Eventually, Chris spoke. 'I'd say under the circumstances . . . your line of thinking was . . . understandable. Where is your sister now?'

'Safe,' Joel said firmly. 'I was finally able to encourage her to move here from WA. Away from her old life and habits. I've set her up in a place on the Central Coast, and I'm staying with her for a while to help with the baby.'

Chris cleared his throat again. 'And your business?'

'Isn't going anywhere. Neither am I, apparently. Nate is keen to continue working together.'

'I see.'

'I never told anyone about my dad. About him trying to rape Mia. She still won't talk about it. It's all just so . . .' He closed his eyes. 'Horrifying.'

When Joel opened them again, Chris's expression was more thoughtful than suspicious.

'You should tell Emily everything.'

Joel raised his eyebrows, surprised. 'I know you're right, but it doesn't make it any easier. Em's so . . . precious to me. Does it sound weird to say that I'm worried some of the darkness inside of me will rub off on her?'

Chris swiped a hand across his face and released a breath. 'My girl is strong. So is the light inside of her. You can tell her. Then let her decide.'

Joel stilled. It wasn't a blessing exactly, but it was an acknowledgement of his daughter's free will. That had to count for something, surely?

'Thank you for listening to me,' Joel said, meaning it.

'Regardless of what happens with you and Emily, I'll be talking to Nate about having you work with us on the contract again.'

'He'll appreciate that. *I* appreciate that,' Joel corrected.

He turned to go, still wondering if he'd said too much. Speaking about his past never got any easier.

'Joel? Nate laid into me, you know. After I requested that you be taken off the contract. He explained that things between you and Emily had started long before she'd taken the job there. That you wanted to keep things quiet until she'd settled in. Notwithstanding the, ah, compromising position we found you in that day, of course. That was . . . unfortunate.'

'It was wrong,' Joel said firmly. As much as he loved Em,

they never should have gotten carried away like that on work premises. 'It shouldn't have happened.'

'I was young once, and I know what it's like to get carried away.' Chris cleared his throat. 'Anyway. Nate suggested I was letting my personal views affect my business decisions, and that you were serious about my Emily.'

An odd feeling swelled in Joel's chest.

'He was right,' Chris went on. 'I can see now that I was wrong to question his unwavering faith in you.'

Joel's eyes stung with something suspiciously like tears. Unconditional support wasn't what he was used to, although he'd recently discovered that he'd had Nate's all along.

Now he needed to know if Em felt the same.

Chapter Thirty-Eight

'WHEN ALL ELSE FAILS, open a bottle of wine,' Kat announced, holding up the red they'd selected from the storage area located inside Em's garage.

'Or mocktails,' Jess added.

'I'd prefer the wine myself,' Ana told her, then shrugged. 'But you know, breastfeeding.'

Em shared a grateful smile with her sister. 'Thanks so much for coming, you guys. I know you're all so busy. I just needed . . .'

Em wasn't sure what she needed. A distraction? Ever since seeing Joel stride past her at the office today without so much as a second glance, it was like her world had crumbled. First she'd called her sister. Then Kat had called, and Em's dreadful day had spilled out. Now they were all here in a show of support.

'Hey.' Reading her sister's expression, Ana came over and put an arm around Em's shoulders. 'Busy? It's definitely Theo's turn to mind Isabella. I deserve a few hours off.'

Em's niece was only a month old, and Em had to admit

that while she didn't know much about babies, Isabella was rather special.

Kat nodded seriously. 'You certainly do. There's no way I'd have agreed to having this baby if Matt wasn't totally on board.' Kat paused and eyed her growing stomach suspiciously, like she still didn't quite believe it was real.

'Matt's an obstetrician!' Jess exclaimed. 'He's *totally* on board.'

'He just delivers them,' Kat said. 'He doesn't raise them.'

'Well, I know he'll make a great dad,' Jess said firmly.

Kat regarded her stomach with less suspicion this time, her mouth quirking at the edges. 'Yeah, I know he will, too.'

They stood and watched as Kat opened the bottle of red and poured one glass, then handed it to Em.

'Wine for one,' Kat said.

'I feel stupid being the only person drinking,' Em said, taking it but not having any.

'Em, that's a beautifully aged Barossa Shiraz. If I can't drink it, you will.'

Em glanced over at the bottle. 'I feel kind of bad for opening it.'

'Pfft,' Ana said. 'He left the wine here. It's yours now. Enjoy it.'

Em inhaled a shaky breath and forced herself to take a sip of the wine. 'Damn,' she commented after she'd swallowed. 'That's amazing.'

Kat groaned. 'You're killing me, you know that?'

Kat was something of a wine connoisseur and Em took another sip to keep her happy. Not that it was all that hard now she'd tasted how delicious it was.

'Maybe I'll enjoy the whole bottle,' Em mused out loud.

'That's the spirit!' Ana cried. 'Screw Joel.'

Em's face contorted into a frown at the mention of the man she was trying to forget.

Kat shot Jess an "uh oh" expression, and Jess hurried over to Em.

'Come on, let's take this in front of the fireplace. *Your* fireplace.'

Em sniffed and let herself be ushered into the living area. She supposed as far as fireplaces went, hers was pretty stunning. And Jess was right. She'd picked it out and now she owned it, so it was hers.

Everyone sat on the plush sofas, and despite the pain of knowing that this house had been meant for her and Joel, Em still felt at home here.

'At least you've got some closure,' Kat told Em. 'The not knowing wasn't doing you any good.'

'It's not like he's spoken to me. I'd hardly call that closure,' Em replied.

'If he hasn't acknowledged you or the fact that you purchased this house, that's a kind of answer.'

'An, I'm-ignoring-you answer,' Ana finished. 'Which totally sucks.'

'It does,' Jess agreed.

They all fell silent. Em was deeply grateful to have her sister and friends here tonight. She wasn't sure what she'd have done otherwise. Putting the house up for sale again had come to mind, as well as moving back to her parents and renting it out. But that was only the half of it.

'I'm not sure what to do about my job,' Em told them.

One of Kat's dark eyebrows rose. 'If you're thinking of resigning, don't. No man is worth that.'

'Yeah, and you're really enjoying your job,' Jess added.

'I'm just not sure . . . I'm not sure I can be around him if he's back for good.'

'It's not an ideal situation,' Kat agreed, 'but if his plan is to ignore you, then you ignore him too, and have as little as possible to do with him.'

'I know. It just . . . hurts so much.'

Ana sighed. 'I still can't believe that he had no reaction to you buying this house. I mean, even if he wasn't happy about it, some anger would have been good.'

'Joel doesn't like getting angry,' Em said softly.

They all fell silent again.

Jess was the first to speak. 'I think that he didn't let himself love you.'

Kat gave Em a knowing look. 'I think Em may have been in that category herself for a while, too.'

'I knew there was a reason I didn't do relationships,' Em complained.

Jess's expression turned sympathetic. 'When did you know that you were in love with him?'

'It was no one major thing,' Em admitted. 'It kind of crept up on me.'

'I know this is going to sound sappy of me,' Ana told them. 'But despite everything, I'm glad that Em got to experience love.'

'Sappy,' Em shot back. 'And it's not love if it's not recip-rocated.'

Ana crossed her arms and looked as if she was about to protest when the front doorbell rang.

Jess jumped up. 'That will be the food. I'll go grab it.'

'So have you sorted out your maternity leave with the show yet?' Em asked, keen to change the subject.

Before Kat could reply, Jess returned to living room.

'What happened to the food?' Ana asked. While she was no longer pregnant, the breastfeeding made her constantly hungry.

Jess appeared paler than usual. 'It's for you, Em.'

Em stood up, giving Jess a questioning look. 'Who is it?'

'It's probably better if you just go and see for yourself.'

Em shot Jess another look, but walked over to the hall that led to the front door. Em stopped halfway along when she saw who it was.

'Joel.'

He didn't say anything, just stood there looking at her. Really looking at her.

You would think when you loved someone you'd be able to know what they were thinking, but Em had absolutely no clue whatsoever. She didn't move.

'Em? Can we speak outside? I'm sorry if you've got people over.'

Em bit her lip, then nodded and strode up the hall, pushing past Joel.

Funny. She'd thought she'd gotten all of her emotions under control after seeing him earlier today. Sure, she was sad and hurt, but she was dealing with it. At least, she thought she had been until she'd seen him again.

Out on the front porch, Em went over to the railing and held on tightly, pretending to take in the view of the lights twinkling on the harbour when really her entire world was in freefall. 'What do you want, Joel?'

He followed and stood behind her. 'I want to know why you bought this house.'

Chapter Thirty-Nine

JOEL SUPPOSED it wasn't very fair of him to ask Em that question straight off the bat. He was the one who had left without any explanation. But it was the first thing that had come out when he'd opened his mouth.

He saw Em grip the handrail so hard her knuckles turned white. 'Why do you think?'

Joel swallowed. Yeah, he deserved that. 'I've got a few theories, but I'm not sure which one it is.'

'Try me.' Her voice sounded strained.

She had every right to be angry, so Joel decided to be honest. Maybe if he could be honest about this, he'd have the courage to be truthful about the rest.

'You like the house,' he began. 'I know that much. You put in a lot of hard work on the place, too. So maybe when I put it up for sale, you figured why not?'

'That's one possibility,' Em agreed. 'But you're not quite right. I don't just like the house. I *love* the house.'

Joel's heart clenched, because he loved it, too. It had been a painful decision to let it go, but he'd thought that's what he'd had to do in order to move on. But that wasn't the only reason his heart hurt. Until this moment he hadn't appreciated just how much he wanted Em to love him as well.

He stared at her hair in the moonlight. Even in the dim light it appeared alive. He wished she would turn around so he could see her equally beautiful eyes. Was there anger or pain swimming in them? Or worse, hatred?

Joel cleared his throat. 'I can understand that. I love this house, too.'

Like I love you.

But he held his tongue.

'Then why did you sell it?' she asked.

Joel thought carefully about his answer and settled on the truth once more. 'I didn't think I deserved it.'

'That's bullshit. This house is what it is because of you.'

'And you.'

Em released the handrail and walked over to the far end of the verandah. 'It seemed easy for you to give up.'

'No. Not easy. It's the only home I've ever known.'

Em swung around, her eyes flaring with pain. But no hatred, he noted.

'You should have fought harder to keep it then,' she accused.

Joel knew what she really meant was that he should have fought harder to keep her. She was right, and now he was terrified that it was too late.

'Every time I've fought for something in my life, it's ended badly,' he said quietly.

The pain in Em's eyes radiated bright violet. 'That's not true. You've fought to make a better life for yourself. To build a business. To rebuild this house.' She sighed and looked away. 'Why are you here, Joel?'

His heart skipped a beat. It was now or never. He needed all that courage that Nate had spoken of.

'I came here to ask you to marry me.'

Em jolted backwards, like she'd been shocked by an invisible current, and her jaw dropped open. Then she seemed to get hold of herself and she shook her head, like she didn't quite believe what she'd just heard.

'You're proposing marriage?' she asked.

'Yes,' he said, not sure of himself exactly, but not as scared as he thought he'd be.

Em walked over and glared at him. 'You idiot!'

He took a step back, blinking in shock.

Em's eyes narrowed, piercing him with their intensity. 'You think that you can just come back here and it will be alright because you ask me to *marry* you?' She stepped in close again, still glaring.

Em's voice must have carried, because footsteps echoed up the hallway and Kat, Jess and Ana appeared at the door.

'Is everything alright?' Kat asked calmly.

'Oh, fine,' Em spat. 'If you think this jerk asking me to *marry* him is totally acceptable.'

Ana squealed, then clamped a hand over her mouth when Em's death stare settled on her.

Joel took the opportunity to inhale a much-needed breath. Right. So, that hadn't gone exactly as he'd expected.

Em returned her glare to him. 'You don't even *want* to get married.'

Joel didn't hesitate and ignored the others watching on. 'To you, I do.'

'And what makes you think I would say yes?'

She was right. Again. And he was doing this all wrong.

'Because you bought this house,' he told her.

For the first time, her gaze softened, but she didn't say anything so he took the opportunity to continue.

'Our house,' he said. 'Because that's what it feels like, doesn't it? Our house?'

Ana squeaked, and Em shot her sister a firm look.

'It's my house now,' Em corrected.

'But you wanted it to be our house. That's why you bought it.'

'He's on to you,' Ana whispered loudly, and Em's eyes widened in warning.

'Why now?' Em asked, turning back to him. 'I've owned the property for almost two months.'

'Because I didn't look at the contract. To be honest, I didn't want to know who had bought the house, because then it would be real that it wasn't mine anymore.'

Em's eyebrows rose. 'None of this is a good reason to get married.'

'It is when I love you.'

Ana gasped and Kat reached over and tugged on her hand. 'Come on. Let's leave them to their . . . discussions.'

They waited until Em's friends had gone inside.

'You love me,' Em said. It wasn't a question.

'Yes. For longer than I've wanted to admit. I'm pretty sure it was when you were picking out paint colours. It was definitely before you moved in with me.'

Em released a rush of breath and looked heavenwards. 'But you still broke up with me. Then after we got back together, you ran away.'

'Because I was trying to do the right thing.'

'When you love someone, the right thing isn't running away from them!'

'I'm sorry.' For once, the words didn't feel empty. 'I want to tell you more about why I reacted the way that I did. I've told you a lot, but not everything. You deserve to know it all if you choose to be with me.'

Em nodded again, her expression serious. 'I'd appreciate that, and I'd like to hear it. But Joel? I'm not going to marry you.'

EM WATCHED CAREFULLY for Joel's reaction. For once, he was unguarded. Surprise. Sadness. Maybe even despair. Then acceptance.

He nodded. 'OK. I understand. If I were you—'

'That's the thing. You're not me. Instead of asking me to marry you, how about asking me how I feel first?'

'OK,' he said again, sounding uncertain. 'How do you feel about . . . us?'

'I love you,' Em said with certainty. 'More than I fully understand. It made me crazy enough to buy this house. It doesn't make sense to me. I didn't ask to love you, but I do. I just . . . do.'

Joel shoved a hand through his hair. It had grown longer since he'd been away. 'I do, too.'

'But I'm not going to marry you,' Em repeated, then added, 'yet.'

Joel's eyes met hers and he swallowed. Some of his uncertainty had been replaced with hope.

'I can see myself marrying you,' she told him. 'Just so you know. It scares the shit of out me, if we're being honest. I'm definitely not having a stupid big wedding, but you already know that. All of that is beside the point for now. First, you have to love me. Unconditionally. Openly. Honestly. Then I'll consider marrying you.'

Joel took a tentative step in Em's direction. 'I can do that.'

'I know you can,' Em said, also with certainty. 'Whatever you were brought up to believe you are or aren't, I know you're a good person. You just weren't ever given the chance. I'm giving you the chance. Be *my* good man, Joel.'

Joel scrubbed a hand over his mouth, his eyes rimmed with tears. When he removed it, he attempted a smile. 'I can do that.'

'Good. Now it's my turn to ask you something.'

'Yes?'

'Would you like to move in with me?'

Joel's smile intensified, and Em saw it. The sun coming out from behind the clouds. Maybe some of her sister's overly romantic ideals were rubbing off on her. But Em had a feeling that the sun was here to stay, and from now on there wouldn't be as many storms.

Joel took another step towards her and threaded his fingers through hers. 'I'd really like that.'

'Great. Because I need someone to help me repaint that damn garage. Have you seen how big it is down there?'

Joel chuckled and Em basked in the warmth of his smile. If she had her way, she was looking forward to deepening those laughter lines in that gorgeous face of his.

'How about we seal the deal with a kiss?' she suggested coyly.

His eyes darkened, but there was no darkness, only desire, Em observed happily.

Joel drew her in and brushed his lips against hers, but it wasn't enough. It would never be enough when it came to Joel. Just like that first night, Em yearned for him completely, inexplicably, but she didn't care why anymore. She just knew it for a fact. Em deepened the kiss. Joel groaned and then pulled back.

'You have guests,' he reminded her.

Damn. 'I can kick them out.'

'I've got a better idea. Why don't we have a toast to new beginnings?'

'That's a perfect idea. I've got just the bottle of wine for the occasion.' Then she winked and tugged him inside.

Her girlfriends and sister stopped their conversation abruptly when they both entered the room.

'Good news. I'm *not* getting married,' Em announced, grinning broadly while holding Joel's hand. 'It's time to celebrate!'

Acknowledgments

Thank you for reading Daddy's Girl, the final book in the Freshwater series. It's the 13th full-length book I've written, and when I first started my writing journey ten years ago, I never could have conceived writing so many books.

There are some amazing people who have helped me to reach this point. I'm extremely grateful for my lovely beta-readers, Sarah, Donna, Milia and Nicki, who STILL want to read my books after all this time and take the time to dutifully provide feedback. Huge thanks also to my talented editor, Laura, and my eagle-eyed proofreader, Rebekah.

My boys and their loving support means the world to me, and I count my blessings daily that I get to do this life with you both by my side x

Last, but not least, my wonderful readers. I hope that you enjoyed Em's story and I appreciate you purchasing this book. Supporting authors is a big deal, because it means we can keep writing more books. And I've got plenty more to come!

Join Belinda's newsletter

AND RECEIVE A FREE EBOOK!

Sign up to Belinda's newsletter to be kept up to date about her latest book releases, news and specials.

To say thank you, you'll receive a **FREE copy of HEARTSTRINGS a Holly-wood Hearts novella** valued at $2.99, which was rated 'A' by Smart B*tches, Trashy Books!

Sign up here: https://dl.bookfunnel.com/98v02gbzho

About the Author

Belinda Williams is a marketing copywriter who fell in love with romance and writes romantic comedy as well as romantic suspense featuring good guys. She's occasionally tempted by bad boys, but prefers to write strong women characters and men with big hearts.

When she's not writing, Belinda is a music lover who sings lead vocals in cover bands, and her eclectic taste forms the foundation for many of her writing ideas.

Her other love is the water. She can often be found counting laps instead of words at her local swimming pool. Or you might also spot her boating on the harbour with her husband and son in her home town of Sydney, Australia.

Belinda loves to hear from her readers! Connect with her below:

www.ingramcontent.com/pod-product-compliance
Lightning Source LLC
Chambersburg PA
CBHW050143120726
47903CB00002B/477